OTHER BOOKS BY TARA WYATT

If you like Standalone Companion Novels

about One Big Family:

THE PRESCOTTS

Stupid Love

Snow Job

Love Bug

Bad Intentions

Side Effects

Burning Up

Until You

Skin Deep

If you wish Hallmark movies had some spice:

THE GRAYSONS

When Snowflakes Fall

Like Fresh Fallen Snow

Until the Sun Sets

If you like baseball players:

DALLAS LONGHORNS SERIES

Stealing Home

Wild Card

Caught Looking

Moon Shot

Hit and Run

Scoring Position

If you like MMA fighters:

THE BLOOD AND GLORY SERIES

co-written with Harper St. George

Dirty Boxing

Take Down

No Contest

If you like bodyguards:

THE BODYGUARD SERIES

Necessary Risk

Primal Instinct

Chain Reaction

JUST LIKE *Magic*

TARA WYATT

A *Gossamer Falls* NOVEL

"And as she stood beneath the full moon's pearlescent beams, the mist of the falls landed on her cheeks, kissing away her tears. Such was the relief that she felt that she knew it to be no less than a benediction from the angels. A blessing. A promise. A way forward, filled with more love and hope than the poor widow had ever known."

The Legend of Gossamer Falls,
written by Mary Elizabeth Axton,
published 1890

ONE

HAZEL WOODWARD WAS RUNNING from her problems.

And these weren't little problems, like having a bad cold, or getting annoying spam emails, or having shitty wi-fi. In fact, Hazel would gladly trade her problems for a never-ending runny nose, a hundred spam emails a day, and never having reliable wi-fi again. Because the problems she was running from....well.

She was running from the long list of things she didn't want to think about. Things like her ex-husband, her potentially imploding career and subsequent financial ruin, and the best friend she'd thought she'd known. It was a short list, but certainly not lacking in depth.

So, she wasn't running from much. Just, you know. Her entire life.

She settled back in her seat, unwinding the scarf from around her neck. It was sunny and unseasonably warm for the beginning of October, and the interior of the train was stuffy. She tossed it on top of the worn satchel at her feet, the dark brown leather creased with time and use. In it, she had her laptop, planner (although what she was going to need it for over the next couple of weeks she had no idea), a notebook, and an assortment of pens.

Just looking at it made her anxiety spike. But she'd have to get over that because not only did her career and livelihood depend on it, part of the reason for this trip was to get out of the city and clear her head in the hopes that the ideas would start flowing. Hell, she didn't even need them to flow. A trickle would be welcome in the desert of her creativity.

With a snap, the doors closed and the train lurched forward, pulling out of the MTA station on 125th St. The roller bag she'd stashed beneath her seat slid forward, bumping against her heels. In it, she'd packed clothes, toiletries and other necessities for the next two weeks.

Maybe it was foolish to think that getting out of Manhattan for two weeks would really change anything. Two weeks was barely enough time to do anything, never mind figure out her life. Or at the very least, her long overdue book.

God, the book. She didn't want to think about the book. She was tired of thinking about the book. Or rather, the complete lack of a book, despite the multiple extensions granted to her by her publisher. Her gaze flicked to the bag at her feet. She could work during the ninety-minute train ride. She *should* work during the ninety-minute train ride.

She stared at the bag, rubbing her hand over the back of her neck.

It's fine, she told herself, her skin prickly with heat. *You can work once you get settled.*

It was a small reprieve, one of the hundreds, if not thousands, she'd negotiated with herself over the past couple of years. Tomorrow, inspiration would strike. Tomorrow, she'd sit down at the computer and write. But tomorrow never came, always just slightly out of grasp.

The elevated train started to wind its way through Harlem, bright fall sunshine streaming in through the train's windows. Deciding to enjoy the ride as best she could, she popped in her AirPods and cued up her Carrie Clark playlist on Spotify, leaning back against the seat and letting the scenery wash over her.

The sky was a brilliant blue, streaked with wispy white clouds that looked like they were clinging to the tops of the low lying brick buildings in Harlem. The fall colors had already come to the city, the trees lining the sidewalks below having shed their green for soft yellows and burnt oranges.

After a slight curve, the train clattered across the Harlem River and then between graffiti-tagged buildings. Her eyelids felt heavy as the train moved into the Bronx, brown brick buildings closing in around the train and blocking out some of the sunlight. So she let her eyes close, the rocking move-ment of the train and the familiar melodies of her favorite singer lulling her into a dozy nap.

By the time she woke up almost an hour later, the city was behind them. Even Yonkers was behind them. Rubbing her eyes, she returned her attention to the scenery unfolding around her. On the left, she could clearly see the Hudson River, blue and calm. On her right, breathtaking foliage in every single shade of red, yellow, and orange imaginable. These weren't the muted colors of the city. They were bright. Dazzling and warm.

As the train continued north, past Dobbs Ferry, through Sleepy Hollow, the colors only grew in their intensity. With every town they left behind, the trees became denser, the towns sparser and farther apart, the vastness of nature more pressing and consuming. It didn't feel as though New York City was only fifty miles south.

The train took a bridge that went north over the Hudson, crossing lush marshland on the right. To the left, a sparsely populated island was ablaze with fall color, the leaves all rippling their fiery colors in the wind. A few more clouds had rolled in, the play of light and shadow across the endless sea of trees intensifying the bright hues.

Once they were over the island, the bridge continued on over a bay. Gossamer Bay, if she remembered correctly. She knew she was right when the crumbling ruins of a nine-teenth century foundry came into view.

As the train chugged over the bay, the sun burst from behind the clouds, casting sunbeams made of soft, airy gold over the town of Gossamer Falls, which rose up to her left. Ahead, the Hudson Highlands were a softly rolling land-scape of scarlet, saffron, and vermilion, with the occasional towering pine to provide a shot of green. Within the high-lands was the famous waterfall itself, the one that drew tourists from all over the place. The one that had inspired the famous short story that had saved the town from destitu-tion when the foundry had closed at the turn of the twen-tieth century.

The town itself looked cozy and inviting, and as the train slowed, nearing the little train station, Hazel felt her eyes stinging. She couldn't explain it. But for the first time in a very long time, she felt as though she were exactly where she was supposed to be.

Almost like coming home.

But how could a place she'd never been before feel like home? It didn't make any sense.

Then again, not everything in life made sense. Some things were better explained by magic than logic.

The train stopped, pulling into the Gossamer Falls train station, which was a cute little red brick building with red and yellow trim. Old fashioned font scrolled across the side of the building, welcoming visitors to the village of Gossamer Falls, established 1846. Hazel wound her scarf around her neck, gathered up her two bags, and stepped off the train. The air was cooler here than it had been in the city, and fresher too. She inhaled deeply, pulling the cool, crisp air deep into her lungs.

A few other people had disembarked with her, and they were each greeted by friends or family, reminding Hazel just how alone she was. Her parents were retired and cruising the world. Her brother lived in Australia. Her marriage had gone down in flames. Her best friend had betrayed her and caused an irreparable fracture in their little friend group. She had Sarah, her best friend from college, but Sarah lived in Texas with her husband and daughter. They saw each other once or twice a year, and it was great, but...on a day-to-day basis? Hazel was alone. Really, truly alone.

She swallowed around the thickness in her throat. Getting out of the city was doing something to her, as though the tight lid she usually kept on her emotions was loosening.

"Miss Woodward?" came a voice from behind her, and Hazel whirled, almost knocking over her suitcase in the process. A young woman rushed forward, auburn hair flying behind her as she raced to right the suitcase. She flashed her a grin and then held out her hand. "I'm Autumn Shephard, customer relations at the Shephard Inn. I'm your ride."

"Oh, really? You didn't have to do that. I could've just..." Hazel trailed off. This was a town of just over a thousand people. Maybe there weren't any cabs or Ubers or even busses.

"It's my pleasure," said Autumn easily, tucking a strand of her long hair behind her. She was extremely pretty, in a very wholesome way. She had stunning blue eyes and a heart-shaped face, with high cheekbones and a wide smile. "We always meet our guests at the train station." She wrapped her hand around the handle of Hazel's roller suitcase and started walking toward the parking lot.

"So. First time in Gossamer Falls?" she asked as she led the way to a plain black van. She hoisted the suitcase into the back. Hazel nodded.

"Yeah. I was looking for a place to get away, and...you're going to laugh at me."

Autumn smiled earnestly at her. "I pinky swear I won't." She held up her pinky and with a small laugh, Hazel hooked hers around it.

"I was looking through this magazine, and—do you mind if I sit up front with you?"

"No problem." Autumn held the passenger's side door open for her, not closing it until Hazel was buckled in. Autumn slid into the drivers' seat and turned the van on. Carrie Clark came blaring through the speakers, and she jolted forward, turning the music down. "Sorry about that."

"You don't ever need to apologize for blasting Carrie Clark, as far as I'm concerned," said Hazel. "*My Kinda Heroine* is a hugely underrated album."

Autumn grinned at her and turned the music back up a little. "I couldn't agree more." She turned out of the parking lot. "So, you were reading a magazine and...?"

"Right. It was some free magazine I found in a coffee shop, about tourist destinations in New York State. You know, Lake Placid, the Adirondacks, that kind of stuff. But then the weirdest thing happened. I was sipping my coffee and a gust of wind blew in the door of the coffee shop, flipping the pages of the magazine. And it landed on this."

She reached into the pocket of the chunky cardigan she was wearing and unfolded the ad she'd torn from the magazine. It featured a shot of the famed Gossamer Falls, surrounded by fall foliage, and the slogan *Gossamer Falls: Where magic happens.*

"And I just knew I needed to come here...It felt like a sign," said Hazel, blood rushing to her cheeks. "This is the part where you laugh at me."

Autumn shook her head. "It probably *was* a sign. They're everywhere, if you know where to look." They came to a stoplight and Autumn turned, her gaze suddenly scrutinizing. "How old are you?"

"Um. Oh, I'm thirty-nine."

Autumn nodded, suddenly taking on the air of a detective questioning a suspect. "Are you single?"

"Um, yeah, but I'm not...I'm divorced and not really...but yeah, I'm, I guess I'm single."

"What do you do for a living?"

Hazel unwound the scarf from around her neck, feeling a little warm. "I'm a writer. I write fantasy novels." *At least, I used to.*

"Oh, that's so interesting!" she said, and the wholesome

girl next door was back. "How many books have you written?"

"Um, three."

"Anything famous?" she asked, waggling her eyebrows.

"Um. Well. My first book was *A Revelation of Enchantment.*"

Autumn swerved and pulled over abruptly. "Shut. Up! No way! Didn't they make that into a TV show?"

Hazel nodded, feeling a little embarrassed, even though she knew she shouldn't. But it was hard to feel proud of her success when her future was so uncertain. "A miniseries, yeah."

"That is so cool. What are you working on now?"

"I don't know yet," she said, deciding that she had nothing to lose being honest with Autumn. After all, she hadn't laughed when she'd told her the magazine story. "I originally told my editor that I was working on a new book featuring one of the characters from the trilogy."

"Like a spin off," said Autumn, and Hazel nodded.

"Exactly. But I just couldn't make it work. So I came up with a proposal for a new trilogy, about a pair of vampires who are fated to find each other again and again, across time."

"Wow. That sounds so romantic."

"That's what I was going for. But...I don't know. It's not working either."

"Oh."

"That's actually why I'm here. I wanted to get away from the city and focus on writing."

Autumn nodded and pulled away from the curb. "So,

since this is your first time in Gossamer Falls, how about a little tour?"

Hazel nodded. "Perfect."

"So, this is Foundry Bridge Road. It crosses Gossamer Bay and runs along the shore. The old foundry is right on Gossamer Bay. It was the town's lifeblood way back when, but at the beginning of the twentieth century, demand for iron was drying up thanks to the rise of steel. It's a protected landmark now, and a vital part of the town's history." Hazel nodded. She knew some of this from what she'd read, but she found herself wanting to learn more.

Autumn turned right and continued speaking. "This is Main Street, the central part of town. It crosses Chestnut Avenue in an X, and where they meet is what you'd consider our downtown." They passed a gas station styled like it was the 1950s, and it shared a parking lot with a small FoodTown grocery store. Quiet, tree-lined streets branched off of main, with names like Hickory Street and Balsam Drive. "Up ahead is the pub, Pour Decisions. If you want to check it out, I'd be happy to take you one night. My brother Beckett is the bartender there, so I'm sure we could score some free drinks."

Hazel nodded. She couldn't remember the last time she'd gone out for drinks. "Yeah. I'd like that." And she wasn't just saying that. There was something immensely appealing about Autumn's vivacious, warm energy.

She blinked slowly as they passed Pour Decisions. The exterior looked like a proper English pub, with a black lacquer façade, the name written in a fancy serif font in gold paint across the front. Below the name, massive windows looked out onto the street, and several baskets of yellow and orange fall mums hung between the panes.

Autumn slowed as they came to Main and Chestnut, the main thoroughfare. "There's the bookstore, up there on the left," she said, pointing to a cozy looking shop on the corner. The name All Booked Up was painted in red and gold on a black placard, and Hazel smiled to herself. This was starting to feel like something out of a movie set. It was *too* cozy. *Too* perfect. Even better than she ever could've imagined. "Down to the right there are a couple of cute clothing shops, an antique store, a few little restaurants." They continued up Main Street. "Up ahead on the right is the coffee shop and the bakery. The coffee shop is called Deja Brew, and the bakery is called You Little Tart. They're run by Sienna and Laurel Radley—they're twins and also my besties."

"Those names are adorable," said Hazel, already making plans to visit all of the cute places Autumn was pointing out to her. On their left, a large town square opened up, filled with charming old buildings and cobblestone streets. The buildings were clustered together, but not so tightly as to make it feel claustrophobic. Just cozy. Warm and inviting.

"That's Hemlock Square. That's where you'll find the library, the post office, town hall, the police and fire station, the museum, and the Odeon, our movie theatre. It only shows second run movies, but it's cheap and it's fun. Plus they have the best popcorn you've ever tasted. I don't know what they put in it, but it must be crack or something."

Hazel laughed. "What are they showing right now?"

"*The Mummy*. Not the Tom Cruise one," she added quickly. "The good one. With Brendan Fraser."

"Oh, that is a good one. Honestly, I think that movie was part of my sexual awakening."

Autumn laughed, the sound bright and loud in the confines of the van. "Girl, you are speaking my language." She pointed at a larger, newer building. "That's the condo building where Beckett and my brother Oliver both live. Not together. In their own apartments."

"So you have two brothers?"

Autumn laughed again, but not unkindly. "Oh, God. No. I have five."

"Five?"

"Yep, and I'm the baby."

"What was that like?" asked Hazel, unable to wrap her head around the idea of having five siblings. She had one, and they'd never been close.

"Good, mostly. No one ever messed with me growing up, I can tell you that much."

"With five older brothers, I wouldn't think so," said Hazel with a little laugh. "Do they all live in town?"

"All except one." Something flickered across Autumn's face, and then she changed the subject. "There's also a farmer's market every Saturday morning in Hemlock Square," she said, returning to her tour. "Lots of fresh food, baked goods, local artists. Definitely worth checking out." As they passed Hemlock Square, they came to another stoplight. "If you turn right, that's Cemetery Road, and the town cemetery is down at the end. Here on the corner, there's a shop called The Mystic Muse. Have you ever had your tarot cards read?"

Hazel shook her head. "I can't say I have."

"Do you believe, Hazel?" she asked, turning to look at her.

"Believe?"

"In magic? In things we can't explain? In coincidences so coincidental that there has to be more to them? Signs?"

"Um...maybe? I don't know."

"That wasn't a no."

"No. It wasn't a no."

"Good enough for me."

"I take it you believe?"

Autumn nodded, an earnest expression on her pretty face. "When you live in a place like this, you can't help but believe. You'll see for yourself, if you open your eyes."

Goosebumps erupted across the back of Hazel's neck, and she felt dizzy, just for a second. She felt acutely aware of everything around her, as though it was the most important thing in the world to soak it all up.

A laugh bubbled up inside her, and she let it out. Autumn smiled at her.

"This is Oak Street," she said, gesturing down to the left as they continued up Main. "This is where I live. With my mom. For now."

"I'm not judging," said Hazel, lifting her hands.

They passed Pine another residential street lined with pretty houses, large trees and wide sidewalks. Autumn hung a left onto Cedar, driving past several more cozy, colonial-style houses before turning down a large, winding drive at the end of the street.

"Here it is. The Shephard Inn, proudly run by my family since 1948."

TWO

"WOW," Hazel breathed. She'd seen pictures of the hotel online, but seeing it in person hit different. A sprawling mansion rose up before her, sitting serenely on the top of a softly sloping hill covered in lush, green grass. A gabled slate roof sat atop the enormous house, which was encased in pale limestone. French windows dotted the walls at even intervals, and twin stone chimneys rose up on either side of the massive gable.

"You sound impressed," said Autumn, a smile in her voice. Hazel nodded, tucking a wayward strand of hair behind her ear.

"I am. I mean, I saw the pictures online, but I don't think they fully captured just how amazing this place is." Now Hazel understood why Gossamer Falls only had the one hotel. Because even though she hadn't seen the inside yet, she knew there was no way anything could possibly compete with this. It was beautiful and peaceful, warm and welcoming.

Autumn pulled the van around the circular drive and

under a porte cochere stretching out from the main entrance. "Here we are," she said, cutting the van's ignition. She hopped down from the driver's seat and quickly retrieved Hazel's bag from the back. Hazel followed her inside, and it was as though every single ounce of tension in her body just melted away.

They stepped into a wide hall with gleaming wood floors and warm lighting. To the left was a dark wood staircase with an elaborately carved banister, with what looked to be the reception desk nestled beneath it. Straight ahead, she could see a room with a wall of windows facing what looked like a pond.

"That's the sunroom," said Autumn, pointing straight ahead. "And even though it's called the sunroom, it's my favorite place to be when it's raining, especially if Adam lights the fireplace."

"Adam?"

Autumn grinned, something almost mischievous twinkling in her eyes. "Yep. My oldest brother. He's the manager of the hotel."

"Gotcha. Do you like working with him?"

Autumn rolled her lips inward. "Mostly, yes. And he needs me. So this is where I'm supposed to be." She swallowed and then gestured to a large room on the right. "That's the lounge. Go take a look and I'll get your room key."

Hazel walked slowly toward the double doors, the floors creaking in welcome beneath her feet. Wood beams ran along the vaulted ceiling, and a collection of leather couches sat grouped around the biggest stone fireplace Hazel had ever seen in her life. Floor-to-ceiling windows framed it on either side, looking out onto the property and the Hudson Highlands in the near distance. A wrought-iron chandelier hung from the ceiling's apex, casting a soft, warm glow over the area. On the mantel, there were candles, books, and aging maps of the area, framed and tilted against the stone. She turned slowly, taking it all in. A small bar sat against the far wall, set up for coffee or something stronger. But it was the wall at the opposite end of the room that had her gasping and rushing over. Built-in bookshelves spanned the entire length of it, and there was even a rolling ladder attached to a rail that ran along the top.

Hazel found herself letting out a giddy little laugh as she approached it, pushing her finger against the wood and giving it a tentative slide. Then, glancing over her shoulder, she let out another giggle as she stepped on and whooshed down several feet. The ladder stopped with a sudden, jarring halt, almost as though someone had grabbed it.

"Must've snagged," she murmured to herself, glancing up at the rail. Her eyes landed on a worn copy of something familiar, and forgetting about the snagged rail, she reached forward and pulled the heavy book off the shelf. It was a copy of *The Mists of Avalon*, a book she'd read and loved as a teenager. In fact, it was one of the books that had made her want to be a writer in the first place, and she couldn't remember the last time she'd read it.

A slight coolness slid over her skin, almost like a draft, except it felt almost like a caress. But it must've been a draft because the book's cover flopped open in her hands, right to the very first page of the story. Hazel gently closed the cover and took the book with her back into the hallway.

"Is it okay if I borrow this?" she asked Autumn, who was

typing away at the computer behind the dark wood desk. Autumn glanced up and then nodded.

"Sure. Did you pick it, or did the ladder?"

"What?" asked Hazel, even though she was pretty sure she already knew what Autumn was talking about.

Autumn stopped typing and looked up. "So...some people think the hotel is haunted. But good haunted."

Hazel stepped closer, intrigued. "Really? Haunted how?"

"With benevolent spirits. Two, actually."

"Benevolent spirits...as in spirits who try to help people?"

Autumn beamed at her. "Exactly. There's Reginald, one of the original owners of the house. He likes to fix things, locate lost items, stuff like that. And the other is Mary, my grandmother. She and my grandfather bought this place after the Second World War and turned it into the Shephard Inn. They were newlyweds at the time, barely twenty years old. Can you imagine? Taking something like this on right out of high school?"

"I can't. I feel like I can barely keep my apartment together, never mind a place like this."

"Right? Anyway, Grams died in 2016, and not long after that, things started happening."

"Like what?" Hazel asked. She wasn't normally one for ghost stories, but she had to admit, this was intriguing.

"Little touches. A bouquet of wildflowers sitting on the desk in the morning, before anyone was here. Sometimes you can smell things, like cinnamon or chocolate, even when there's none around." She leaned forward on the desk, pointing at the book in Hazel's hands. "She gives people the book she believes they need the most."

Hazel glanced down at the book in her hands, goose-bumps once again crawling over her skin.

"I thought the rail got stuck," she said quietly, and Autumn let out a little laugh.

"Nope. Not stuck." She stepped out from behind the desk, a key with the number two attached to it in her hand. "Come on, I'll show you to your room. Things are a little quiet right now. We have ten rooms total, and rooms three, five, seven, and nine are currently booked out."

"How would we go about—" came a male voice from behind a closed door Hazel hadn't noticed behind the reception desk. There was a small placard on it that simply read *management*.

"You don't," replied a second male voice, this one quieter, but somehow deeper and richer. "There's no such thing as ghosts, and I won't have you make a spectacle of this hotel. I respect that you're just doing your job, but the answer is a firm, unequivocal no."

"But if we could just—" said the first voice again, and once again, he was cut off by he of the lovely, deep voice. Hazel wondered if he'd ever considered a career narrating audiobooks because there was something about the timbre of it that made her want to lean in and listen.

"You can't. I'm sorry to disappoint you, but you'll have to look elsewhere. Now, if you don't mind, I have work to do."

Hazel glanced over at Autumn, who was listening to the exchange with an amused expression on her face. "Adam is the best guy you'll ever meet, but he doesn't believe in ghosts or magic or any of it," she said, tipping her head in the direction of the library. She thrust the key into Hazel's hand. "Here. I'd better go see what's going on. It takes a lot for him to lose his cool, but when he does..." She mimed an explosion. So, Adam Shephard was he of the sexy voice. Noted.

She mounted the stairs, coming out on an airy landing carpeted in an orange and red patterned area rug. The large hallway was T-shaped, with wings stretching out in both directions. She started down the hallway, delighted to find that each large window contained a small alcove with a window seat and recessed shelves containing plants, candles, framed pictures of the falls, and more books.

She found her room easily, and slipped the key into the lock.

"Oh, wow," she whispered, stepping into the room. She'd stayed in plenty of hotels, but she'd never had a hotel room that looked like this. A queen-sized bed sat against the wall to her right, flanked by twin night stands decorated with plants and candles. Strands of delicate twinkle lights hung on the wall behind the bed, disappearing behind the light wood headboard. Soft looking linens in orange and cream looked inviting, along with the plush pillows resting against the headboard. Across from the bed, a TV was mounted to the wall, and below it were shelves with more books, more candles, and a couple of soft looking throw blankets. Past the TV, a door led to the bathroom, where more plants hung from the ceiling. There was a large, glassed-in shower and a soaker tub that had Hazel wondering if she should start running a bath right now.

On the far side of the bed, a gas fireplace was nestled into the wall, and beyond that, a large bay window that looked out over the pond and the Hudson Highlands, fitted with a rounded armchair large enough for two. Another narrow bookshelf sat against the opposite wall. A large bouquet of sunflowers with a small note folded at the base of the vase sat on the built-in ledge. She picked it up, reading the masculine scrawl.

Hazel –

Welcome to the Shephard Inn. If there's anything you need, just ask.

Adam Shephard, manager

She traced her finger over the ink, feeling the ridges against her skin. The sudden sensation of static electricity raced through her, and when there was a sharp knock at the door, she squeaked, then set the card back down.

"It's Autumn," came the voice from the other side. "I have your bags."

Hazel hurried to let her in. "Thank you," she said, helping Autumn with the bags and setting them on the end of the bed. "So…I know it's none of my business, but what was that about? Downstairs, with Adam," she asked, not wanting to pry, but curious all the same. Hazel was normally someone who minded her own business, but she felt a comfortable kinship with Autumn already. She wouldn't have asked the question if she didn't.

"Oh, that," she said with the wave of her hand. "A ghost hunting documentary crew is dying to investigate the hotel. They've been asking for years, and Adam refuses. He thinks it's the wrong kind of publicity for the hotel."

"What do you think?" asked Hazel. "I mean, you obviously…"

"I believe in ghosts, but I agree with Adam. This isn't a haunting. They're more like caretakers, in my opinion. Their show is about spooky voices and unexplained bangs. It's entertaining, but it's the wrong vibe for us. And it would attract the wrong kind of clientele. How do you like your room?" she asked, glancing around, as though making sure everything was as it should be.

"It's amazing. Even better than I could've imagined. It's so warm and homey and comfortable, and that view...the colors are amazing." She returned to the window, eyes roving over the sea of gold and crimson, soothing something inside her.

"Were you planning to visit the falls?" asked Autumn, and something in her voice had Hazel turning. That shrewd look was back on her face, the one that made Hazel feel as though she were being tested in some way.

"I was," she said, somewhat hesitantly.

"Good. I run an organized tour for guests, and we're actually going tonight, if you wanted to join. It's a full moon, which is the most magical time to see them."

"Magical, huh?" said Hazel, returning her gaze out the window.

"Have you ever read the story? *The Legend of Gossamer Falls*?"

Hazel shook her head. "I can't say I have."

"I bet there's a copy in here somewhere..." She started skimming the titles on the shelves below the TV. Suddenly, a book slipped off the shelf by the window, landing on the floor with a thud, making Hazel jump.

Autumn smiled. "Thanks, Grams."

"No way," Hazel said, shaking her head. "No way."

Autumn picked up the book, but then frowned. "Oh. Well, not the right one. But that's okay. She pointed us in the right direction," she said, sliding the book back onto the shelf and slipping another one off. It was old and worn, the fabric cover frayed at the edges. She handed to Hazel, who traced her fingertips across the gold-foiled title, faded and scratched with age and use.

"Anyway, you should read it."

Hazel nodded. "I think I will."

Autumn checked her watch. "I have to get going. But we're meeting out front at eight for the trip to the falls."

"Is it far?"

She shook her head. "No. It's only about a ten minute drive from here. Then we hike in, about another ten minutes. Don't worry, the path is paved and well-lit, so even though we're going at night, it's perfectly safe." Hazel nodded, and then Autumn continued. "If you're hungry, there's a restaurant attached to the hotel called Our Place. You can eat there or have food sent up. Alternatively, you can walk back down to the main strip and there are options there, too."

"Great, thank you."

Autumn started toward the door, but then turned, hesitating. "Hazel?"

"Yeah?"

"I'm glad you're here."

And then, with a funny little smile, she turned around and left Hazel alone in her room. She let out a sigh and sank down onto the cozy chair by the window, her attention held rapt by the riot of fall colors rippling before her. The clouds from earlier had mostly cleared, bathing the trees in a soft, golden light. It would be a clear night tonight, perfect for visiting the falls under the full moon.

Her gaze darted to her laptop bag on the bed, and that nagging sense of what she *should* be doing swamped her, and she sank back against the chair. She suddenly felt too heavy to do anything but sit in her snug room and just be. Besides, she knew that all that was waiting for her on her laptop was a blank page, increasingly frustrated emails from her editor and agent, and readers wondering if she would ever publish again. She didn't usually answer those emails because she didn't know what to tell them.

So she left her computer where it was, and returned her attention out the window, pulling in deep breaths and letting the fiery landscape soothe her anxiety. Looking around the room and out the window, it felt almost surreal that she'd been in New York City, the place she'd called home most of her adult life, just a few hours ago. Gossamer Falls felt so far removed that it was hard to believe it had only taken a short train ride north to get here.

She mused over the town's slogan: where magic happens. Did she believe in magic the way Autumn so clearly did? In signs and ghosts and legends?

She didn't know. Everything she'd experienced today could be chalked up to coincidences and timing. Drafts in an old mansion. Randomly picking a place out of a travel magazine. Finding an old book she'd loved long ago.

Maybe the better question was this: did she *want* to believe?

And the answer was that, yes. Maybe she did.

Maybe what Hazel needed most in the world was a little magic.

THREE

SUNDAY NIGHT DINNERS at the Shephard house were an all-hands-on-deck affair. Everyone was expected to bring something—wine, a side dish, a dessert—and no one was allowed to leave until the last dish was dried and put away. It was something they'd always done, a tradition that went back to when Adam's grandparents had still been around and they'd hosted everyone for the Sunday feast. After Gramps had died fifteen years ago, the tradition had shifted to his parents' house to alleviate the burden on Grams.

Adam had driven over with Autumn from the hotel just a couple of blocks away. After dinner, he'd drive her back so she could run her tour, and he'd head home to his cabin on the edge of town. On the edge of the Hudson Highlands, really. It was just secluded enough to feel cozy and private without being far from town and his family.

"You know, our new guest overheard you telling those ghost hunters to get lost," she said nonchalantly as they pulled up to the curb in front of the sprawling colonial where they'd both grown up. He knew what Autumn believed, and that was fine. But Adam knew for a fact that there was no such thing as ghosts. Just like there was no such thing as magic. It was a pretty story that brought people to the town, and for that he was grateful, but there wasn't more to it than that.

"Oh. I hope it didn't make a bad impression, or scare her off thinking the place might actually be haunted," he said as he shut off the ignition. Not that the hotel was hurting for guests—they weren't—but Adam hated the idea of making a bad impression on someone, especially a newly arrived guest who was staying for two weeks.

"I don't think so. She seemed more concerned than anything. I really like her, actually. Her name's Hazel, and she's from the city." She leaned in, elbowing Adam. "She's a famous writer."

His eyebrows went up at that. "Interesting."

"Isn't it?" she asked, a naughty gleam in her eye, and Adam had a feeling he knew what she was up to.

"No. Before you say anything more, before you ask, before you do anything, the answer is no." Adam had a hard and fast rule that he didn't get involved with hotel guests. Not only was it hugely unprofessional, but they were inevitably from out of town, so there was no hope of a future. And casual hookups weren't really his thing.

Autumn feigned shock. "I have no idea what you're talking about."

"Good." He swallowed, drumming his fingers on the steering wheel. "And thank you. For helping her get settled."

"That's what I'm here for." She beamed at him and he reached across and ruffled her hair, just like he'd done when they were kids. While Autumn was the baby of the Shephard family, Adam was the oldest, with fourteen years between them. But the gap didn't make them any less close. In fact, one of Adam's favorite childhood memories was when his parents had brought home that tiny bundle wrapped up in a soft pink blanket and told the boys that they finally had a sister, and that it was their job to look after her and protect her. He cleared his throat as it thickened at the memory of his parents, especially his dad.

There was a sudden, sharp rap of knuckles against his window, and Adam rolled his eyes, turning to look out his driver's side window. Gossamer Falls' chief of police stood there, still in uniform, looking every inch the part with his navy uniform and aviator sunglasses.

"What seems to be the problem, officer?" asked Autumn sweetly, comically batting her eyelashes at him.

"What are you guys talking about?" asked Jack Shephard, Adam's younger brother by two years. He leaned against the car, bracing his hand on the roof of Adam's Subaru. "Got any good gossip?"

"Please, you know a lot more town gossip than we do," said Autumn. "We deal with strangers all day."

"We were actually talking about you," deadpanned Adam, who never missed a chance to give his brothers a hard time. Granted, they all gave as good as they got.

"Oh, yeah? What about me?" he asked, taking off his aviators and narrowing his eyes at them.

"That you should definitely grow a mustache," said Autumn, eyes once again twinkling.

"Oh, yeah?" he repeated, stroking a hand over his clean-shaven jaw. "Is that what the ladies prefer? Mustaches?"

Autumn's grin grew, and just as she opened her mouth,

Adam shook his head. "Nope. I don't want to hear about mustache rides or whatever filth is about to come out of your mouth." It wasn't that Adam didn't appreciate filth—he did —just not from his baby sister.

"Aw, he hasn't had sex in a long time," said Jack in mock sympathy. "What's it been, like a decade?"

"Fuck off," Adam muttered, undoing his seatbelt and stepping out of the car, forcing Jack to take a step back. "It's not my fault you've poisoned the dating pool. Is there a single woman over thirty within a fifty-mile radius that you haven't hooked up with since your divorce?"

"Are you calling me a slut?" asked Jack, a smart ass smirk on his face.

"Hey, if the shoe fits," said Adam. Truly, he didn't care what his brother did with other consenting adults. It was just fun to give him shit for it.

Jack stepped a little closer. They were nearly the same size, with Adam only about an inch taller, but with Jack just as broad shouldered. They stared each other down for a second before laughing and hugging.

It hadn't been a decade since Adam had last had sex, but it had been a long time since he'd been with someone. Mostly because unlike Jack, or Beckett, who was twenty-seven and single, he didn't do one-night stands. He'd tried the meaningless sex thing, and it wasn't for him. For him, sex was emotional. It always had been, and it always would be. He wasn't able to compartmentalize the way Jack did, and sometimes he envied him for it.

Adam had had his share of serious relationships over the years, but none of them had ever worked out in the long term because of one simple fact: Adam loved Gossamer

Falls. This was where he'd been born, and it was where he was going to die. His family was here. His business was here. His entire life—a life he quite enjoyed, most of the time—was here. And the women he'd been in relationships with had always found Gossamer Falls lacking. Too small, too far from the city, too boring. Jenny had been ambitious, and there hadn't been much for her to do with her MBA here. Haley had found the town too boring to think about making a life here. Melissa had decided she wanted to see the world, with promises she'd come back after slaking her wanderlust. Spoiler alert: she hadn't. There'd been a few less serious ones that had ultimately fizzled out. Elizabeth, Christina, Laura. After his last relationship had died the slow painful death all long-distance relationships do about two years ago, he'd called it quits on dating entirely.

As sappy as it sounded, he wanted what his parents had had. What his grandparents had had. He wanted roots and stability and the comfort of trust and familiarity. And if he couldn't have that, then he'd make do on his own, and take solace in his family and the town he loved so much.

"Let's go inside," said Autumn, somewhat impatiently. "Mom said Oli's making his Bolognese sauce tonight and I want some before Beckett eats it all."

Adam grabbed a bag from the back that contained two bottles of red wine and a pumpkin pie from the town's bakery, and then they headed inside. His stomach let out a loud rumble as they all stepped through the unlocked door, the scents of garlic and fresh baked bread wafting in the air. Soft jazz—his mother's favorite—played through the speakers in the living room. The large foyer opened up onto a formal living room on the right, and a dining room that led to the kitchen was on the left. Straight ahead was a set of wood stairs that led to the four bedrooms, and beyond that, a cozy den that looked out onto the backyard. The house was large, but it always felt small when everyone was home. Currently, only his mother and Autumn lived in the house, but he knew his mother never thought about downsizing. She lived for these Sundays, when everyone—well, almost everyone—came together.

"Hi, Dad!" Chloe, Jack's eleven-year-old daughter, came barreling down the stairs and straight into her father, who received her with an exaggerated "oof!" sound as he wrapped his arms around her. "I have something to show you!" She pulled her newly acquired iPhone out of her pocket and practically shoved it in his face. "There's a rumor that Carrie Clark might film a music video in Gossamer Falls!" She jumped up and down and then tugged him into the kitchen.

A fire crackled in the living room as they passed, moving down the hall to the kitchen, where Oliver was chopping onions and his mother was humming along to the music while she tossed a salad. Beckett leaned against the island, nursing a beer.

"Oh good!" she said, looking up and wiping her fingers on the tea towel she'd tossed over her shoulder. "The rest of my babies are here."

Adam set the pie on the island, then bent to kiss his mother on the cheek.

"Hey, Mom," he said, passing her the two bottles of wine.

"Oh, thank you, honey. But what's everyone else going to drink?" she teased, dimples flashing. She reached up and ruffled Adam's curls, the ones he'd gotten from her, but where his were (mostly) still a dark brown hue, hers were heavily streaked with silver. She kissed Jack on the cheek and then moved to retrieve wine glasses from a cabinet in the corner, playfully bumping hips with her only grandchild as she did.

"You want some chocolate milk, honey?" she asked, and when Chloe nodded, she pulled down a glass for her, too.

"Hey, where's my kiss?" joked Autumn, and Julie turned, smushing Autumn's cheeks between her hands.

"Right here, even though I just saw you at lunch." She kissed the tip of Autumn's nose and they both laughed. Sometimes it amazed Adam that despite the fact that there were six Shepard children, their parents had always had more than enough love and attention to go around to make sure everyone felt seen and secure. To make sure each of them knew they were valued and appreciated for who they were.

Adam ambled over to where Oliver was tossing ingredients into a saucepan, pulling the heavenly aroma into his lungs. His stomach let out another loud rumble, and Oliver shot him a grin. It was nice to see him smiling more after all of the loss he'd endured over the past couple of years.

"I swear, that wasn't me," said Beckett, looking up from his phone. He had the same dark blond hair and light blue eyes as Jack. The same dark blond hair and blue eyes their father had had. The rest of the Shephards—Adam, Oliver, Finn, and Autumn—had their mother's chestnut curls and hazel eyes.

"Would you put that away?" said Julie, shaking her head as she carried the salad she'd just finished to the large table in the dining room. Given that there were so many of them, they'd always eaten around the old farmhouse table there.

"Just finalizing some plans," said Beckett, his brow furrowed. Adam had a feeling he knew what kind of plans Beckett was finalizing, and he was surprised at the pang of jealousy he felt. He wished he could be free like that, just have no strings attached fun. But that wasn't who he was. He was quiet and serious, like Oli. The flirty, outgoing genes seemed to be connected with the blond haired ones, although Autumn was outgoing and friendly, too. Then again, Autumn had never met a rule she didn't twist or outright ignore, depending on what suited her best.

"I'm going to make a no phones at Sunday dinner rule," she said, the *don't argue with your mother* tone they were all extremely familiar with creeping into her voice.

"Sorry," said Beckett, shoving his phone into his pocket.

"Can you chop those cremini mushrooms on the counter?" Oli asked, and Adam nodded. He wasn't the stellar cook that Oliver was, but he knew his way around the kitchen.

"School still going well?" he asked his brother, who taught art, history, and literature at the local high school.

Oliver nodded. "So far, yeah."

"Tell him about your show!" said Julie, returning from the dining room.

Autumn whirled around from where she'd been teasing Beckett. "Did you get into Skywalk?" she asked, her face lighting up as she mentioned the prestigious art show in Lake Placid every fall.

Oliver blushed slightly and then nodded. "Yeah, I did."

"Oli, that's amazing!" she said, running over and wrapping her arms around him.

"Congrats," said Adam, clapping his hand on Oliver's shoulder. While he loved teaching, Oliver's real passion was sculpting, and he had a real talent. A gift for making something out of nothing.

It was the kind of gift Adam had once thought maybe he'd had, too, but...no. He was fine where he was. He liked running the hotel. Liked using his hands to fix things and care for the building that meant so much to him and his family.

Chloe scooted by with her chocolate milk and disappeared into the den, a video of Carrie Clark playing on her phone.

"The fandom gene is strong with that one," he commented to Jack, who sighed.

"Tell me about it. Her room is plastered with posters —Carrie Clark, K-pop groups, Harry Styles. That kid loves music like you wouldn't believe."

"How are her piano lessons going?" asked Julie and Jack smiled, his pride evident.

"Good. She practices every night. I bought a keyboard so she can practice at my place, too, not just at Norah's."

Norah was Jack's ex-wife, and Adam was impressed at how they'd handled their split. They were on friendly terms and co-parented Chloe pretty seamlessly. They'd gotten married young, and had figured out that they were better off as friends than as husband and wife. Norah was happily dating a man named Ian, who worked as an architect a few towns over, while Jack was sleeping his way through the female population of upstate New York on the nights he didn't have Chloe. He was always careful to keep his personal life private where she was concerned.

Adam tossed the mushrooms he'd sliced into Oliver's saucepan and then accepted a glass of wine from his mom. She offered one to Autumn, but she shook her head.

"I'm taking a couple of guests out to the Falls for the full moon after dinner, so I'd better not." She leaned in closer to Julie. "Our newest guest is a famous writer."

FOUR

JULIE'S FACE LIT UP. "Really? How interesting." She glanced over at Adam, who pretended that he was too busy looking for oregano to notice.

"Maybe she could give Adam some tips," said Beckett, his grin falling when both Oli and Autumn shot daggers at him with their eyes.

"It's fine," he said quietly, because it was, mostly. Not every dream was meant to come true.

"I'm taking her to the Falls tonight along with the other guests," said Autumn, letting Beckett's comment lie.

"Maybe she'll write about getting kissed by the mist in her next book," said Julie, sipping her wine. "You'll have to make sure she gets a keychain or something to remind her."

"I don't think she'll need a keychain to remember," said Autumn. "It's a pretty unforgettable experience."

Julie sighed, a wistful expression on her face. Adam let Oli take back control of his sauce while he set about boiling water for the pasta. "It is. And I don't care what other people say. The legend is true."

Adam snorted. "No, it's not."

"How would you know?" shot back Autumn. "It's not like you've ever been."

"Maybe not. But I don't even know how many times you've been, and you're not exactly living it up with your true love."

Autumn held up her finger. "The legend doesn't say that you'll live happily ever after. All it says is that if you're kissed by the mist under the light of the full moon, your true love will be *revealed* to you before the next full moon."

"And has your true love been revealed to you?" Adam asked. Autumn's expression flickered, sadness pulling at her pretty features, instantly making him wish he could take it back.

"As a matter of fact, he has," she said quietly. "But it's...complicated."

"Do I need to beat someone up?" asked Beckett, bracing his palms on the island.

Autumn laughed, her eyes gleaming. "I'll let you know."

Conversation fell to regular topics as they finished getting dinner ready—hotel business, the changing season, the upcoming fall festival, books and movies. Finn, and if anyone had heard from him. As usual, no one had.

Once dinner was ready, they all carried it into the dining room. Adam avoided looking at the empty place at the far end of the table that had always been his father's spot. It had been just over two years since the sudden heart attack that had taken John Shephard's life, but for Adam, the pain was still so raw. So real and sharp and awful.

But at least he'd stayed. Unlike Finn, who hadn't been able to handle it and had run, burying himself in work and trying to single handedly solve the climate crisis. Adam thought Finn was a coward, afraid of his grief. Afraid to face the truth that their father was gone.

But he couldn't say that he'd faced his grief head on, either. Two years, and he'd never been to his father's grave, despite nagging from Autumn and gentle encouragement from his mom.

If Finn was a coward, then maybe so was he, just in a different way.

Beckett poked him in the arm, bringing him back to the present, offering him the basket of fresh baked bread slathered in garlic butter.

"You good?" he asked, helping himself to another piece once Adam had taken one. Somehow, Beckett managed to pack food away like he was still a teenager. "You seem quiet tonight, even for you."

Adam sighed and put some salad onto his plate. "Yeah, I'm good. Just a long day. Those stupid ghost hunters were back, and Autumn's trying to fix me up again, this time with a guest. But I'm good. The hotel is great, and I'm having Sunday dinner with my family. Life isn't perfect, but it's good."

And it was true. Even though he was forty years old, Adam couldn't imagine not having Sunday dinner with his family. They were his anchor.

They were his heart, right along with Gossamer Falls. Everyone and everything he needed was right in this room.

"What about you?" he asked, turning the tables on Beckett. "You good? You seemed really absorbed in that text convo earlier."

Beckett pushed a hand through his short hair, leaving it a bit dishevelled. "Yeah, it's all good. Nothing time won't fix."

"What did you do?"

He grinned sheepishly. "Juggled one too many dates."

"Rookie mistake," said Jack, and Beckett flipped him off.

"Hey, none of that at my dinner table," said Julie from the other end, rolling her eyes and biting back a smile.

"No middle fingers!" said Chloe around a mouthful of salad. "If I can't do it, you can't either, Uncle Beck."

He raised his hands in a placating gesture. "Fair enough."

"If anyone's the rookie here, it's you, not me," said Beckett, somewhat defensively. "I've been single way longer than you have."

"Maybe there's a reason for that," teased Autumn. Beckett made to throw a piece of garlic bread at her, but set it back down after a withering look from Julie.

Adam grinned. He loved that no matter how grown up and responsible they all became, they could still all tease and goad like they were kids again. It felt good. Like coming home, not just in a physical sense.

This sense of belonging, of having his heart connected with all of theirs, was another reason he'd never leave Gossamer Falls. His family and the town were everything to him, and always would be.

They ate and talked until their stomachs were full and the wine was nearly gone. They divided up the pumpkin pie Adam had brought, and his mom set out cupcakes from You Little Tart, the bakery on Main by Hemlock Square. Adam rubbed a hand over his flat stomach, knowing he'd pay for this on the rowing machine tomorrow. Not only was he forty, so was his metabolism.

"I need to get going to get organized for the tour," said Autumn, standing up from the table and stretching. "I'm going to have to grab a coffee in order to fight off this food coma. It was so good, Oli."

He raised his almost empty wine glass to her. "Thank you."

"Yes, compliments to the chef!" said Julie, and as was family tradition, they all balled up their paper napkins and pelted him with them while laughing, Chloe's laugh ringing out above everyone else's. Oli tried to bat them away, but gave up, letting out a mock shriek of indignation when one landed in his wine.

"I'll make you a travel mug," said Julie to Autumn. "What time do you think you'll be home?"

"Ten-ish?"

Julie nodded and cleared several plates, disappearing into the kitchen with them. While Autumn waited for her coffee, Adam helped to clear the table and then said his goodbyes, hugging his brothers and giving his niece a squeeze. Jack's radio crackled to life, a call about some kids spray painting a bench in Hemlock Square.

"Ooh, that's a serious one," said Adam, flashing his brother a grin. After everything Jack had been through in Iraq and Afghanistan, it was probably nice to have such low stakes problems to deal with.

Jack shook his head. "I swear to God, if it's Liam Miller and his little posse again, I'm gonna be real pissed after the break I cut them last time." He popped into the kitchen. "Mom, I gotta go to work. Is it cool if Chloe hangs out here until Norah can pick her up in an hour?"

"Of course it is. We can put a movie on."

"Can we make more friendship bracelets?" Chloe asked eagerly. "If Carrie Clark is really coming here to Gossamer Falls, we'll need a lot of them."

Julie laughed and nodded, and Jack kissed his mother on the cheek and headed out.

Autumn appeared beside him, travel mug in hand, the aroma of coffee in the air. "I'm ready."

After a final goodbye, they returned to Adam's Subaru. Night had fallen while they'd eaten, the white glow of the moon beaming down on the quiet street. A soft breeze rustled the crisp leaves, and Adam pulled in a deep breath of cool air before getting in the car. Spending time with his family was like refueling, like a battery recharging.

"Good night for the tour," he said as he steered them back toward the hotel, the moonlight touching absolutely everything, like a luminescent blanket.

"You should come," she said, her tone plain and sincere. There was no teasing or joking. Just a simple suggestion, and for a second, he thought about it. He'd never been, and the moon tonight was beautiful, with a clear sky, blanketed in stars surrounded by the soft velvet darkness.

"I don't think so," he said.

"Oh, come on," she said. "It's a Gossamer Falls tradition and you're like, Mr. Gossamer Falls. You know everything about this town, and you love it more than just about anyone. And yet, you've *never* done the falls under the full moon." She paused. "Why is that, Adam?"

He swallowed, curling his fingers around the steering wheel. "Because it's a silly tourist thing," he said. The lie stuck in his throat like a pill lodged sideways.

"What are you scared of?"

He didn't answer, and he focused on the road as they drove back to the hotel, which was no easy feat given the way Autumn was scrutinizing him the entire time. He pulled the car to a stop under the porte cochere.

"I think I know," she said, and he turned to look at her with what he hoped was a flat expression. "I used to think it was that you didn't believe in magic, or maybe just not in the idea of true love. But I don't think that's true."

"Yes, it is. I don't believe in legends or ghosts or magic. They're stories. Great stories, but that's all they are."

She grinned, shaking her head slowly. "I think you believe more than you'd like to let on." She leaned in closer. "I think you're scared that you'll find your true love, and she'll leave, just like the others. So you'd rather not know."

Her words slammed into him, tightening his chest.

"What's the point in knowing if they leave?" he asked quietly, and her expression softened.

"Because knowledge is power. And besides, maybe the one—the real one—won't want to leave. The real one will love Gossamer Falls as much as you do. The real one will love you the way you deserve."

Adam's throat thickened, and he coughed, the sound too loud in the quiet car.

"Enjoy your tour," he said, reaching across and opening her door for her.

"Oh, I most definitely will," she said, and with a wink, she took her coffee and stepped out of the car.

FIVE

HAZEL LOOKED up from the book in her lap to check the time, tossing the book aside and leaping to her feet when she realized she was supposed to be downstairs in just a few minutes to leave for the visit to Gossamer Falls. She'd been so engrossed in *The Legend of Gossamer Falls* that she'd totally lost track of time. She'd even forgotten to get something for dinner, and now her stomach was rumbling thunderously.

Her mind was whirling, buzzing, as she got her things together and rushed downstairs. She could just imagine Sarah Benjamin, the young Civil War widow from the story, in a house like this, skirts swishing as she rushed down the stairs at the sound of the front door, hoping for news of her husband, Union soldier Samuel. And eventually, news did come. The news she'd been dreading.

In the story, Sarah, heartbroken and alone, visits the town of Gossamer Falls with two other widows, looking for peace and healing. Solace in nature. Trying to understand how such senseless violence could take place on such a beautiful planet. Hazel had just gotten to the part about the actual legend—about being kissed by the mist under a full moon—when she'd had to put the book down.

Autumn greeted her with a smile as she came out onto the landing. "Ready? The others are already in the van."

Hazel nodded. "Yeah, sorry. I was reading and I lost track of time."

"Did you get to the part about the legend yet?" she asked. Autumn seemed to have this uncanny ability for knowing exactly what was going on in someone else's mind, like some kind of psychic spy.

"I just finished the first bit about it."

Autumn grinned. "Good. Because you're about to experience it for real."

Hazel suddenly froze. She wasn't someone who normally put much stock in ghost stories or legends or anything like that. But being here, in this place, with its sparkling, soothing energy and funny little coincidences had her second guessing her beliefs. Which meant, *if* the legend was true, and she was visiting the falls under a full moon, that within the next month, her "true love" would be revealed to her.

Did she want that? Was she ready for it? Even though the divorce was final and had been for over a year, things still felt very unfinished between her and Seth.

She knew that they weren't unfinished for him. He was currently dating Grace Visser, she of the blond hair and red lips and massively popular YA fantasy series. When she'd first met Seth through her agent, he'd told her he was completely disinterested in YA as a genre and preferred to focus on adult books.

He'd changed his mind when he'd met Grace and become her editor. It was as though he was starting his cycle all over again—the charming, handsome editor who makes the writer in his care swoon and fall for him. When she'd first started dating Seth, it had felt so terribly romantic—a writer and editor falling in love. And then he'd upgraded to Hazel 2.0. Grace was prettier, a little younger, far more successful. She was the new and improved version, and ultimately Seth had opted out of the marriage.

So now he was starting over with Grace. But this time, things were different, because Hazel was still in his orbit, given that he refused to transfer her to another editor. She knew she should make a stink about it. But standing up for herself wasn't something that came naturally to Hazel. She hated conflict hated making waves, hated inconveniencing others. Just the thought of it made her itchy and nauseous.

Her hands were also somewhat tied by the way the publishing world worked. Even though she was the creator of the work, ultimately the publishing house had all the control. The editorial and marketing teams made decisions without consulting her, and even if she didn't agree and her agent pushed back, ultimately they could do what they wanted. She hadn't realized before she was published just how predatory the industry could be. Writers poured their hearts and souls onto the page and hoped the publishing house would do right by the book.

Pushing the thoughts away, she stepped into the van and said hello to the others. Jeff was in his late fifties, gay, and a garden designer. Melvin and Viola were older, gray haired and slightly bent. Two women in their sixties, Beverly and Dolores, completed the group.

Hazel took the empty seat next to Jeff for the short drive to the falls.

"Hoping to find your true love?" she asked, and he laughed.

"Maybe, if there is such a thing."

"I know what you mean," she agreed.

Autumn put on some soft acoustic music for the drive, and the chatter died away as they drove through the town, the streets dark and sleepy, the businesses closed. After they'd passed Hemlock Square, she turned down Chestnut, and then right along a winding road that followed the edge of the Hudson Highlands.

Nestled into the trees at the edge of the forest, there was a cabin that caught Hazel's eye. It was beautifully built, and lit up from within, with white smoke curling from the chimney. An odd tingling sensation worked its way over her skin as she watched it recede into the darkness, followed by an overwhelming sense of wanting to go back. As though she belonged there.

Okay. This place was officially getting to her.

They rolled up to a small guardhouse with an illuminated green placard that welcomed them to Gossamer Falls. Autumn said something to the security guard, he laughed and then waved them through. They drove down a gravel road, passing by grassy areas dotted with picnic benches. Autumn pulled smoothly into a parking space and then hopped out, the guests following.

The sound of the waterfall filled the air, even though it wasn't visible yet, and Hazel pulled in a deep breath of crisp, fall air, excitement buzzing through her. Whether she believed in the legend or not, this was a cool experience, one she wouldn't likely forget. The gentle wind rustled the leaves in the trees, the dry rasp brushing over her face almost like a caress. Above, the moon shone down, illuminating everything in a soft glow, casting everything in shades of silver and pewter.

"The walk in is just under a mile, but it's easy terrain. Follow me, and if you have any questions just ask," said Autumn. They followed her as she headed left out of the parking lot, down a gently sloping grassy hill, and then along a paved path. The sound of the falls grew louder as they walked, and Hazel could feel the moisture in the air. She tried to imagine it as it would've been all those years ago when Mary Elizabeth Axton would've visited and been inspired to write her famous story.

A set of stairs appeared on their left, and Autumn guided them down. The stairs were concrete, wide and even, and all the breath whooshed out of Hazel's lungs at the sight before her. The stairs were flanked by silvery trees, while directly ahead was the waterfall, misty and glorious as it poured out of the craggy rocks surrounding it.

"It's bigger than I expected," said Hazel, marveling at the way the moonlight caught the mist and cast shiny moonbows that disappeared as quickly as they manifested.

"It's 215 feet high, which makes it over thirty feet higher than Niagara Falls," said Autumn proudly. "It's the highest single-drop waterfall east of the Rocky Mountains."

Halfway down the stairs was a lookout, and the group stopped there. Below, Hazel could see others closer to the falls. The scene before her was breathtaking, the moonlight glinting off of the falls, the creek below flowing rapidly, like liquid silver. The air was fresh and cool, with an almost sweet smell to it. Rocks and trees surrounded them, as though sheltering them from the rest of the world. Cocooning them in magic.

"Welcome to Gossamer Falls," said Autumn. "I'm going to give you a brief overview of the history and the legend, and then if you want to walk further down to be kissed by the mist, we can walk on the paved path that goes quite close to the base of the falls."

"To find our true love..." started Jeff, shifting back and forth on his feet, "do we have to like, make a wish or something?"

Autumn shrugged. "If you want. Personally, I think that you just have to believe." She let everyone enjoy the majesty of the falls for a moment before speaking again. "The town of Gossamer Falls was originally settled in 1730, but it was nothing more than a small settlement until the foundry opened in 1818. You probably saw it on your way into town, on the edge of the bay. It still stands, even though it's in ruins now. Some say it's haunted," she added with a gleam in her eye.

"By the 1840's, the foundry was building huge ships, and the influx of workers created more housing and businesses. Gossamer Falls officially became a village in 1846, more than a hundred years after the first settlements. The foundry produced munitions during the Civil War, as well as steam engines and pipework for New York City's water system. The community was built around the economic prosperity from the foundry.

"But at the turn of the century, the rise of steel making lessened the demand for cast iron, and in 1911, the foundry closed for good. If you want to learn more about that part of our history, the local museum has a large exhibit dedicated to the foundry and its impact on the evolution of the town. But the most interesting part of our history, I think, is the story written by Mary Elizabeth Axton.

"She visited Gossamer Falls in 1888, and was inspired to write her tale. Some say she wrote it as a way of explaining what happened to her here, as she is said to have visited the falls under a full moon and within six months was married. Everyone should have a copy of the story in your rooms back at the inn, but I'll summarize it quickly for you now, and then we can go down for a closer look." She took a breath and a sip of coffee from her travel mug. "Oh, that reminds me. If you're interested, we'll have hot chocolate and decaf coffee in the main lounge around the fire when we get back to the inn. Anyway, the legend," she said, glancing over her shoulder at the falls.

"The *Legend of Gossamer Falls* is about a young Civil War widow named Sarah Benjamin who visits the falls after the death of her husband. She feels the mist of the falls on her face and describes it like the tears of angels weeping with her for her lost love. With her heart open, she wishes for a new love, a true love. And the following week, she meets a handsome doctor, to whom she's engaged before the next full moon."

"And what do you believe?" asked Dolores, arms crossed, a skeptical slant to her mouth. "Do you think the magic is real? Or did the story's popularity make people see what they wanted to see?"

Hazel felt a little uncomfortable at Dolores' confrontational tone, but it didn't seem to faze Autumn at all.

"Obviously no one knows for sure if magic is real or not.

It's like faith—it's real to those who believe, even without proof. Personally, I think life is short. Why not invite a little magic in?" And with that, she turned and started down the rest of the stairs that led to the paved path.

Melvin and Viola stayed huddled together at the lookout while the rest of the guests followed Autumn down the remaining steps. Hazel glanced over her shoulder at them, her heart twisting itself into a knot at the sight of their wrinkled fingers intertwined. She'd thought she'd found that, once. She'd thought that she and Seth would grow old together. She wouldn't have married him if she hadn't seen a future for them.

Now, she just felt like a fool for thinking happy endings existed outside of books and movies. Not ones where men and romance were concerned.

Which, okay, yes, sounded very jaded. But her heart had been battered and bruised, then pureed in a blender. Slowly, she'd been trying to piece it back together, but it was never going to be the same. It couldn't be, because she wasn't the same.

And yet here she was, reading stories about magical waterfalls and true love and it was hard not to get swept up in the magic of it all. New York was lots of things—glamorous, loud, exciting, big—but it wasn't magical. Not like this. Hazel could see how a place like this would inspire someone to believe in things like legends and ghosts and true love.

Hazel could feel the moisture in the air intensifying, and the roar of the falls grew, drowning out all other sound. The paved path ended, and there was a rocky outcropping a few others were standing on.

"It's safe to stand on the rocks, just tread carefully," said Autumn, hanging back. "It can be a little slippery."

Slowly, Hazel moved closer and closer to the falls. Everything was bathed in moonlight. Glowing. Ethereal. Beautiful and far more perfect than anything humans had ever made. The air felt different so close to the falls. It felt... transformative. It felt hopeful.

"So, Hazel, single and not looking," said Autumn quietly from beside her. "What do you think?"

She smiled at Autumn. She felt as though she'd known her so much longer than just a few short hours. There was already an easy familiarity that, if they'd met in Manhattan, would've made Hazel instantly distrustful. But, things felt different here.

"I think it's beautiful, and I think the story is compelling. I was reading it in my room before we left, and I skipped dinner because I needed to get through it."

"But do you believe?"

She hesitated, biting her lip. "I don't know."

Autumn tipped her head towards the falls, where a spot closer to the edge of the rushing creek had opened up. "Maybe you need to test it for yourself."

"Seeing is believing?"

Autumn grinned at her. "Something like that."

Hazel took a step forward, but then hesitated again. What if the legend was true? What if her true love was going to be revealed to her before the next full moon? Was she ready for that? She rubbed a damp palm over the back of her neck, feeling almost dizzy with the sudden shot of anxiety rocketing through her. The idea of being with someone again filled her with a sense of panic.

Autumn's eyebrows rose as they made eye contact, and while she felt comfortable with her, she wasn't ready for full blown, ugly, messy honesty.

"I...was with my ex for several years. The idea that I'd have to be naked in front of someone new for the first time kinda makes me want to throw up."

Autumn laughed, the sound echoing off of the stones for a second before being swallowed up by the white noise of rushing water.

"But if it's with the right person...the perfect person, which your ex clearly wasn't..." she shrugged. "Getting naked might not be so scary."

Hazel swallowed, not entirely sure she agreed with Autumn. She closed her eyes and sucked in a breath, the air cool and damp as she pulled it into her lungs.

She was tired of being scared. Tired of being alone. Tired of feeling lost, like a boat without an anchor, endlessly floating and at the mercy of any current that came her way. But she was also terrified of getting hurt again.

She thought about Sarah Benjamin, who'd loved and lost. Who'd visited the falls, been kissed by the mist, and found her true love. Maybe the reason she was so drawn to the story—she'd forgotten to *eat* she'd been so engrossed in it, and Hazel loved food—was because it was like a beacon of hope. A promise that there was more waiting for her, if she just opened herself up to it.

She pulled in another deep breath, and then stepped closer to the falls. The mist landed gently on her face, speckling her with fresh, clean water. A sense of peace came over her, and she looked up at the full moon, hazy through the veil of moisture. The sense of peace grew, the tightness in her muscles easing as a soft smile spread across her face. Her limbs felt pleasantly heavy, as though she could stay right in that spot for hours and be content. As though it was exactly where she was supposed to be. No one spoke, or if they did, their voices were muted by the pounding of the falls, the sound enveloping her.

And then, she heard it. The faintest whisper, right in her ear.

Make your wish

Find your love

She whirled, but there was no one near her. Not near enough to whisper right in her ear. A warm sensation worked its way through her chest and down her spine, making her feel as though she was melting into this place.

"I want to find my true love," she whispered, and tears sprang to her eyes. She let the tears fall, overcome with emotion. Overcome with the beauty of this place, with a sense of hope and renewal.

Conscious of not wanting to monopolize a prime spot, she stepped back, the mist still clinging to her cheeks, her eyelashes, her hands. She didn't want to wipe it away. If magic was real, it lived here, and she wanted to absorb as much of it as possible.

It was unlike anything she'd ever experienced in her thirty-nine years, and she knew she'd never forget it.

Less than an hour later, they were back at the Shephard Inn, their little group quiet, as though everyone was processing their own experience at the falls. They'd returned to steaming mugs of hot chocolate and decaf coffee, just as Autumn had promised, and were gathered around the gently crackling fire in the lounge.

Hazel curled her fingers around her mug, letting the warmth seep into her. A sense of contented drowsiness was pulling at her, and she knew she'd have to go back to her room soon. But she wasn't ready quite yet. Tonight felt special, and she wasn't ready to end it. She felt as though something was shifting inside her. A sense of openness she hadn't experienced in a very long time was expanding in her chest, making her want to try new things, explore new ideas, and keep an open mind about things like ghosts and magic.

She'd only been here for a few hours, but already, Gossamer Falls was leaving its mark on her.

"That was...not what I was expecting," said Jeff quietly from beside her, sipping at his hot chocolate. A fleck of whipped cream clung to his lip, and he wiped it away with the back of his hand.

"Do you feel different?" Hazel asked, leaning back into the impossibly comfortable couch.

"I do. I can't explain it. I feel more..." He trailed off, his face scrunched as he tried to find the words.

"Hopeful?" she suggested, and he nodded.

"Yeah. That's it, exactly. Hopeful. I don't know what it is about this place, but it's different."

"It's special," Hazel agreed. Melvin and Viola sat together on one of the loveseats, murmuring softly as they gazed at the fire. Even skeptical Dolores seemed subdued, sitting quietly in an armchair while Beverly talked to Autumn about the selection of books in the lounge.

"Can you imagine, if this was everyday life?" asked Jeff quietly. "Books and magic and warm drinks by a fire? The most breathtaking scenery you've ever laid eyes on, conversations with kind people, shopping in adorable little stores?"

Hazel laughed softly and shook her head. "I can't, actually. It seems too good to be true."

"I keep waiting for Lorelai Gilmore to poke her head around the corner."

Hazel laughed into her hot chocolate. "I know exactly what you mean." She took a sip, the chocolate velvety and luxurious on her tongue. It warmed her all the way down, and even though her limbs felt heavy and tired, she also felt at peace for the first time in a long time.

Maybe now the words would finally start flowing.

She chatted with Jeff a little more as they finished their drinks, and once her mug was empty, she placed it on the tray Autumn had left on the large table in front of the couch.

"I'm going to head up to bed," she said to her new friend, and she realized then that that's exactly how she was thinking of Autumn—like her new friend. She couldn't remember the last time she'd connected with someone so easily. Everyone in the city was so closed off, so absorbed in their own lives and problems. Too wrapped up in their own lives and ambitions to ever look outwardly at those around them.

Autumn nodded, sending her a warm smile. "Sleep well, Hazel."

She made her way back up to her room and flicked on the light, casting a soft, warm glow around the room. The floorboards creaked quietly beneath her feet as she padded across the room to turn on the gas fireplace. It flared to life and she smiled. She moved to close the curtains, and then paused. Normally, she'd never leave the curtains open after dark, but here, she wanted to let the morning light in, and besides, it's not like anyone could see her up here.

She changed into her favorite pair of comfy pajamas and then dimmed the lights and climbed into bed, leaving the fireplace on for now, enjoying the play of light and shadow it created from the corner and the gentle warmth that it was spreading through her room. Her eyelids were heavy and she didn't feel like reading, but she wasn't quite ready to say goodbye to the day yet, so she curled up in bed and turned on the TV. It was a smart TV, with access to multiple streaming services, and she was drawn to the ones she didn't have. She opened up Disney Plus and immediately knew what to watch, tucking the blankets around her as the opening strains of *Hocus Pocus* played. She couldn't remember the last time she'd watched this movie, but it had been one of her favorites growing up.

She glanced over at her nightstand, where the slim volume of *The Legend of Gossamer Falls* sat on top of the brick that was *The Mists of Avalon*.

Funny how she'd had to come to a new place to start finding her old self again.

SIX

THE NEXT MORNING, Adam arrived at the Shephard Inn bright and early, as usual. He'd always been a morning person, and during the time he'd been a writer, he'd gotten used to getting up at five AM to get his words in before heading to the hotel. By the time he arrived around 7:30 or 8, his father had already been there for at least an hour, going through his usual morning routine as the hotel's manager.

Things were different now—his father was gone and Adam was the manager, and he hadn't written anything in a long time—but he was so used to getting up early that it was ingrained in him.

It was shortly after six when he stepped inside the quiet lobby, turning on lights as he moved toward the front desk. Jamie, the older woman who worked the desk at night, yawned and scrubbed a hand over her face, smiling wearily at the sight of Adam.

"Quiet night?" he asked, and she nodded.

"Not a peep."

He smiled at her and tipped his head toward the door. "I'm here now. I know you're on until seven, but you can head home. I'll sign you out at seven."

She smiled gratefully and laid a hand on his forearm. "You're one of the good ones, Adam Shephard. Just like your dad."

Adam's smile faltered slightly at the mention of his father. He hated how raw that still was. Hated how stuck he felt in his grief.

"Get some sleep," he said, his voice a little hoarse, and he cleared his throat. Jamie seemed oblivious to the effect of her words on him, and she yawned again.

"Gladly. See you tonight." She worked the front desk from eleven at night until seven in the morning Sunday to Thursday, and Adam was grateful for her and how reliable she was. Overnight help wasn't easy to find in a small town, but the schedule suited Jamie just fine. She spent her nights reading and knitting, went home and slept, and then watched her grandkids after school.

She signed off the computer and then gathered her things, flicking a tired wave over her shoulder. Adam logged himself on and took a quick look at the day ahead. It was going to be a quiet one, with no checkouts and no new arrivals. He checked his email quickly for anything urgent, and then began his daily walkthrough of the hotel, starting with the lounge. He arranged a few of the throw pillows on the leather sofas, straightened a picture on the mantel. He loved this room, with its warm wood beams crisscrossing the ceiling, the gently worn leather furniture, the wall of books.

He frowned when he noticed two books sitting on a side table near one of the arm chairs, stacked haphazardly on top of each other. His frown deepened when he saw what they were, the familiar covers making him swallow hard. He picked the first one up, tracing his fingers over the embossed lettering.

The Wicked Season: A Robert Brady Mystery

By Adam Shephard

He thumbed through the pages, the scent of paper and ink wafting up. The urge to sit down and open it, to let his eyes rove over the words he'd written almost ten years ago, was strong. But he knew what lay down that road. Regret and bitterness, a feeling of failure. The death of a dream. Hope dashed, and a passion lost.

He cleared his throat again, and without looking at the second book, he slipped them back on the shelves. Maybe someone else would read and enjoy them, even if all he saw was disappointment when he looked at them.

Pushing all of it aside, he stepped out of the lounge and continued down the hall toward the restaurant at the back of the hotel. The dining room had originally functioned as a greenhouse or conservatory, and it still had the same curved glass ceiling. The sun wasn't up yet, but the sky was lightening, morphing from black to a soft blueish gray. The chairs were still stacked on top of the tables and the lights were off, but Adam could hear the sounds of softly clanking pots and pans from the back. He moved between the round tables and to the swinging doors that led to the kitchen.

Logan Huxley, known by almost everyone as Hux, was the restaurant's head chef, and Adam was surprised to see him in so early. He normally left the breakfast shift to his staff and handled the lunch and dinner rushes himself.

"You're in early," he said, leaning against the wall.

Hux shrugged, then shoved up his sleeves, exposing the colorful tattoos on both of his forearms. "Couldn't sleep. Figured I might as well go do something useful." He held up the gleaming copper pan in his hand, clearly the recipient of a vigorous scouring.

Adam tilted his head, studying the slightly younger man. He'd known Hux since they were kids. He'd been best friends with Adam's brother Finn ever since kindergarten. He wondered if he heard from Finn more often than they did, but he figured Hux would tell him if he had something to share about Finn.

"Everything okay?"

"Yeah. Just…nothing I can't handle."

Adam's eyebrow arched. "You know if you need help, we've all got your back."

Hux hadn't grown up in a warm, loving family the way Adam had. He'd been raised mostly by his grandmother here in Gossamer Falls, with occasional stints all over the country with his mom—when she took an interest—or his biker father, when it was convenient for him. Adam didn't know what he'd do without the support system of his mom and his siblings. He couldn't imagine it.

Hux flashed him a tired grin and pushed a hand through his dark hair. "All good, man. Life's just shit sometimes, you know? And even when there's nothing you can do about it, it still…" He paused. "It eats at you."

Adam pushed off the wall and crossed to Hux, laying a hand on his shoulder. "Sounds rough."

"I…" He trailed off and then shook his head, and Adam recognized the look of a man pushing away shit he didn't want to think about because he did it, too. "Heard from Finn lately?"

Adam shook his head. "No. I mostly keep up with him on his YouTube channel."

"Me too."

Finn Shephard was an independent documentarian with a journalism degree from NYU. He'd always been passionate about the environment and conservation, and he made a living from his YouTube channel where he created mini-documentaries about various eco issues.

"Last I saw, he was somewhere in Alaska."

"Yeah, up in the fucking tundra, picking flowers." Hux didn't try to hide the bitterness in his voice, and Adam couldn't blame him. They all felt abandoned by Finn, even if they understood that it was what he needed to do. Hux snorted. "Has he at least reached out to Sienna?" he asked, bracing his hands on the stainless steel counter top.

Adam shook his head. "I don't think so, but you'd have to ask Autumn. She's friends with her."

Sienna and Finn had been together for about a year and a half when he'd taken off shortly after their father's death. According to Autumn, she'd thought he was going to propose. Instead, he'd left.

An easy silence fell between the two men and then Adam crossed to the coffee maker and poured himself a cup, adding just a splash of milk and then stirring it. When he crossed back towards where Hux was standing, he laid his hand on the man's shoulder again.

"Seriously. If you need anything...time off, money, a friendly ear, I've got you. You don't need to tell me what it is."

Hux sighed. "I might need some time off. I have some shit to figure out...with my dad."

Adam nodded and gave Hux's shoulder a friendly squeeze. "Anything you need, man. We'll figure out the restaurant."

Hux nodded, looking slightly less world weary than when Adam had first stepped into the kitchen, and he considered that a win. He took a sip of his coffee and started toward the swinging doors.

"Hey, Adam," Hux called and Adam turned, catching the swinging door with his foot before it smacked him.

"Yeah?"

"Thanks. For being..." He shook his head. "Just...thanks."

Adam smiled. "Welcome."

He walked back through the hotel as the light filtering in through the windows lightened, revealing a pale, overcast sky that promised cool air and possibly rain. He set out the newspapers in the lounge, turning on a few lights as he went, and then headed toward the sunroom at the back that looked out over the grounds. A wall of French doors led out onto a covered patio where he and Autumn had hung a few hammocks. She'd decorated the space for fall with pumpkins of various shades and sizes, and several outdoor lanterns with electric candles were strewn about. A large fireplace sat on the edge of the space, and Adam frowned slightly when he noticed that the metal bin that normally held firewood was empty. He'd have to chop some later.

Autumn kept trying to convince him to chop wood in a plaid flannel shirt so that she could take a video for their social media, saying something about a "hot lumberjack vibe."

He'd told her no. Obviously.

He stepped back inside, sipping his coffee as he walked slowly down the hall, making sure everything was as it should be. Just as he slipped behind the front desk, the phone started to ring.

"Front desk, Adam speaking," he answered, setting his coffee down on the desk, watching the steam rise in swirling whorls.

"Oh, um, hi. I'm so sorry to bother you so early. This is Hazel Woodward in room two."

Ah, the famous writer. "It's not a bother at all. What can I help you with, Miss Woodward?" There was silence on the other end of the line. He frowned slightly, glancing down at the display screen on the phone's cradle to make sure the call was still connected. It was.

"Miss Woodward? You still there?" he asked, and then he heard a shuddery breath on the other end of the line.

"Yeah. Sorry. Um. Your voice is…wow, okay. I clearly cannot function without coffee. The reason I called is that I think there's something wrong with the shower in my room. I can't figure out how to turn it on. I'm not sure if it's user error, or…"

Adam grinned. Was she flustered? Just by the sound of his voice? What on earth had Autumn been filling her head with?

"I'll be up in just a moment. Can I bring you a coffee as well?"

She let out a sound that sounded almost like a moan. "Please."

"Be up in a minute."

He headed back to the kitchen and quickly poured a steaming cup of coffee, then grabbed a few packets of sugar and containers of milk from the fridge before snagging his tool chest from his office. Less than five minutes later, he was knocking on the door of room two.

SEVEN

"IT'S ADAM SHEPHARD," he called, and the door swung open.

If he was a smart man—and he usually thought he was—he would've googled Hazel Woodward before coming up here. Maybe then he could've prepared himself. He could've done something to brace himself for the sight of an adorably sleep rumpled woman wearing nothing but a white robe. Her golden brown hair fell just past her shoulders and stuck up at the back of her head. She peered at him with enormous brown eyes from behind large black-framed glasses, blinking slowly enough that he could appreciate the way her thick eyelashes fanned against the tops of her rounded cheeks. A small smile pulled at her full lips and she stepped back slightly.

But he hadn't prepared, and now he was staring. Staring at Hazel, with her golden hair and golden skin and golden everything. His stomach did a slow turn, and he knew he really needed to stop staring, but he couldn't seem to tear his eyes away.

"Hi," she said, and then cleared her throat, her cheeks going pink as she stared at him, her eyes roving from his face and down his body and then back up again. "*You're* Adam."

"I am," he nodded. "And you're Miss Woodward."

"Hazel. Just Hazel, please."

A heartbeat passed between them as they both stared.

"Can I come in? I have coffee," he said, holding up the mug in his hand.

"Gimme," she said, practically lunging forward and taking the mug from his hands. She took a long swallow before he could say, "I have milk and sugar if you want."

She shook her head. "Black is fine. Thank you. So, um, the shower..." She gestured toward the open door of the bedroom. Her eyes met his, and it was like an electrical current passed between them.

Jesus fucking Christ, Hazel was beautiful. She was the kind of beautiful that inspired art, that inspired poetry.

That inspired all kinds of things Adam wouldn't allow himself to entertain because she was a guest at the hotel, which meant she was completely off limits. Because she was from out of town, and he'd already read that book. He knew how that story ended.

"Right. Let me see what I can do, but if it's truly out of commission, we can move you to another room right away."

"Oh," she said, sounding a little disappointed. "Well, I hope you can fix it, because I love this room. I had the best sleep of my life last night."

Adam grinned as he hefted the tool box in his hands and moved toward the bathroom. "I'm glad to hear it."

He rolled up the sleeves of his gray Henley and started

fiddling with the knobs. Sure enough, nothing happened. Hazel leaned against the door jamb, arm banded across her waist as she sipped her coffee, humming appreciatively. When he glanced at her, she lifted her gaze from his ass and blushed.

"Really good coffee," she said, but there was a hint of flirtiness to it that had him blushing in return.

Did women flirt with him regularly? Yes. Yes, they did. Did any of them look like Hazel Woodward, with her warm brown eyes and big smile and adorably oversized glasses? No. No, they most definitely did not.

"I'm just going to take a look to see if the valve is broken," he said, doing his best to concentrate on what he was doing.

"The valve?" she asked, still watching him.

"There's a rubber ring around the valve that can get corroded. If the shower's not turning on, that might be the culprit. But, if the actual cartridge is broken, I'll need to replace the entire valve, and I'm not sure I've got the parts handy."

"I see," she murmured, her lips pursing as she blew steam away from the rim of her mug, and he dropped the wrench in his hand with a loud clang.

"Sorry," he muttered, ducking down to retrieve it, and then smacking his head on the faucet. Hard.

"Oh my God!" Hazel said, moving toward him as embarrassment licked at his body like flames. "Are you okay?" she asked, stepping over the toolbox. He pressed a hand to his head, wincing slightly.

"Unless you can die of embarrassment, I think I'll live."

She rolled her lips inward, clearly biting back a smile as she stepped into the tub with him, laying a hand on his shoulder. "Let me see."

He slowly lowered his hand from his throbbing head, forgetting the pain entirely when she gently probed at his scalp with her long fingers. "I don't feel a bump," she said quietly, and their eyes met.

Another one of those electrical currents passed between them, making the air feel charged and alive. Adam couldn't remember the last time he'd responded this way to a woman he'd just met.

He was pretty sure he never had, actually. Was this what people meant when they talked about sparks? About hearts skipping a beat?

She smiled softly at him, her fingers still in his hair. He smiled back, fighting back the urge to lean into her touch like some kind of affection starved cat.

And then the shower turned on. Warm water pelted them both, making Adam groan and Hazel laugh in delight.

"You fixed it!" she said, removing her hand from his hair and looking up at the showerhead. When she looked back down, his heart slammed against his ribs. Water was dripping down her hair, over her face, slipping off of her nose and lips. They were so close that he could see the smattering of freckles on the bridge of her nose, the flecks of gold in her eyes.

Kiss her, the water seemed to hiss. He noticed that she was staring at his mouth as warm water soaked them. She leaned forward, so close that he could feel the wet fabric of her robe against him and then…reached behind him and turned the shower off.

"Sorry," he said, wishing he'd thought to do that. Duh.

"Don't be. You fixed it," she said softly. He really needed to stop staring at her mouth. This was so inappropriate and unprofessional and bad. Bad, bad, bad.

God, maybe if he'd just go out and get laid the way Jack and Beckett did, he wouldn't be drooling over the first pretty woman who'd touched him that he wasn't related to.

"At least we know it works," she said a little breathlessly as she pushed to her feet. She stepped out of the tub, leaving a little puddle on the tiled floor. Her white robe was plastered to her body, leaving absolutely nothing to the imagination. The fabric clung to her full breasts and the flare of her hips, emphasizing her feminine curves. The tips of her dark pink nipples poked against the fabric and Adam wasn't sure if his head was swimming because he'd slammed it against the faucet, or because all of the blood in his body was moving south.

"Sorry," he said again, wishing he could think of something else to say. But there wasn't enough blood in his brain to make it work. His clothes stuck to him uncomfortably as he pushed to his feet, trying to subtly adjust the bulge in his soaked jeans. She sucked in a sharp breath as her eyes skimmed over his body and the way his shirt was plastered to his chest. He rubbed a hand over his stomach in an attempt to conceal himself, somehow.

"Nothing to apologize for," she said, handing him his wrench, then crossing her arms over her breasts, her cheeks a shade of pink that made him want to pull her into his arms.

He stood to his full height and rubbed his hands down his thighs, instead. "Well, if there's nothing else I can do for you, I think I'll leave now with what remains of my dignity."

Her gentle laugh was like sunshine, warm and soft, and for a second, he forgot that he was sopping wet.

"Don't be embarrassed. It's not every day a man makes me wet without even trying." Her eyes went wide and she slapped a hand over her mouth. "Oh my God. Can we pretend I didn't say that? I don't normally...say..." She glanced at him, wincing slightly, her cheeks bright pink. "Well. There goes my dignity, too, so I guess we're even."

He laughed, warmth filling him up, and he shook his head, sending droplets sliding down from his hair—which would be a mess of curls now, thanks to the water—and over his neck. She tilted her head, seemingly following their path, and drawing his attention to the long swoop of her delicate neck.

He cleared his throat and gathered up his tool box. The room felt warm, almost dizzying. "I'll be at the front desk if you need anything. It was nice to meet you, Hazel."

She grinned at him. "Likewise, Adam."

He trudged down the hall and back to the stairs, his boots squelching as he walked. When he reached the front desk, Autumn was standing there, arranging chrysanthemums in a vase.

"What the hell happened to you?" she asked, eyeing him with an arched eyebrow.

"I took a shower with Hazel Woodward," he deadpanned, and Autumn jumped on the spot and clapped her hands together.

"I knew it! I knew it!"

"Don't get too excited," he said, stepping behind the desk and putting his toolbox back in his office. He opened a small closet and pulled out a spare shirt and pair of jeans. "I was just fixing her shower."

"I know, but Adam, last night she went to the falls under the full moon, and she—"

He stepped out from his office, peeling his wet shirt off over his head. "Autumn," he said, his voice low. "The legend isn't real."

She stepped behind the desk, her arms crossed in front of her, her floral arrangement forgotten. "Yes, it is."

"No, it's not. And you know I don't get involved with hotel guests." He pulled his dry shirt on over his still slightly damp skin. "So whatever it is you're doing or you're trying to do, stop. Please."

"But what did you think of her? Isn't she pretty?" she asked, and heat licked at his insides as he remembered just how pretty Hazel was. The lust that had slammed into him earlier hadn't dissipated yet, still simmering low in his gut.

"I didn't notice. I was busy fixing the shower."

"Adam Shephard, you are such a liar!"

He quickly swapped his wet jeans for dry ones, grimacing when he realized he didn't have dry boxers to change into. This would have to do until he could go home at lunch and change.

"Don't you have something to do?" he asked, squinting at her as he stepped out of the office. "Tours to arrange? Pillows to fluff? A different brother to pester?"

She continued as though she hadn't heard him. "And she's a writer, too. And she's so sweet and I think she has a good sense of humor. I also think she's been hurt in the past, and…"

He tuned out then, his stomach clenching, cold and hard, at the thought of someone hurting Hazel. Who he didn't even know. Who was a guest at his hotel. In a couple of weeks, she'd be nothing but a memory.

"…find what she's looking for," finished Autumn breathlessly. "Which I think, is you. You just don't know it yet. But trust me, once the magic starts to do its thing, there's nothing you can do. Just go along for the ride."

"You're a nut," he said, pointing a finger at her. "Why don't you go see if Hux needs any help in the restaurant?" He lowered his voice, gentling his tone. "He's having a tough time, and he might have to take some time off soon. I'm sure he could use a friend."

Autumn licked her lips, swallowing visibly. "Right, a friend. Sure."

Adam stared at her expectantly.

"Fine, I'll go. But only because I'd rather drool over Hux's food and tattoos than argue with your stubborn ass anymore." She stuck her tongue out at him and spun on her heel, heading for the restaurant.

Adam shook his head, letting the *drooling over tattoos* comment slide. He accepted that Autumn was a grown woman, and that she probably had a sex life that he—thank God—knew nothing about. But as far as Adam was concerned, no matter how old they got, she would always be his baby sister.

He sighed and pushed a hand through his damp hair, his mind flashing back to the way Hazel had gently threaded her fingers into it, checking for a bump. The still simmering lust ramped back up, even though he did his best to ignore it. To push it away. Because while Hazel was beautiful and sweet and honestly pretty fucking charming, for the good of his own battered heart, nothing could happen.

Legends and myths and whatever else be damned.

EIGHT

HAZEL STARED at the blinking cursor on the screen in front of her. The blank page filled up the entire screen of her laptop, and the longer she stared at it, the more anxious she felt. She had four chapters of...well, honestly, of total crap. With a frustrated sigh, she clicked back to her notes, reading over the character sketches and plot notes she'd made for this book. Usually, returning to her notes gave her clarity, or at the very least, she could figure out a place to start. But looking at the pages and pages of notes—notes that had taken her weeks and weeks to put together—she didn't feel anything except anxiety and frustration and the gnawing sense that this story just wasn't working.

The concept was solid—two vampires fated to find each other again and again across time—but the characters felt flat. The chemistry, the supposed bone-deep connection between them wasn't coming through, and she didn't know how to fix it.

Maybe she just didn't know how to write about love anymore. She'd written the second book of her trilogy—the most romantic of the three—while falling madly in love with Seth. But now that she knew how that love story ended, the magic was gone, and she couldn't find it within herself to write about sparks and passion and racing hearts.

She'd hoped that if she got out of the city and away from everything that was weighing on her, that the words would start flowing. But while she was quickly falling in love with the town of Gossamer Falls, the words were still very much stuck. She blew out a breath, closed the lid of the laptop and flopped back onto the bed, spread out like a starfish as she stared at the ceiling. She turned her head to the side, her gaze landing on the little stack of books on her nightstand.

The slim volume containing *The Legend of Gossamer Falls* sat on top. She'd finished it last night, and she was already planning on re-reading it. There was something about the story that spoke to her—the magic, the hope, the healing after grief—it was special.

The phone on her bedside table started ringing, startling her out of her thoughts. Immediately, her heart leapt into her throat; she hoped it was Adam. Sexy, droolworthy Adam Shephard, with his dark curls and dimpled smile, his broad shoulders and arms the size of tree trunks. Seriously, the guy looked like he lifted refrigerators, not weights. And his voice, oh God, his voice. Deep and melodic, smooth, almost lilting. She could listen to him read a thesaurus and never get bored.

She'd thought she wasn't interested in dating after the way her marriage had gone down in flames, so she was surprised to find that she was, in fact, *very* interested in Adam Shephard. She didn't really know if anything would come of it, especially given that she was just visiting. What she did know was that she was crushing. Hard.

"Hello?" she asked, trying and failing not to sound overexcited, because now she was remembering the way his wet Henley had clung to his muscular torso.

"Hey, it's Autumn. I'm finished early for the day, so I was wondering if you'd be into grabbing a late lunch and seeing some of the town. Unless you're busy, of course," she added.

"No! I'm not busy at all," said Hazel, pushing up off the bed. "And that sounds perfect. I'd love to see more of the town."

"Great. I'll meet you in the lobby. Ten minutes?"

"Perfect."

Hazel quickly changed out of her oversized sweatshirt and leggings and into a cute off-white sweater and a pair of jeans. She brushed her hair, slicked on a coat of mascara and a little blush, and then grabbed her jacket and her purse. As she made her way down the stairs, her heart picked up its tempo slightly. Then, at the sound of Adam's voice, it pushed right up into her throat.

"...for four nights? Let me see what's available," he said, and she could see him typing on the computer behind the front desk, the phone cradled between his ear and his shoulder. Their eyes met, and she lifted her hand in a wave. He'd been so adorably flustered earlier, and Hazel had wanted to jump up and down and squeal with delight at the thought that a man like Adam Shephard would get all twisted up over her.

He smiled at her and she bit her lip, trying to think of something to say to him when he finished his phone call. He stopped typing and picked up a pen, twirling it expertly between his fingers as he listened. God, those fingers. It was as though every part of him was big and strong and capable.

She missed the last step and stumbled awkwardly forward, taking several steps to regain her balance. Blood rushed to her cheeks, but she turned around, faced him, and hit the pose gymnasts always struck after landing a tumbling pass, arms stretched above her head. Normally, she played her cards close to the vest, but she found she didn't mind if Adam knew that he flustered her as much as she did him.

He grinned at her, tilting his head. "You okay?" he mouthed.

She nodded and started to approach the desk when Autumn came bounding out from the lounge.

"Hey, you're early. Ready?"

Adam had returned his full attention to his phone call and was once again typing on the computer. She hadn't thought of the front desk as small yesterday, but it looked tiny with Adam standing behind it, all tall and broad, and God, look at the way his hair had gone so curly...

"Hellooooooo," said Autumn, waving a hand in front of Hazel's face. Then she realized who Hazel was staring at and a wide grin spread across her face. "That's right, you met Adam this morning, didn't you?"

Hazel groaned, letting Autumn lead her out of the hotel's front door. "You heard about the shower incident?"

"How on earth did Adam wind up getting soaked?" she asked, leading them toward a small blue Honda Civic. "I figured we'd drive since it looks like it might rain," she said, pointing to the overcast sky.

"I don't mind a little rain," said Hazel, slipping into the passenger's seat. "In fact, I kinda love it."

"Me too! There's something so cozy and atmospheric about a rainy day. It just makes me want to curl up with something warm to drink and a good book or a favorite movie."

"I know exactly what you mean."

Autumn turned the car on, once again having to hastily turn the music down. "So how did Adam get soaked?"

"I couldn't get the shower to turn on, so I called down to the front desk and he came up to fix it. He dropped his wrench and then he hit his head on the faucet—"

Autumn burst out laughing, a loud, joyful guffaw that filled the car's cabin. "This is my new favorite story. Continue."

"I went to check on him, you know, because he hit his head and there...was a moment? I don't know how to describe it."

"A moment? Like...a pull?"

Hazel nodded. "Like...a sudden awareness. And then all of a sudden, the shower came on, seemingly all by itself."

Autumn laughed again. "I knew it! I knew it. I absolutely knew it."

"Knew what?"

"You'll see," she said cryptically, and Hazel just laughed and shook her head.

"You know, you didn't tell me your brother was like a swoony, Henry Cavill-esque lumberjack who belongs on the cover of romance novels."

Autumn laughed again. "Oh, he's going to love that."

Hazel blushed, wondering if she'd overstepped. On the one hand, she felt incredibly comfortable talking to Autumn. There was an ease to their connection that made her feel as though she'd known her for months, not just a couple of days. Maybe it had something to do with how open Autumn was. Everyone Hazel knew back in the city was so closed off, meaning she never fully knew where she stood with them. But she knew where she stood with Autumn, and it made everything feel natural and easy.

Autumn giggled. "You're not the first person to make that comparison, you know."

"I don't mean it in a bad way. I just mean...dang, girl. That man is gorgeous. Sorry if that's weird because he's your brother." She had absolutely no idea what she was doing when it came to dating or flirting or reading signals. She'd always been a bit clueless in the dating department.

She shook her head. "It's not weird." They came to a red light and she glanced over at Hazel, her expression earnest. "Hazel, I *want* you to like him, okay? But once things progress past kissing, leave out the details," she added with a wink.

"Wait, what?" said Hazel, her head whipping around to face Autumn. "I feel like I missed something here. Or several somethings? I didn't say anything about kissing..." She trailed off as butterflies erupted in her stomach at the thought of kissing Adam, with his full lips and big, capable hands, and...

Autumn laughed. "You might not have said it, but I can tell you're thinking it right now."

"Yeah, because *you* said it!" Hazel shot back while laughing.

The light changed and they proceeded through the intersection, gray clouds following them as the wind picked up slightly. A perfect, orange maple leaf smacked against Autumn's window. The adorably cozy downtown came into view, and Autumn pulled into a parking lot off of Hemlock

Square. Despite the gloomy weather, dozens of people milled about, exploring the shops and taking in the scenery.

"Listen," said Autumn, suddenly serious as she turned to Hazel. "I know that you and I are still getting to know each other. But I have a feeling about you. I've had it since the moment I met you."

Hazel's eyebrows rose. "A feeling?"

Autumn nodded. "And then when you told me about the ad in the magazine...I knew I was right." She met Hazel's eyes. "I think you and Adam are meant for each other."

Hazel's mouth formed a small *O*. "What?" Confusion pulled at her, making her feel too warm.

"Let's look at the evidence," she said, spreading her hands in front of her as though she had something physical to present. "You're the same age. You're both single. I think you have a lot in common, including the fact that you're both authors."

"Adam's an author?" Hazel asked, tilting her head.

"Well, not exactly. Not anymore, anyway." Hazel had questions, but before she could ask them, Autumn charged ahead. "And then there's the more...magical evidence. Like the fact that you went to the falls under the full moon, and the very next morning, Adam went to your room to fix a shower that wasn't even broken."

"But it was," said Hazel, shaking her head slowly as she tried to take all of this in. "It wouldn't turn on."

"Until Adam got there and the two of you laid eyes on each other and then boom, shower suddenly turns on."

Hazel's mouth opened slightly as goosebumps erupted across her arms. The sudden chill worked its way through her. When she didn't say anything for a moment, Autumn smiled kindly at her. "Because Adam's the one for you. He's dated in the past, had relationships, but none of them have ever lasted. Not long-term. He thinks it's because none of them wanted to stay in Gossamer Falls, which is maybe partly true. But I think the real truth is that none of them were you."

Hazel let out an uncertain laugh. "That's very flattering, but you don't really know me," she said gently.

"Not yet. But I do know how to read signs. And they're all pointing at one thing. You and Adam."

Hazel sucked in a breath. "Listen, Autumn. I appreciate your enthusiasm for matching me up with your ridiculously gorgeous brother. I do. But...well, it's complicated. I got divorced about a year and a half ago, and I haven't dated since then. I mean, yes, he's hot and I'm totally crushing on him, but jumping to there being a 'me and Adam' is kind of a lot of pressure."

Autumn nodded. "I get that. I do. Okay, how about this. Why don't you just see where the next two weeks take you?" She shrugged and reached for her purse. "If I'm right, it'll become obvious all by itself anyway."

Hazel grinned. "Deal." She didn't think Autumn was right, and she was still fairly certain she didn't believe in magic or legends, despite the experiences she'd had since arriving just yesterday. But she also knew that she was stuck in a rut—it was part of the reason she'd gotten out of the city and come here in the first place.

"Let's grab sandwiches at You Little Tart," said Autumn. "You can meet my bestie Laurel while sampling the world's best brie and pear grilled cheese."

Hazel nodded. "Sounds absolutely delicious," she said,

her stomach giving a little grumble. The wind whipped around them, and they walked a little faster to the other side of Hemlock Square.

"Afterward we can check out Deja Brew next door. Laurel's twin Sienna runs it, and even though they're a few years older than me, we've been close for a while now. Things got a little weird when Sienna started dating my brother Finn, and then even weirder when he left, but we managed to find our footing."

"Finn? You mentioned one of your brothers doesn't live in town. Is that him?"

Autumn nodded, her expression tense. "Yeah. My—our —dad died about two years ago, and Finn couldn't handle it. He took off."

Hazel bit her lip. "Oh, wow. I'm sorry."

Autumn sent her a watery smile. "Thank you. Finn and I were close, so having him leave so soon after Dad..." She swallowed thickly. "It was hard. And he broke Sienna's heart in the process, so he's on a lot of people's shit lists."

"Where is he?"

Autumn shrugged. "The arctic somewhere, last I saw. He's a documentarian, and he's hellbent on saving the planet. He runs a successful YouTube channel, so I mostly keep up with him through his videos."

Hazel could see the hurt and the loss written all over the younger woman's face, and she reached out and slung an arm around her shoulders. It wasn't something she normally would've done, especially with someone she'd only known for about twenty-four hours, but she liked Autumn.

And there was something about this place, away from the city. As though here, she had the space to be a better version of herself. One who was less afraid, less riddled with self-doubt and insecurities, one who wasn't so scared of vulnerability.

"What kind of desserts do they have at this bakery?" she asked. "Because I'm thinking maybe we need to start with that."

Autumn laughed softly and leaned into her. "I think that's the perfect idea. Laurel makes these cinnamon rolls that are like the size of your head."

"The size of my head, you say? Lead on."

NINE

AUTUMN AND HAZEL walked down the sidewalk made of interlocking red brick and reached a cute building clad in white shiplap style siding with two doors standing side by side in the middle of it. Above one hung the sign for You Little Tart, with its adorable pie-face logo and orange script. The door beside it was emblazoned with a soft yellow coffee cup covered in pink hearts with the name Deja Brew Coffee Shop Co. beneath it. Hazel could see customers sitting at cozy looking tables, large mugs cradled in their hands.

Her mouth started to water the second they stepped inside the bakery. The scents of cinnamon, chocolate and fresh-baked buttery bread filled the air, and she pulled in a deep breath.

"It smells like heaven in here," she said to Autumn, who nodded. The far right side of the store was taken up with enormous display cases, all softly glowing and showcasing the treats within. Hazel stepped closer, drooling over the pumpkin swirl bread, the cinnamon muffins, the pumpkin pies with intricate pastry leaves, the cranberry white chocolate chip cookies bigger than the palm of her hand.

To the left of the display cases was a wooden counter where customers could place their order. An enormous black chalkboard hung on the wall behind it, listing what was available. The walls were covered with art—an eclectic mix of paintings and photographs of varying sizes and shapes. Below the counter, wooden crates housed other items for sale—local jams, You Little Tart branded cake and muffin mixes, branded tote bags, even a small collection of candles with scents inspired by the shop's treats.

"Hey, Autumn!" shouted a woman from behind the counter. Her long dark brown hair was swept up into a high ponytail, with her long bangs almost obscuring her eyes. She wore a dark blue T-shirt with the shop's logo on it, and when she smiled, it was wide and bright, showcasing the slight gap between her front teeth.

Autumn tugged Hazel over to the counter. "Hey!" she called out. "We're here for lunch. We were going to have sandwiches but then decided cinnamon rolls were a better choice."

Laurel laughed. "You're in luck. I just pulled a batch of pumpkin walnut ones out of the oven." She turned her attention to Hazel and then extended her hand across the counter after wiping it on the khaki colored apron tied around her waist. "Hey, I'm Laurel."

"Hazel. I'm staying at the Shephard Inn."

"Ooh, lucky you. I'm not sure what's better. The view of the Highlands, or the view of Adam Shephard." Her eyebrows bounced and Hazel laughed. She had to agree, because both the scenery and the hotel's owner were equally appealing.

Laurel gestured toward an empty table that had just opened up beside the rain spattered window, and Hazel and Autumn hurried over before someone else snagged it. A few minutes later, Laurel appeared with two plates, each bearing an absolutely mouthwatering cinnamon roll that smelled like heaven. Hazel was pretty sure she was drooling.

"I have a few things to finish up, but…Oh, look who it is," she said, waving as an identical carbon copy of herself stepped inside. For some reason, when Autumn had mentioned that Laurel and Sienna were twins, Hazel had assumed that they weren't identical, but they clearly were. The only difference in their appearance was their hairstyle. Where Laurel's was long and dark with a thick fringe of bangs, Sienna's was a lighter coppery color, shorter, and without bangs. Thankfully, it made them easy to distinguish.

"Oh, no," said Sienna as she approached where Hazel and Autumn were sitting. "Oh, this won't do at all. Hang on." She held up a finger and then dashed back out the door.

"What…" started Hazel, just as Laurel pulled up a chair to join them.

"She's going to get coffee," she said easily. "So, Hazel. What brings you to Gossamer Falls?"

"Well, a few things. The beautiful views, obviously. But mainly, I'm here to work on my book."

"Are you a writer?" asked Laurel, leaning in eagerly. "Sienna and I are both total bookworms."

Hazel grinned, happy to have a way to dodge the question. A few years ago, she'd been so thrilled to talk to anyone and everyone about her career, her books, her process. Now talking about it felt like poking a bruise, dull and vaguely painful.

"What kind of books do you like to read?"

"Mostly smutty romance," said Laurel easily. "Ana Huang, Lauren Asher, Lucy Score, Elsie Silver."

"She's leaving out the monster and alien porn," said Sienna, who'd returned in record time with four paper coffee cups emblazoned with Deja Brew's cute logo. She lifted them one by one out of the tray, then reached into her pocket and unceremoniously dumped sugar and milk packets onto the table before sinking down into the remaining vacant chair. "Hey," she said, nodding at Hazel. "You must be Hazel. I'm Sienna. Autumn has already told me so much about you."

Hazel blushed slightly, but before she could think of what to say—thank God, because she was painfully out of practice when it came to getting to know people and friendships and, well, fun—Laurel pointed at Sienna with a stir stick.

"Please, you're the one who got me reading that stuff." She turned to Hazel, eyebrows once again bouncing. "If you like alien peen, you need to read *Ice Planet Barbarians*," she said, nodding sagely.

"I can honestly say I've never read, um, alien peen, but color me intrigued."

"Hazel's actually a pretty famous author," said Autumn.

"Really?" the twins asked in unison, and once again, before Hazel could speak, Autumn spoke for her.

"She wrote *A Revelation of Enchantment*," said Autumn.

"Seriously?" squealed Sienna, slapping her coffee cup back down on the table and then helping herself to a torn off hunk of Autumn's cinnamon bun. "Oh my God, so good," she mumbled as she chewed.

"Um, yeah," said Hazel. She shifted in her seat, feeling uncomfortable with the attention, with the weight of eyes and expectations on her. It struck her then that these women were younger than her—Autumn by a good ten years, Laurel and Sienna by a little less—but she felt young sitting with them, and not in a good way. Young in an immature, inexperienced, what am I even doing here way.

But the feeling dissipated quicker than morning fog over the Hudson Highlands as Autumn reached over and squeezed her forearm. "I'm optimistic you'll find the inspiration you're looking for here."

Hazel shot her a small smile and picked at her cinnamon roll. "Thanks. It's been..." She blew out a breath. "A challenge."

Instead of judgement or pat advice, the women just murmured in understanding. They weren't judging her as a failure or a fraud because of her struggle to write something new.

"Your shop is amazing," she said to Laurel. "And I can't wait to visit yours," she added to Sienna. "When did you open them?"

"About five years ago," said Laurel. "We'd always known we wanted to stay in Gossamer Falls and run our own businesses. I went to school for culinary arts, and I knew I wanted to run a dessert shop. Originally, I'd wanted to set up a tea shop, but no one can compete with Play Oolong. So when Connie retired and said she wanted someone to take over her bakery, I knew it was perfect. And then six months later, the lease on the shop next door came up, and we figured that nothing goes better with desserts than coffee, so we managed to secure loans and raise enough capital to make it happen."

"Did you always want to run a coffee shop?" Hazel asked, moaning softly and earning a round of laughter as she bit into her cinnamon bun, taking a big, buttery, sticky bite.

Sienna laughed. "God, no. For most of my twenties, I had no idea what I wanted to do. I came back after college with an English degree, hoping something would fall into my lap. I bounced around, working at the library, the museum. I was even a mail carrier for a while. But eventually, I figured out that I wanted something that was mine, and the coffee shop just made sense. It was like everything in my life was falling into place, with the shop and F—" She cut herself off abruptly and took a long sip of her coffee.

Autumn deftly changed the topic, and they spent the next half hour chatting about books, TV shows, movies, and music. As they talked, Hazel relaxed, bit by bit, her shyness thawing like ice in the sun. It felt good to sit and talk and just be. To not have to worry about secrets they might be keeping, waiting to lob them at her like casually thrown bombs.

She swallowed thickly, tightness gathering in her chest as she thought of her last conversation with Leah. The one where she'd blown their fifteen-year friendship to smithereens so cavalierly that Hazel wondered if they'd ever been friends at all. She'd already been trying to pick up the smoking remains of her life after finding out that Seth was leaving her for Grace, that he'd been carrying on an affair with her for almost a year.

And then she'd found out that Leah had known. That

she'd known almost from the start. And that she'd decided to keep his secret instead of telling Hazel. That she really didn't think it was a big deal that she hadn't told her. That she had a working relationship with him to protect, and so she'd had her own priorities.

In that instant, Hazel had felt sick. Sick, and dizzyingly alone in the world.

And utterly, completely humiliated.

"So, can I ask what your new book's about?" asked Laurel, leaning her elbows on the table, her expression kind and full of open interest. It pulled Hazel back to the present, and she was grateful for it. She didn't want to think about Leah and how she'd flushed fifteen years of close friendship down the toilet. How she hadn't mattered enough to her to come first.

Hazel didn't think she'd ever come first with anyone. Not her family. Not her friends. Not her husband.

She blinked rapidly, trying to dispel the stinging in her eyes. "Well, I guess it's about vampires."

"Oooh, yes!" said Sienna, a wide grin on her face. "I love a good vampire story."

"The premise is that they're fated mates, destined to find each other again and again across time, using different monumental events in history as touchstones. It opens during the fall of Rome, when everything is in chaos and their lives are torn in different directions."

"But?" asked Laurel gently, her head tilted.

Hazel's shoulders slumped and she shook her head slowly. "But, it's not going well, and I can't for the life of me figure out why. Is it the characters? The premise? The voice? Is the entire story just wrong?" She took a long sip of her coffee, the warm liquid calming her. Soothing her. "I'm stuck."

"I bet you'll figure it out while you're here," said Autumn warmly, her voice full of kindness.

"Absolutely," agreed Sienna. "Come by Deja Brew anytime; coffee's on the house. It's writer fuel, right?"

"Wow, thank you," said Hazel, touched by the woman's kindness. They'd only known each other for an hour and she was already treating Hazel with more compassion than most people in her life back in the city.

"Don't mention it," said Sienna, waving away Hazel's thanks. "It's just what we do, here. We cheer each other on."

"Well, I'm grateful. I'm going to need a *lot* of coffee if I have any hope of figuring this book out." She paused, opened her mouth, closed it, and then decided she wanted to share. That it was safe to share. "My publisher has given me extension after extension, and now, if I don't hand in the first 100 pages by Halloween, they're going to cancel the contract and ask for the advance back. Which is a bit of a problem because I've been living off of it for the past two years, so I don't exactly have it anymore. So, if I can't hand something in, I'll be broke, unemployed, potentially homeless..." Anxiety set her insides quivering, a slow wave of nausea rolling through her.

Laurel winced. "Talk about having your feet to the fire."

"No kidding. And the cherry on top is that my ex-husband, who edited my first three books, is still my editor." She hadn't planned to bring Seth up, but there was something freeing about opening herself up to these women who'd welcomed her so easily and warmly.

Three mouths fell open in unison, and Hazel laughed. "I know. I know, I know."

"Can't you like..." Autumn's hands fluttered in front of her. "Request someone else?"

"Oh, I've tried, both through my agent and directly. But he won't pass me to someone else. He...he had an affair, and even though he won't admit it, I think he feels guilty. And I think he manages that guilt by pretending there are no hurt feelings between us. That everything is fine. If he passes me to another editor, it's like admitting wrongdoing on his part."

"But everyone knows he's your ex, right?" asked Sienna, and Hazel nodded.

"Oh, they do. Publishing is...not the place to make friends. Everyone is overworked and underpaid, out for themselves, and no one wants to hold an author's hand."

"You know, that sounds really similar to something Adam once said," said Autumn. "Although I think there were a few f-bombs in there."

"You mentioned earlier that he was an author, too," said Hazel, tracing her finger through the crumbs of her cinnamon bun on her plate. "What's the story there?"

Autumn grinned, her eyes twinkling in that mischievous way. "That's something you should ask him about."

"Have you met him yet?" asked Laurel.

"They had a shower together this morning," said Autumn before Hazel could answer and immediately, all eyes at the table were on her.

"He was fixing my shower. It's nothing like that," she said, her face burning as she spoke.

"I took Hazel to the falls last night," said Autumn breezily. Something unspoken seemed to pass between the other three women as they glanced back and forth between each other and Hazel.

"Is he not the hottest guy, like, ever?" asked Laurel, looking over at Hazel, whose cheeks were once again on fire. Which was stupid. What was she, sixteen?

"He's definitely attractive," she agreed.

"He's super swoony," continued Laurel. "Not only is he gorgeous, but he's smart, and kind, and he loves his family. He's one of the good ones, for sure."

"You always had such a huge crush on him," said Sienna, shaking her head.

"I did. And alas, he was never interested. What kind of man only dates women his own age?" she said, and they all laughed.

"I'm surprised no one's snapped him up," said Hazel, and Autumn laughed.

"They've tried. But no one can compete with his love of this town." She leaned in close, her shoulder brushing Hazel's. "Except maybe you."

"You're so sure about that, but I've had one conversation with him, like ever," said Hazel, warmth pouring through her chest like sunshine at Autumn's words. At the idea that she, who'd never been enough, could be enough for him.

Absolute lunacy.

Autumn shrugged. "Time will tell if I'm right. Come on, there's one more place I want to show you before we head back to the Inn so you can get some work done."

TEN

AUTUMN AND HAZEL dashed down the street, the rain falling from the sky in a solid sheet of water. They both shrieked as they ducked and ran, dodging puddles and other umbrella-wielding pedestrians. By the time Autumn pulled her inside a little shop on the corner of Main and Hemlock Square, not far from where they'd parked the car—thank God—Hazel was soaked, her sweater clinging to her skin, her hair plastered to her face. Immediately, her mind jumped back to that morning, when the shower had soaked both her and Adam. More specifically, her mind jumped back to the way his clothes had clung to him, exposing his frame, thick with muscles. The feel of his soft curls between her fingers. The droplets of water collecting at the base of his throat.

The way his jeans had—

"Here we are!" said Autumn enthusiastically, pulling Hazel out of her heated thoughts. The scent of incense filled the air, making it feel thick and warm, but not cloying. More like a hug. A welcome blanket on a cold day. "Welcome to The Mystic Muse, my favorite shop in town."

To her left was a large fireplace, the wood inside crackling softly and casting a warmth through the space. On the mantel sat bottles of essential oil, bags of herbs, a collection of books, and several candles. To the left was an enormous floor-to-ceiling bookshelf, crammed full with more books. Hazel stepped in, wiping her feet on the mat with the store's logo, a hand with an all-seeing-eye nestled in its palm. Directly ahead were several large round tables, laden with crystals of all shapes and sizes. Gorgeous art hung on the walls, depicting the full moon, lushly drawn fairies, goddess figures.

Everywhere Hazel looked, there was something magical waiting to be discovered. And while she never would've thought that things like crystals and spell books would appeal to her, she found herself pleasantly intrigued. Happily curious.

"It's a metaphysical shop," said Autumn quietly, her voice mingling with the gentle music playing from a speaker somewhere. "If you're looking for magic, you'll find it here."

"How fun," said Hazel with a grin. "Show me around."

Autumn clapped excitedly and then pushed a strand of wet hair out of her eyes. She showed Hazel beautiful crystals, intricately drawn tarot decks, tea cups suited for reading tea leaves, dried flower crowns, miniature cauldrons, and salts in every color of the rainbow. And every single item was just as intriguing as the last.

A sense of peace came over Hazel as they browsed, probably a combination of the warm air, the scent of the fire mingling with the incense, the beautiful art. In this little shop, she felt safe. As though her worries about her book and her finances and her life in general were nothing but wispy fingers that couldn't reach her.

"Autumn? Is that you?" came a thin, raspy female voice from somewhere toward the back of the shop. Autumn's face split into a wide grin, and she tugged on Hazel's arm, pulling her away from a display of ceremonial daggers that had Hazel's mind dancing with potential ideas for her story.

"Just a sec," she said, pulling her phone out of her bag and opening the notes app so she could jot down the ideas before they evaporated. Once she was finished, she dropped her phone back into her bag and followed Autumn through an arched doorway that led to a smaller room.

A woman who appeared to be in her fifties sat before a round table covered in a white tablecloth. Her mane of blond and white curls was unruly, frizzing around her like a halo, probably thanks to the rainy weather. She wore enormous, thick glasses that made her blue eyes look luminous. Bangles and beaded bracelets ran from wrist to mid-forearm, and she wore a fringed red scarf as a cardigan. She stood up as the two women entered, the scent of herbs and incense heavy in the air.

"Hazel, this is Fiona Crowley, the owner of the Mystic Muse. Fiona, this is Hazel. She's staying with us at the Shephard Inn."

Fiona offered Hazel a warm smile and an extended hand, which Hazel shook.

"Hi, it's—" Hazel started, but the words died on her lips when instead of letting her hand go, she flipped it over, peering intently at Hazel's palm, lips moving wordlessly, fingers tracing with a featherlight touch.

"Mmmm..." she said, nodding as she tapped gently on Hazel's palm. "Heartbreak, yes. And things out of your control, hmm. Very interesting indeed." She gave Hazel's hand a squeeze and then let it go, looking up at her and blinking through her glasses.

"Have you ever had your cards read, dear?" she asked, patting her sweater as though looking for something. She reached in somewhere below her left armpit and pulled out a deck of worn, almost frayed Tarot cards.

Hazel shook her head. "No, um. I can't say I have."

"You should," said Autumn encouragingly. "Fiona's the best, and the cards can help provide clarity when you're feeling lost."

She glanced over and met Autumn's gaze. There was empathy and understanding in the younger woman's eyes, as though she could see right through Hazel.

"Okay," she said. "Just tell me what to do."

Fiona gestured at an empty chair on the other side of the table. "Please."

A bolt of excitement ran through Hazel, making her sit up a little straighter. A week ago, if someone had asked her if she believed in magic and legends, in signs and ghosts, she would've said absolutely not. But here, now?

She couldn't say she *didn't* believe. The way coincidences had seemed to pile up on top of each other like bricks in a wall was too much to ignore. And she couldn't deny the emotional experience she'd had at the falls, either.

And then there was the whole thing with the shower that morning...Butterflies unfurled long dormant wings in her stomach at the memory of Adam.

"How...how does this work?" she asked, watching as

Fiona fanned out the cards before her on the table and then waved a smoldering incense stick over them.

"Since you've never had your cards read before, I suggest starting with a simple three-card pull. Then, we can pull more cards for clarification, or if you think of questions you want answers to."

"Oh, I have questions. A lot of questions."

"Good," said Fiona, gathering up the cards in a smooth, practiced movement. "Then let's get started."

She shuffled the cards with nimble fingers, and Hazel leaned forward, her stomach fluttering in eager anticipation. Then, she laid out three cards face down, flipping over only the one farthest to the left.

"These three cards represent the past, present, and future," she said, tapping on each one. "When we look at the past card, it shows us the energies and events in your past that are still affecting you. It shows us how your past is holding you back, or blocking you from what you need. It can also show us what you need to learn from the past." She pursed her lips, glancing down at the card she'd flipped over. "The Five of Wands. Conflict, tension, lots of arguing. There was a great battle, I think," she says slowly. "Friends were lost, alliances shredded. Your goals did not come to fruition as you'd hoped."

Hazel let out a small laugh. "Yeah, I'd say that about sums it up. I divorced my husband, I lost my best friend, and my career is..." She shook her head. "Stagnant, I guess."

Fiona nodded and turned over the second card. "This card represents the present. What's happening right now, what energies are around you, current opportunities and challenges. This is the King of Pentacles." She tapped it softly. "Money. Career success. A loyal and dedicated romantic partner."

Hazel's eyebrows inched up. "I don't know about that. I don't have much money, and my success is all in the past. And I'm very much single."

"The loyal and dedicated partner is in your life, currently. And this card is telling me that you can translate your vision into something real—you're a writer, yes? That's what Autumn told me?" When Hazel nodded, she continued. "This card indicates creative fulfilment, perhaps attached to the person it represents."

"Creative fulfilment attached to this loyal and dedicated partner?" Hazel couldn't keep the note of skepticism out of her voice.

"This is your present. The idea you need is within you already. The person you need is around you already. The energies are converging in a positive way. When you trust your instincts, everything you touch will turn to gold. Stop fighting against yourself so hard," she said softly, indicating the Five of Wands again. "Success is yours for the taking. Love is yours for the taking."

"Love," she repeated quietly.

"Yes. With someone steadfast and somewhat traditional, who has financial stability and wants to be in a committed relationship. This man," she said, tapping the card again, "is a good provider, and would make an excellent husband. This man is good-natured, but firm when he needs to be."

Autumn let out a little squeak, and Hazel knew she was thinking of her brother. Funny, Hazel was thinking of him, too. Even though she barely knew him, his face was swimming through her mind. She tried to remind herself that the power of suggestion was indeed a powerful thing, that maybe she shouldn't let herself get caught up in all of this. Tried, but failed.

"Now, the final card represents the future. The outcome of the present, the direction things are moving in. It can also reveal what you truly want, which we're not always honest with ourselves about." She flipped it over, and a rumble of thunder purred in the distance. A shiver ran down Hazel's spine.

"The Two of Cups," said Fiona, smiling. "A happy outcome, indeed."

"Yeah?" asked Hazel a little breathlessly.

"Oh, yes. The Two of Cups symbolizes unity, love, partnership, and really great sex."

Hazel's heart thundered against her ribs, drowning out another crash from outside.

"You will heal, Hazel, and you will find new love. This new love will be a deep connection, and there's a partnership of sorts...perhaps a business venture. It's all tied together. This new love will share your values, will love you as you are, and will give you more orgasms than you know what to do with." She laughed, a bright tittering sound.

Hazel blushed. "Well, that certainly sounds promising."

"This partnership will be mutually beneficial. A win-win situation, one fueled by your romantic connection. You will feel giddy. Weak in the knees. Butterflies in the stomach. All of that. And it's real, and it will be here to stay. There is another marriage in your future."

Hazel sucked in a breath, her lungs tight because of the hope expanding inside her for the first time in a long time. "And what about the book? About my career?"

"I see a new partnership in that aspect, too. This relationship is filled with positive energy. Lots of inspiration."

Hazel smiled. A new partnership could only mean one thing—Seth was finally going to let her go. Halle-freaking-lujah. He was finally going to see reason and let her write for someone else. It was infuriating how much control Seth had over her career.

She bit her lip, hesitating as something occurred to her. "My ex-husband is my editor...are you saying I'm going to get involved, like, romantically, with another editor?" she asked. She licked her lips, her mouth dry. She'd promised herself that she'd never mix her professional and personal lives again. It was too messy when it all came crashing down. Too complicated and tangled. Going through the divorce and still having to work with Seth was killing her, creatively. She couldn't open herself up to that again. She wouldn't.

"Let's ask the cards," said Fiona with a little smile. She pulled a card from the top of the deck, deft fingers flipping it over. Hazel's skin burned at the words on the card.

The Fool.

She was going to do something foolish again, wasn't she?

Her heart sank and she immediately wanted to distance herself from all of this. From Tarot readings and legends and ghosts and any of it.

"Now, now, don't panic," said Fiona gently. She reached forward and laid her hand over Hazel's. "This doesn't mean you're a fool."

"What does it mean, then?" asked Hazel.

"The Fool is a card that signifies beginnings. Enthusiasm. Taking risks and having fun. Being free-spirited. You're at the outset of a new journey. Have an open, curious mind because you don't know yet where this journey is going to take you. If you don't want to make the same mistakes, you won't. But don't close yourself off to something new, either. If something scares you, do it anyway."

"Easier said than done," said Hazel, relief filtering through her.

"True, but The Fool is one of the major arcana cards, meaning this energy will be tremendously influential. When it comes to romance, The Fool encourages you to be vulnerable in getting to know someone. In your career, it signifies a fresh start. So no, I don't think you're going to fall in love with another editor. There is love in your future, and that love will impact your career, but it sounds as though you've learned the lessons of the past," she said, indicating the Five of Wands. "So keep an open mind as you move forward." She folded her hands in front of her. "What else would you like to ask?"

"I...I can't figure out what my book should be about. I have a premise and an outline, but something about it isn't working for me. Am I on the wrong path? Am I writing the wrong story?"

Fiona nodded and flipped over another card. "The World. Another major arcana card, how interesting."

Hazel leaned forward again, fully re-engaged now that she knew she wasn't doomed to repeat the mistakes of her past. "What does it mean?"

"The World denotes the completion of something. A cycle, an accomplishment, a phase of life. Perhaps you need to write something different. What you were writing before, that was the old phase. It's time for a new one, especially if you're not finding fulfilment where you are right now."

"Okay...so...a new genre? A new pen name?"

"Only you can figure out what your next steps are. But know that the past is done, that phase of your writing career is done." She moved her finger back over to The Fool. "It's time to be open to new ideas. Be curious and follow that curiosity. That's where you'll find your answers. Instead of pushing, go where you're pulled."

Hazel immediately recognized the truth in Fiona's words. She'd come to Gossamer Falls because she'd felt pulled here. She'd gone to the falls for the same reason. Maybe what she needed to do most was to stop trying so damn hard.

She thanked Fiona for the reading, who refused to take any payment for it. Hazel bought a Tarot deck and a book about the ghosts of Gossamer Falls, a little bit out of obligation, but mostly because she was following her curiosity, as Fiona had suggested. Fiona rang up her purchases and then plucked something from behind the sturdy wooden desk. She pressed a small velvet bag into Hazel's hand.

"It's a rose quartz pendant. Rose quartz is known as the love stone. Wear it to attract love, receive love, and give love."

Hazel smiled. "Thank you. That's a lovely message." She slipped it into her little paper bag stamped with the shop's logo, and then put the bag into her purse. The rain had eased up while they'd been inside the shop, but it was still drizzling out.

"Come on," said Autumn, linking her arm through Hazel's. "Let's head back to the inn. I have it on good authority that the fireplace is roaring and there's a fresh batch of chocolate chip cookies coming out of the oven. Maybe a cup of tea to go with it?"

Hazel bumped her shoulder against Autumn's. It was incredible to her that she'd only known her for a day. It felt like much, much longer, in a good way. There was an ease that she wasn't used to. Then again, maybe she'd been the problem all along. Maybe she'd always been trying too hard to force things instead of letting them happen organically. As they were meant to.

"You read my mind," said Hazel, a smile on her face as they headed back to Autumn's car through the gloomy weather.

ELEVEN

ADAM MOVED through the main area of the hotel, turning on lights even though it was only mid-afternoon. The rain had descended earlier and the clouds were still low in the sky, blocking out any trace of yesterday's sun. As he turned on a lamp on the table in the lounge, he frowned, noticing something glinting at him in the light. Reaching forward, he pulled out a small gold hoop. Someone had lost an earring. Hopefully it belonged to a guest who was still staying with them.

As he returned to the front desk, preparing to put the earring into an envelope for safe keeping, the front door opened, bringing with it a gust of damp, fall air. Autumn and Hazel stepped inside, laughing as they pushed the door closed against the gale.

"Oh, my gosh! Is that my earring?" Hazel asked, stepping forward, her eyes zeroing in on the gold hoop between his fingers. "I realized that I lost it yesterday and I assumed it had fallen off at the falls. Where did you find it?" she asked, taking it from him. Their fingers brushed, sending a current of electricity up Adam's arm. The rush of awareness he'd felt this morning was suddenly back.

He cleared his throat softly before speaking. "In the couch cushions in the lounge."

"Really?" asked Autumn, her eyebrow cocked. "Because I cleaned in there earlier, and I didn't see anything."

Adam shrugged. "I guess you must've missed it." He wasn't looking at Autumn as he spoke because his eyes were still very much glued to Hazel—the wet strand of hair plastered to her cheek, the droplets of rain on her glasses.

"Well, thank you," said Hazel, slipping the earring into her pocket. "I'm glad you found it."

Out of the corner of his eye, Adam saw Autumn slinking away towards the lounge.

"You got caught in the rain, I see," he said, and before he could stop himself, he lifted his hand and brushed the wet tendril away from her cheek, tucking it safely behind her ear. She inhaled sharply, and when he dropped his hand, the tips of his fingers were tingling. He wasn't normally so...so forward, but he couldn't seem to help himself when it came to Hazel. It was as though he looked at her and everything inside him unravelled.

"Oh," she breathed. "Um...rain. Yes. It's raining."

"I know." She was adorably flustered, and he felt as though he'd evened the playing field slightly after his little debacle this morning.

God, that white robe plastered to her...Fuck.

"Um...how's your head?" she asked, blinking up at him.

"I'll live. Lucky for me, I've got a hard one."

"I bet you do." In an echo of that morning, she slapped a

hand over her mouth. "You must think I'm such a pervert. Everything I say seems to come out wrong around you."

"Does it?" he asked, cocking his head. "I hadn't noticed." He leaned forward, lowering his head so that his lips were only inches from her ear. "And for the record, I don't think you're a pervert. I think you're fucking adorable."

She made a soft sound in the back of her throat. Something about that sound chipped away at his resolve to treat her with polite, professional indifference. Normally, he had his rules, and he stuck to them. He didn't get involved with tourists or hotel guests. He didn't do casual hookups. He didn't even flirt much, usually.

But Hazel...God, he barely knew her, but something about her made him want to break his rules. Made him want things he knew would only end badly. He couldn't explain it. All he knew was that he wanted more of her.

"Do you have plans tonight?" he asked, the words falling out of his mouth before he could stop himself. A voice somewhere in the back of his head told him to stop, but a much louder one told him to go for it. He couldn't deny that he was drawn to her. That he wanted to get to know her.

"Um...no?"

"I have a cider tasting to go to. For the Inn. Totally fine if you're not—"

"Sure. Yes. I want..." She bit her lip and shook her head, swallowing whatever she'd been about to say. "Yes. A cider tasting sounds fun."

"Great. Meet me down here at seven?" he asked. He hadn't been planning on going home to change, but now, obviously, he was going to.

"Uh huh, yep. Seven. Seven is good." She started to walk

backwards towards the stairs, tripping over her own feet and righting herself quickly. "Seven!" she said and then dashed up the stairs.

Autumn emerged from the lounge, where she'd clearly been eavesdropping. Of course she had.

"What about tea and cookies?" she called up after Hazel.

"Another time!" she called back, and Hazel laughed, her gaze zeroing in on him.

"Adam Patrick Shephard! Did you just ask a hotel guest out on a date?"

He rubbed a hand over the back of his neck. He didn't understand what had come over him, but he found that he didn't want to analyze it. Flirting with Hazel felt good.

"Mind your own business, Autumn," he said, moving behind the front desk.

"Never," she said with a laugh.

Adam spent the next few hours doing what he did best: overanalyzing. After all, he hadn't ever asked a hotel guest on a date before, so why had he broken his rules now? He couldn't deny that he felt drawn to Hazel, but was that only because Autumn was in his head? Was it because he was a little lonely? Was it because he wanted to prove to himself that Autumn was crazy and there was nothing between him and Hazel?

He didn't know. But he wasn't going to back out now. He was a lot of things, but rude wasn't one of them.

What he did know was that he'd asked a woman out for the first time in a long time, and he didn't regret it.

The rest of the work day crawled by. All he could think about was Hazel up in her room. That she was literally a flight of stairs away. But he forced himself to stay downstairs. To wait. When Jamie came in for her shift, he passed everything over to her, did a final—but quick—walkthrough of the hotel, and then jumped in his car and sped back to his cabin to change.

Up in his bedroom, he opened his closet, stared at the clothing inside, and then sank down on the bed. He felt like a rusty hinge, creaking to life, unsure of his movements. Unsure of so much. With a sigh, he pushed a hand through his hair and then pulled his phone out of his pocket, texting Jack.

Adam: What does one wear on a first date?

Jack: Depends. Where is one going on this date, and what are one's intentions?

Adam: My intentions are to get to know her. Which is generally the intention of a first date.

Jack: If you say so.

Adam: And we're going to a tasting at Three Brothers.

Jack: Are you not going to tell me who you're going on a date with?

Adam: No.

Jack: You know I'll find out anyway.

Adam: I know. But making you work for it is more fun.

Jack: Wear something simple and classic, but not too dressy. You don't want to look like you're trying too hard. Do a sweater with jeans or dark pants. Nice shoes. Shave.

Adam: I was planning to shave.

Jack: Okay, I gave you fashion advice. Now tell me who this date is with.

Adam: No. And thanks for the advice.

His phone buzzed again, but he ignored it, instead

peeling off his clothes and padding into the adjoining bathroom to take a quick shower and shave.

By the time he got back to the hotel, it was just before seven, and Hazel was already waiting in the lobby. She turned as he stepped inside, and it was as though the entire world dropped into slow motion. Her hair shone like bronze in firelight as it cascaded over her shoulders in shiny waves. She was wearing a white cable knit sweater dress that hit just at the knee, and knee-high brown leather boots. His steps faltered slightly as he drank her in, her eyes like melted chocolate, her mouth full and heart-shaped. God, she was beautiful.

Her cheeks went pink as she stared at him, heat trailing in the wake of her roving gaze that moved over his shoulders and chest, down and then quickly back up to his face.

He couldn't deny that the physical chemistry between them was real. But he needed to know if there was more than attraction between them.

"You look lovely," he said, stepping closer to her. He wanted to hug her, to kiss her cheek, but held back. Out of nerves or self-preservation, he wasn't sure. He wasn't sure about anything: dating a hotel guest, letting himself get tangled up with yet another woman who was leaving, if there was anything more than hormones and loneliness at play here.

"Thank you," she said, her eyelashes fanning against the tops of her cheeks as she glanced down briefly. "You look nice, too."

He'd picked out a dark blue sweater and a pair of black pants, following Jack's advice. He inclined his head toward the door. "Shall we?"

She nodded, allowing him to hold open the door for her and then following him to his car, where he held open the door for her again.

"So, um. Where exactly are we going?" she asked once she was buckled in and they'd pulled out of the inn's parking lot.

He let out a small laugh. "I guess I should've given you more details. There's a cider house and brewery on the outskirts of town called Three Brothers Brewing. It's run by Cole, Cameron, and Easton Miller. Some of my younger brothers went to high school with them."

"It must be nice, having a big family like that," she said, her head rolling as she looked out the window at the passing scenery. It was already full dark, but the moon was full and bright, leaving everything in delicate silvery shadows.

"It is. Usually," he said with a small smile. "The brewery provides all the beer and cider for the inn, and they have a new fall menu, so Cole invited me to come for a tasting."

"Oh, so this isn't like...an event?"

"No. It'll just be us, and Cole." He frowned slightly. "I probably should've mentioned that. If you're not comfortable, we can go back—"

She cut him off with a shake of her head. "No, no. It's fine. If you murder me, I won't have to finish my book, so..." She made a show of weighing out two things in her hands. "There are worse things."

"Is that what brought you to Gossamer Falls? Getting away to work on the book?"

She shrugged, and the movement made her thick sweater dress slip down her shoulder, exposing a slim section of smooth skin. He couldn't help but notice that there wasn't a bra strap visible, meaning she was either wearing a strapless one, or none at all. She adjusted it absentmindedly as she talked, and his blood heated in his veins. "Sort of. I was hoping that a change of scenery would jar something in me, spark some creativity, you know? I saw an ad for it in a New York State tourist magazine and decided to take a chance."

He turned down a winding road enveloped by trees. "And how's that going for you so far?"

"Not great."

"How come?"

"Because everything I write is flat, emotionless crap." She shifted in her seat, turning towards him. "I have an idea. I have an outline. I have character sketches. But the story has no spark. At all."

"What's the story?" he asked, keeping his eyes on the road as he navigated through the dark.

"It's a romance of sorts about vampires fated to find each other throughout different time periods."

"Great premise," he said, tilting his head as he listened.

To his surprise, she threw up her hands in what seemed like frustration. "That's what everyone says! But every time I go to put words to paper, what comes out is all wrong."

"Someone needs to invent a machine that you hook directly into your brain, and it sucks the book out, fully formed, right onto the page."

"Yes!" she said with a little laugh. "My kingdom for a brain sucking thought depositor."

"We might need to come up with a catchier name, though."

"You're right. Maybe..." She pursed her lips, tapping her finger against them, and his chest filled with warmth. This felt so easy. So natural. There was no stilted awkwardness, no pregnant silences. "Oh, I know! What about the Story Sucker?"

"I like it, but a product with 'suck' in the name might be a hard sell."

"Story Belcher," she offered. He laughed and shook his head.

"I'm not sure if that's better or worse," he teased.

"What about...the Mindjaculator?"

He laughed again, harder this time, and nodded. "Perfect. A brain orgasm where ideas spurt out."

She howled with laughter. "I mean, it is a romance." She glanced at him, her bottom lip caught between her teeth and a bolt of heat raced through him. Fuck, she was cute. Cute and sexy and funny. She was like sunshine bursting out from behind clouds on a rainy day, a bright, shiny rainbow of surprise. "Autumn mentioned that you used to write?"

He nodded, and then pulled the car into the brewery's parking lot. As he jogged around the front of his car to open her door for her, he weighed how much to get into about his failed writing career. If she was struggling with her book, she probably didn't need to hear about his failures. Then again, it might feel nice to commiserate with another writer.

He opened her door for her and then offered her his hand to help her out. He knew he should probably drop it, but he didn't want to. So he kept it, and she seemed perfectly content to stroll forward towards the brewery with her much smaller hand nestled in his. Heat slowly worked its way up his arm.

"This is Three Brothers," he said, her steps slowing on the gravel path as she took in the building before them. It looked like a miniature version of a mountain lodge, with its peaked roofs, wood plank walls, and intricately scalloped sign. A firepit surrounded by Adirondack chairs sat dormant tonight, and off to the side was a pergola decked out in fall mums. To the left was a building that housed the brewing equipment and storage areas, and to the right was a large room reserved for tastings. Large windows looked out onto the garden from one side, and into the adjacent forest on the other.

"Very cozy," she said. At least, he was pretty sure that was what she'd said. He was finding it hard to concentrate on anything besides her hand in his.

He led her to the front doors, and then, once they were inside, to the right, their steps echoing against the stone floors and soaring ceilings. A few other patrons sat at tables in the tasting room, flights of beer or cider in front of them.

"Adam!" Cole came out from behind the bar, a towel slung over his shoulder. "Glad you could make it!" His gaze drifted to Hazel, and he cocked a subtle eyebrow. Then he extended his hand. "Cole Miller, one of the three brothers of Three Brothers."

"Hazel Woodward," she said, shaking his hand while still holding Adam's.

"She's staying at the inn," said Adam, unsure if that semi-clarification would make things less awkward or more.

"Well then, welcome to Gossamer Falls," said Cole smoothly. Of the three Miller brothers, he was the one with the best people skills, which was why he was in charge of tastings, tours, and relationships with vendors and restaurants. Cameron was quieter and ran the more administrative side of the business. And Easton was a grumpy bastard who wanted to be left alone with his hops and his kegs. He was also an award-winning brewmaster. "Let me show you to a table, and I'll bring the first flight out. I think you're going to be impressed," he added to Adam, who nodded. He was picky about what he brought into the inn, only wanting the best of the best. But he had a feeling Three Brothers wasn't going to disappoint. They never did.

The table he showed them to was nestled in the corner, adjacent to the fireplace and beside a window looking out on to the forest behind the property. Strings of lights hung from the trees, glowing orange in the night. Adam swallowed, watching the way the firelight bounced off of Hazel's skin. Her hair. Her luminous brown eyes he wanted to lose himself in.

He held out her chair for her, fighting down the urge to dip his head and inhale deeply. Her perfume was light, but intoxicating, smelling of oranges and flowers and something warmer, something almost woodsy.

He moved around the table and sat down, wondering what the everloving fuck was going on with him. He wasn't looking for a relationship, especially not one with a hotel guest who was on her way back to the city in less than two weeks. He didn't normally get moony over women he barely knew. Women he'd just met. He was more of a slow burn kind of guy, taking the time to get to know someone and building up to physical intimacy.

But with Hazel...he couldn't explain it. Everything felt different. As though someone had pressed the fast forward button on his brain. On his heart. Most definitely on his dick. Every time he looked at her, he felt like he was sliding slowly down a cliff towards an inevitable ending.

And he was powerless to do anything but go along for the ride.

"You asked me about writing," he said, rolling up his sleeves and bracing his elbows on the table. He watched her eyes dip to his forearms, trace from his elbows to his wrists and back down again. Goosebumps trailed in the wake of her gaze.

"Right," she said, licking her lips and giving her head a small shake. The light caught her hair again, making it flicker and glow in the firelight. It was both fascinating and thrilling that he seemed to have the same effect on her as she did on him.

She's leaving. Don't get attached.

The voice seemed to whisper from somewhere in the back of his mind, but for once in his life, he wasn't paying it any heed.

TWELVE

"WHAT AUTUMN TOLD you is true. I used to write. It had always been a dream of mine to write a book, and when I turned thirty, I decided it was time to get serious about it," Adam said.

Hazel smiled, the corner of her lush mouth pulling up. "That sounds familiar."

"I wrote a couple of books, and they were both terrible. We're talking God-awful, never see the light of day, let's pretend they don't exist books."

She laughed. "Me too. I have this horrendous historical fiction about Jackie Kennedy that was just…it was a mess."

He nodded, something loosening in his chest. "But then I figured out what I wanted to write, and where I'd gone wrong in the other manuscripts and I wrote *The Wicked Season*."

"What's it about?" she asked, leaning forward, her fingers laced together, her eyes dancing with interest.

"It's a mystery novel that takes place in a small town in New York similar to Gossamer Falls. The main character is a detective who works for the state police, and he's dispatched to solve a murder. The town is full of quirky characters and hidden secrets."

"Can I read it?" she asked, and it was like sunshine had just socked him in the chest. Just then, Cole returned, balancing a plate of appetizers on one hand, and two cider flights on the other. He set everything down carefully and then wiped his hands on the dish towel still over his shoulder.

"Okay," he said, rubbing his hands together. "I brought you something to nibble on," he said, indicating the large plate he'd placed at the end of the table. "Mini quiches, bacon-wrapped chicken skewers, cheddar with apple slices, and roasted cauliflower bites."

Hazel inhaled and then bit her lip. "It smells amazing," she said, and Adam realized that the way she was looking at the food, ravenous and excited, was exactly how he wanted her looking at him.

What the fuck was wrong with him? He was going to kill Autumn for weaseling into his head like this.

"And the ciders. From left to right we have our pumpkin cider, our fall craft cider, which is made with pears and raspberries, our sour apple cider, our vintner's cider, which is made with apples and pears and then aged in wine barrels, and finally, our honey cider, which is made with honey crisp apples, blueberries, and honey. Enjoy, and let me know if you have any questions." He nodded and then returned back to the bar.

"Should we go left to right?"

Adam nodded. "Yeah. Let's sip and compare in order."

They started tasting, each one more delicious than the

last. Adam reached for a mini quiche at the same time as Hazel, their fingers brushing. They both went completely still, eyes locking, awareness zapping between them, just like it had that morning. When she'd been wearing a soaking white wet robe and he'd seen the delicious outline of her breasts and—

She pulled her hand away slowly. "Can I read your book?" she asked again, her voice soft.

He nodded. "If you want. There's a copy in the lounge at the inn."

She grinned. "I can't wait." They both chewed and sipped for a few minutes before she asked, "So...what happened?"

"Ha, well," he said, shaking his head. "I found an agent, who sold the book to a publisher in New York. The deal was for three books. The money wasn't great, but I didn't really care. I had my foot in the door, you know? The beginnings of something." She watched him, rapt as he spoke. Before he could talk himself out of it, he reached across the table and brushed a crumb away from the corner of her mouth. She let out a tiny gasp that went straight to his dick, and he let his thumb linger on her warm skin, just for a second. "Sorry, you had a little something."

"Don't be sorry," she said breathlessly. "It's...it's fine." She took a breath, and then asked, "So then what happened?"

"The first book came out and didn't do very well. Granted, it didn't receive much promotion, but still. I never earned out the advance, and the large print run bit me in the ass because there were a lot of returns."

Hazel winced. "Isn't it wild that bookstores can do that? I can't think of any other industry where stores can basically take products on consignment and then return them if they don't sell them."

He sighed. "The print run for the second book was smaller, which meant even less promotion. By the time the third book came out, I knew the series was dead in the water. They declined the option book in the contract and let me go. I pitched several more ideas to my agent, but he said that I'd have to start over with a new pen name and everything in order to get anywhere because of how poorly the series had sold." He felt as though a weight were pressing down on his shoulders, and a cold, hard ball that he recognized as bitter grief sat in the middle of his chest.

Hazel reached across the table and laid her hand on his. "I'm sorry, Adam. That's brutal. Publishing is brutal. I think sometimes they throw spaghetti at the wall just to see what sticks. And if you don't stick, you get brushed aside. But I really hope you don't take it as a reflection on you or your books. You persisted and wrote something worthy of an agent's attention, worthy of an offer from a publisher. That's not nothing. Most people who want to write don't make it that far." She gave his hand a gentle squeeze, sending warmth pouring through him. "Do you still write?"

He shook his head. "No. That dream...it didn't work out." He forced a grin to his face. "But I'm happy running the hotel. It's more than enough for me."

"Do you miss it?" she asked, tilting her head.

He paused, mulling that over. Did he miss it? "Yeah, sometimes. I miss the excitement of creating characters. I miss losing myself in a world of my own creation. I don't miss the bullshit of publishing."

She smiled softly. "I get that. Publishing is definitely bull-shit a lot of the time."

"But it's worked out for you," he said, eyebrow slightly arched.

"It has," she conceded. "But I might be about to go up in flames, too." She gave a little shrug.

"What do you mean?"

She bit her lip, tracing her finger around a ring of condensation on the table, left by one of the cider glasses. "After the success of my last trilogy, they offered me a lot of money for whatever I was going to write next. They didn't even care what it was. They just wanted to lock me down, which I know sounds great. They gave me the money and six months to come up with a proposal and a detailed outline. After six months, I had nothing, so I had to ask for an exten-sion. And then another one. And another one. Finally, I had an outline and everything, and as soon as I did, they started asking for the first hundred pages. I could feel the tone shift-ing, you know? It changed from supportive to impatient to flat out irritated. And now, here I am, deadline barrelling down on me, and I still don't have anything." She met his eyes, and he could see the worry and the stress etched across her pretty face. "What if I don't have another book in me? What if those three books were all I'm capable of?"

"When do you need to submit the first hundred pages?" he asked, wishing desperately that he could help.

"Here's the thing. I've used up all the goodwill that my earlier success earned me. So now, if I don't submit the first hundred pages by Halloween, so like...three weeks? Ish? They're going to cancel the contract and ask for the advance back. Which I don't have, because I've been living off of it for the past couple of years. So, I might be really, really screwed if I can't figure this out. Like, we're talking can't pay my rent, totally broke, financially ruined, writing career over."

Adam reached across the table, cupping her face and tilting it so he could meet her eyes. "That's not going to happen. I know we've just met, but I can see that you're a smart woman. I can see that this matters to you. And I don't believe for a second that you don't have another book in you. Maybe you just haven't found the right story to tell, yet."

She leaned her cheek against his palm, her eyes closing briefly. "I hope you're right."

"I'm always right. Ask my siblings."

She laughed, and something tugged at his heart knowing that he'd pulled that golden sound out of her. She reached for one of the small glasses of cider and almost knocked it over. "Sorry. I'm...I'm nervous."

He shook his head. "Don't be sorry," he said, echoing her words from a few moments ago. Their eyes met and held, firelight dancing around them, but the heat Adam could feel wasn't from the flames. Something was building and growing between the two of them. Something he didn't think he'd be able to ignore, even though he should.

But fuck, he didn't want to.

"Why are you nervous?" he asked, helping himself to more food and more cider. Everything was delicious. He knew he should probably be paying more attention to what he liked and what he wanted to bring into the Inn, but he was far more interested in Hazel. How she looked, what she thought, hearing her laugh.

"Well," she said, twisting her fingers together and

blowing out a breath. "This is the first date I've been on since my divorce." Her cheeks went pink and her eyes widened. "I mean...if this is a date, I don't want to assume..."

"Hazel." She trailed off and searched his face. He grinned at her. "This is very much a date."

He could see the relief on her face in the way she glanced down and bit back a smile.

"Can I ask you about your divorce?" he asked, wanting to know. Not to judge, just to understand.

"Well...I don't think I'm supposed to talk about it," she said, nibbling at a mini quiche.

His eyebrows rose at that. "You're not?"

She hesitated briefly before shrugging. "There's this dating coach I follow. On Instagram? And she says to never talk about your exes on a first date."

He made a show of looking around the tasting room. Music floated on the air, mingling with the sound of the softly crackling fire. "Is she here?"

Hazel laughed. "No."

"Then I think you're safe. Unless *you* don't want to talk about it. Which is fine."

She shook her head. "No, I don't mind. It's...I mean, the whole point is getting to know each other and whether I like it or not, this is part of me..." She trailed off, her bottom lip once again caught between her teeth. He wanted to pull that lip free, smooth his thumb over it. Wrap his arms around her to try to absorb some of the anxiety he could feel coming off of her, like heat from a fire. He sipped his cider, not even noting which one it was.

"I met Seth..." She looked up at the ceiling, squinting.

"Sorry, I'm just trying to think of the shortest way to tell this story." She glanced at him. "I've always sucked at writing synopses."

"That's because synopses are an instrument of torture invented by Satan himself," he said, his voice deadpan. She laughed, and he saw some of the tension go out of her shoulders.

"Agreed. Okay, so. I met Seth about eight years ago, through my agent. Seth wound up being my editor for the trilogy, and by the time the third book came out, we were married. But about a year in, things started to feel off. When I finally worked up the guts to confront him about how distant he'd been, how much he'd been working, how off things felt between us..." She trailed off, glancing out the window at the darkened forest. "He admitted he'd been seeing someone else."

"God, Hazel, I'm sorry. What a shit."

Her lips trembled, a small smile pulling them upwards. "Yes. He is a shit. He's charming and smart and connected and a total, complete shit. Anyway, he's with that other woman now and the divorce has been final for just over a year."

"Sounds like good riddance to me," said Adam, his heart aching for what she'd been through. He wasn't a violent man, and he didn't even know Seth, but he wanted to punch him in the face for what he'd done to Hazel.

"Well, it would be if he wasn't still my editor," she muttered, and he stilled, his eyes going wide.

"I'm sorry?" He couldn't possibly have heard her right.

She sent him a sheepish smile. "Yeah. Seth is still my editor."

"No wonder you're stuck," he said, not thinking before the words were out of his mouth.

She tilted her head. "What do you mean?"

"I don't think I'd ever feel comfortable sharing something I wrote with someone who broke my heart. Who showed themselves to be unethical, untrustworthy, and—"

"And a total shit?" she finished for him, an adorable grin on her face.

"Yes. I don't think I could, and I'm only imagining a hypothetical, here."

She sighed. "I've asked to switch to another editor, but Seth won't pass me along. I think it's his way of pretending that everything is fine and that he's not the bad guy in all of this."

Adam put on an overly jocular voice. "See, we're still working together, we're still friends, no harm no foul, nothing to see here."

Her smile returned, bright and flashing in the firelight. "Exactly. That's it exactly."

"Well, I don't know how you're supposed to be productive and creative with that going on." He shrugged. "I know I couldn't be."

"I know, but what am I supposed to do? He won't pass me along. I have to hand something in to avoid having the entire contract cancelled. I just..." Her shoulders slumped. "I don't know what to do. I feel...lost."

"I'm so sorry you're in this situation, Hazel. It's shitty and unfair." He felt drained just thinking about the emotional and professional turmoil she'd been through. Was still going through.

"Thanks. I...it'll be fine. It has to be, right?" He could tell the smile on her face was forced.

He reached forward and laid his hand over hers. "Everything will work out in the end. It always does. If things haven't worked out yet, it's only because the story isn't over."

Her eyes softened. "Thank you. I really appreciate that."

"Maybe you should forget about the outline," he said with a small tilt of his head. "Forget about anything Seth has ever had his hands on. What's speaking to you right now? What's pulling at your curiosity? Write something new. Something different, with no expectations." Adam knew he should probably take his own advice if he ever wanted to write something again. But giving advice was one thing; following through on it was another entirely.

"I'll think about it," she said with sincerity.

They ate and drank in silence for a moment before she said, "It must've been nice, growing up in a place like this."

He smiled. "It was, mostly. Everyone knows everyone, so it's hard to have secrets or privacy, which is less than ideal sometimes. But I wouldn't change the childhood I had for anything. What about you? Are you from the city?"

She nodded. "I grew up in Brooklyn."

"Siblings?"

"One younger brother. He lives in Australia."

"Are you close with your parents?"

"I mean...not particularly? Things were fine growing up, but I wouldn't say we're particularly close as adults. Sometimes it feels as though they've done their job and they're just sort of...done." A shadow flickered behind her eyes and his chest hurt.

"I take it they weren't supportive during your divorce?"

She let out a small laugh. "No. They weren't. And you know, a part of me gets it. They've earned their retirement. They've earned the right to travel and be free."

"Being retired doesn't mean you're not still a parent, though," he said gently.

"Yeah." She sent him a tight smile, and he got the distinct impression it was time for a subject change.

"What's the best book you've ever read?" he asked, steering the conversation in a different direction.

Her expression transformed, a wide smile spreading across her face and making it hard for him to remember to breathe. To blink. Goddamn, she was beautiful. Beautiful in a way that made him ache.

He learned that her favorite books were Agatha Christie's Hercule Poirot novels, especially *And Then There Were None*, but that when it came to comfort reads, her favorite genre was romances, the spicier the better. He learned that her favorite color was green. That she loved Carrie Clark, Beyonce, and oldies. That her favorite movie was *When Harry Met Sally*, and that in sixth grade, she'd gotten a week of detention for starting a cafeteria-wide food fight on a dare. He tucked every little piece of information away, like tiny little jewels that he only wanted to collect more of.

"So, what's the verdict?" asked Cole as he approached their table. Adam blinked slowly, reluctantly pulling his attention away from Hazel. He realized, then, that the tasting room was now empty, the fire down to embers.

"I'll take a case of each," he said, mostly because he couldn't remember which one was which. And frankly, he didn't care.

Cole clapped his hands together. "Awesome. I'll have Cameron bring them over tomorrow."

"Thanks, Cole." He reached into his pocket for his wallet, but Cole waved him off.

"Nah, man. On the house."

Adam shot him a smile. "Thanks. Appreciate it."

"Everything was amazing," said Hazel, her cheeks a little rosy. In the low light, she looked like she was glowing. Lit from within.

"Well, thank you. Maybe we'll see you again sometime."

"I'll have to get a case to bring back to the city with me," she said, and the words were like a bucket of ice water over Adam's overheated system.

For the past couple of hours, he'd managed to put out of his mind that Hazel was leaving. Not leaving. Returning home. Where her entire life was.

And yet...knowing that didn't make him want to back away the way he normally did. Which was weird, because Adam normally questioned everything. Never in his life had he been accused of underthinking something. But the pull he felt toward Hazel was different than anything he'd ever experienced. He didn't have words to explain it. Whatever was happening between him and Hazel felt too precious, too rare, too exciting to toss aside. Already, visions of a long distance relationship or maybe even her falling in love with the town and staying were dancing through his mind.

What the actual hell? He didn't know where any of it was coming from, but he also didn't want to question it. It felt right. As though things were exactly the way they were supposed to be.

They stood from their table, and after he shook Cole's hand, he captured Hazel's much smaller hand in his.

"Thank you for inviting me," she said softly as they walked back to his car. "This is the most fun I've had in a long time."

"Thank you for saying yes," he replied.

They drove back to the Inn in contented silence, their fingers twined together over the center console. He didn't want to stop touching her. He didn't want tonight to end. There was something about being with Hazel…it all just felt so easy. Effortless.

Like magic.

He pulled his car under the porte cochere at the front of the inn, intending to walk her to the door, say goodnight, and then head back to his cabin.

As they stepped out of the car, the still beauty of the night hit him. The moon was still full, lighting up the sky with silvery beams, casting soft shadows along the front of the Inn and the quiet parking lot. The road was deserted, the only sounds the leaves rustling in the trees and Adam's heart pounding in his ears. The breeze picked up, ruffling Hazel's hair, and she leaned against one of the thick, wooden posts of the porte cochere. She smiled at him, one corner of her lush mouth kicking up, and an answering kick echoed, low in Adam's gut.

He braced his hand on the post above her head, sliding his other arm around her waist, the pull he felt towards her utterly irresistible. Like he was hypnotized. "I like you, Hazel. A lot. Maybe it's not cool to say that after one date. I don't know. I don't date much, and frankly I'm too old for games."

She licked her lips, pulling his gaze downward. "I like you, too, Adam."

He lowered his head, waiting for alarm bells to go off. In the past, if something had been this easy, he would've questioned it. He would've had to examine it from every angle, looking for flaws and traps and mistakes waiting to happen. But there were no alarm bells. Only the beating of his heart, loud in his ears, sparks flickering through his veins.

He could feel her breath against his mouth, smell the sweet cider on her breath.

And then a siren erupted from about thirty feet away. They jerked apart as though they were teenagers caught doing something wrong, and Adam let out a groan when he saw Jack's police SUV in the parking lot.

"Get a room," he teased through the megaphone.

Adam was going to kill him.

Hazel laughed and ducked her head. "One of your brothers, I assume?" she asked with a little smirk that made Adam want to kiss the shit out of her, audience be damned.

"Jack, yeah. Do you want to witness me strangling him, or should I save that for later?" he said, a slight groan to his voice.

She laughed again. "Maybe that's our sign to call it a night."

He swallowed. "Yeah, maybe." He held up his hand and flipped Jack off. Lights still flashing, the SUV retreated into the night.

The next chance he had to cockblock Jack, he was taking it.

Hazel started to move toward the Inn's front doors, and it was like something snapped inside Adam. The gentleman in him knew he should let Hazel walk away. Go up to her room.

But for once, Adam didn't want to be a fucking gentleman.

"Fuck it," he growled, and wrapped his fingers around her wrist, tugging her against him. She gasped and her eyes fluttered shut.

"Yes," she whispered, and that was all he needed.

His lips met hers, and she gasped again, her breath shuddering against his mouth, tangling with his own sharp exhale. He slid an arm around her waist, the other tangling into her hair as he pulled her tighter against him. She let out a soft moan, shredding the last of his restraint, and he deepened the kiss, his tongue swiping against hers. He groaned at the silkiness of it, his blood heating to a low, needy simmer. His hand tightened in her hair, and she opened for him even more. Inviting him in. Inviting him to take more of the heaven she was offering him.

She whimpered and clutched at his sweater, holding him close. An intense feeling of possessiveness washed over him unlike anything he'd ever experienced before. He drew back slightly, catching her full bottom lip between his teeth. A low growl pushed up from somewhere deep in his chest, a sound he didn't even recognize.

Fuck, one taste of Hazel and he was gone. Done.

She swayed into him, and he held her tighter, his forehead resting against hers. They were both panting as though they'd just run a marathon. She slowly uncurled her fingers from his sweater, smoothing out the wrinkles she'd made. Wrinkles he didn't give a shit about.

"Holy shit," she whispered, staying exactly where she was.

"Holy shit," he agreed. "That was...unbelievable."

She let out a little laugh. "That's definitely one word for it."

"What word would you use?"

She lifted her head to meet his eyes. "Earthshattering. Life changing. Or maybe knee-buckling. Take your pick."

He laughed quietly, and slowly let his arms fall to his sides. "We should say goodnight."

Her eyes met his again, and he didn't miss the flash of disappointment in hers. "Oh. Right. Yeah." She looked down, suddenly very interested in her shoes. Slipping his fingers under her chin, he tilted her face up to his, forcing her to meet his gaze.

"I want to make something really clear, Hazel. We're saying goodnight right now because I want to keep getting to know you. I don't want you to think that this is just a physical thing for me, because it isn't. It's more, and I think we both know that."

Her lips curved in a smile, and she brushed a lock of hair off his forehead.

"But don't mistake my restraint now for disinterest, because I do want you." He lowered his head and kissed along her jawline, then whispered against the shell of her ear, "I want to kiss you like that again. I want to taste every inch of your skin."

And then, shocking and thrilling the hell out of him, she tilted her head and said, "I want to know what you feel like inside me."

When he met her eyes, he saw the heat and playful

mischief shining at him there. His brain misfired, words failing him.

"I never do this," she whispered. "Date, kiss a man I barely know, say things like I just said."

He pressed his forehead against hers. "I don't either. Holy shit, Hazel, I don't know what this is. I don't know what's different, but *something* is."

"It's scary."

"Hell yeah, it is."

"But, I want it. Whatever it is, this scary thing..." She trailed off, biting her lip. He kissed her gently, the tenderness of the kiss a sharp contrast to how badly his cock was aching.

"I want it, too. I want it so badly that you should go inside before I do something very ungentlemanly."

"I'd hate to ruin your reputation," she teased, pressing a kiss to his cheek. "Goodnight Adam." She slipped away from him and disappeared into the hotel.

Adam stared at the door for several long seconds. "What the actual fuck?" he whispered, giving his head a shake as he took several steps back. "What the hell is happening?"

THIRTEEN

THE NEXT MORNING, Adam moved through the lounge, fluffing pillows, tidying books, watering plants, but his mind wasn't in the present moment. His mind was firmly stuck on last night, and the date he was starting to feel shouldn't have happened. He kept replaying it over and over in his mind. The smell of Hazel's perfume. The sound of her laugh. The taste of her lips against his. The dirty words she'd whispered in his ear.

He let out a soft groan and spilled water on the floor, overfilling the poor potted snake plant sitting on a small table by the window.

"Shit," he grumbled, hustling back out to the lobby to get a towel to clean it up. He'd just finished sopping up the water when the front door to the hotel opened, and Adam's head whipped in that direction so fast he almost popped a tendon. He didn't know what he was going to do or say when he saw Hazel again. He knew, for his sake and hers, that he should let her down gently. Her life was complicated, and she lived in New York City. He was firmly rooted where he was, in this town, in this life.

"I come bearing caffeine and apple cider donuts," said Jack, who was out of uniform this morning.

"Why?" asked Adam warily.

Jack looked at him as though he was speaking another language. "Because I want to hear all about your date. Duh."

"Oh. Right. That." He jerked his head in the direction of the vacant sunroom, and Jack followed. Adam pushed open one of the French doors, leading them out onto the terrace. Mist clung to the field that separated the Inn's property from the Hudson Highlands, and the sun was still slowly making its way into the sky. Adam took the coffee Jack offered him and took a long sip.

"So?" asked Jack, taking a healthy bite of his donut. "How did it go?"

Adam sighed heavily, staring out at the mist. "It was fantastic."

"You say that like it's a bad thing," said Jack, frowning. "I'm a little confused."

"That should be the title of your autobiography," Adam deadpanned, deflecting.

Jack flipped him off. "Why is having a fantastic date with a nice woman a bad thing? Explain it to me, because I don't get it."

Christ, he wasn't going to let this go.

"Because I like her. A lot. And in two weeks, she's going back to her life in New York City. Because I like her, and it can't go anywhere. Because I kissed her and it was fucking amazing and it can't happen again." The words tasted like sawdust in his mouth, dry and crumbly, and he took a sip of his coffee to try to chase it away. "I'm already halfway—" He cut himself off, shaking his head. He knew what he'd said, how he'd acted with Hazel last night. It was as though being with her had slashed all of his brake lines. He'd been so absorbed in her that he'd forgotten about reality.

"Oh my God, dude. You need to get out of your head and just have some fun. When was the last time you didn't worry about the future and just did what felt good in the moment? What felt right?"

"I—" He opened and closed his mouth. "Just because that's how you live your life, doesn't mean that's how I want to live mine."

A murmuration of starlings swooped across the field, dipping and diving in an intricately choreographed flight pattern.

"I'm not saying you have to live like me. Believe me, there are downsides. But when was the last time you had fun? Felt good?" He leaned closer, his forearms braced on his thighs. "Because I don't think you have since Dad—"

"Don't," said Adam sharply, shaking his head. "This has nothing to do with Dad."

"Doesn't it?" asked Jack, one eyebrow arched. "You've been in a complete rut since he died. It's like you're frozen. You're not writing anymore, you don't date, you barely have a social life." He lowered his voice. "That's not what he would want. Not for you, not for any of us. Even though he's not here, he'd want you to live your life and be happy. Not..." He waved a hand in Adam's direction. "Whatever it is you're doing right now. Existing in a holding pattern."

Adam sipped his coffee, not saying anything as Jack's words hit home, socking into him like cannon balls.

"Yesterday, you were completely into this date. You're telling me you had a fantastic time. And now…what? You're just going to drop it? You need to get out of this rut you're in. Even if it's just a temporary thing, you need to let yourself have some fun."

"Yeah. Maybe."

"Stop thinking so much," he said, and Adam snorted out a laugh.

"Classic Jack advice if I've ever heard any."

"I'm serious. You need to get out of your head and out of this rut. Start living your life again. I know you like running the Inn, and that's great. But what about writing? What about a relationship?"

"I don't know," said Adam, a little snarl making its way into his voice. But Jack didn't flinch. He just sipped his coffee and watched the starlings swooping above the mist.

"Tell you what," he said after a moment. "See where this thing with Hazel goes. Give it the two weeks. Don't run scared because it's not perfect or whatever. Get out of your head."

"And when it blows up in my face?"

"If it does—which I don't think it will—I'll…I'll shovel your driveway all winter."

Adam's eyebrows inched up. He hated shoveling snow. "Fine, whatever. Deal." He glanced over at his brother, who was smiling smugly at his coffee. "What do you think's going to happen?"

Jack shrugged. "Dunno. Maybe you'll get laid and stop being such a pill. Maybe something more will develop." He tilted his head. "Autumn said she took Hazel to the falls, and the very next morning you were soaking wet in her mysteriously malfunctioning shower. So…" He wiggled his fingers. "Maybe the magic's working."

Adam rolled his eyes. "Christ, not you, too. I didn't think you believed in Autumn's woo-woo stuff."

Jack shrugged slowly. "I don't know, man. But one thing I can tell you is that you'd never in a million years catch me at the falls under a full moon."

"Wimp."

"You've never gone either."

"Because it's stupid."

"Right," said Jack, stretching out the word.

The French doors on the other side of the patio opened and Adam's heart kicked against his ribs when he saw Hazel step out, her hair up in a messy bun, glasses on, wearing a *Nightmare Before Christmas* themed sweatshirt and a pair of leggings.

"Good morning," Jack said after a minute, making Adam realize he'd been staring. Something seemed to happen to him every single time Hazel was around. It was as though his brain disconnected from his body and all he could see, all he cared about was her.

Hazel let out an adorable squeak and then turned from the other side of the terrace. "I'm sorry, I didn't see you sitting there," she said. "I'm…I'm not used to all this quiet. It's almost unnerving sometimes." She walked over, self-consciously tugging on her sweatshirt.

"I'm Jack, Adam's brother," he said, extending his hand. "Sorry about the, uh, the siren last night."

Hazel's eyebrows went up. "Oh, that was you?"

"Just having a little fun at my brother's expense," he said, clapping Adam on the shoulder. Adam grunted. "Anyway, I'm going to head out. Nice to meet you."

"How did you..." Hazel started and then swallowed, her gaze darting back and forth between Jack and Adam. "How did you know it was me? Last night I looked...not like this... and it was dark, and..."

He elbowed Adam. "His reaction when you stepped out." He winked at Hazel and offered her the bag that still held a couple of donuts. She took it, watching him with an unreadable expression on her face.

After he left, she opened the bag and practically shoved her face inside. "Oh my God," she moaned in a way that made Adam's blood heat. "These smell amazing."

She pulled one out and took a bite, and Adam felt as though he was mesmerized. He'd never experienced anything like this before, and he already knew that his resolve to keep his distance from her was in tatters.

Maybe he *should* take a page out of Jack's book and stop thinking about everything so much.

"What's the plan for today?" he asked her. She stilled when he reached up and brushed a crumb away from the corner of her mouth with his thumb. She licked her lips, and there was an answering tug in his gut. God, he wanted to kiss her again. Kiss her and so much more.

"Open manuscript. Stare at manuscript. Question every life decision I've ever made to get here. Drink too much coffee. Resume staring at manuscript."

He laughed. "That sounds both torturous and familiar."

"You know what's weird? People always assume that I must love writing. That I live for it. But...I don't think I do. I don't enjoy the actual writing, but I always enjoy having written."

He laughed again. "Like exercise. Or cleaning."

A pretty smile spread across her face, making his heart feel wobbly. "Exactly." She shook her head. "I like talking to you about writing. You...you just get it."

"Maybe a change of scenery would help? You're welcome to set up in here," he said, gesturing at the sunroom behind them. He knew from experience that it was a peaceful place to write. He also knew that if she worked there, he'd get to watch her all day.

"I might. Then you can have a front row seat to me tearing my hair out."

The sudden image of his fist in her hair seared through him, and he cleared his throat. "You know, I was thinking about your book last night."

"You were?"

He nodded. "I could read what you have, if you want."

She sighed. "Maybe. There isn't much to read, honestly. You know, I was thinking about your advice from last night."

"Oh?" he asked, trying to remember what he'd said. His mind was too full of Hazel to remember his own words.

"Yeah. I think I might just...write. Whatever comes to mind. See where it takes me. Plus, I do think it would be freeing to write something Seth has never seen or had his hands on. If I do that, do you think you might...you might read it?"

"I'd be honored."

Her eyes went wide. "Speaking of, I need a copy of your book. Since you said there's one here."

His heart did a weird little stuttering motion in his chest

at the thought of Hazel reading his book. He nodded and tipped his head toward the sunroom. "Follow me."

The palm of his hand tingled as she walked beside him, their fingers brushing slightly. She made a soft humming noise in the back of her throat that he almost wasn't sure he'd heard. The tingle spread outward from his palm and up his arm until it felt as though it was vibrating.

They stepped into the lounge, but at the threshold, Hazel tripped slightly, catching her toe on the sill. On instinct, he reached out to steady her, wrapping his fingers around her wrist. The buzzing inside him settled as soon as he had his hand on her.

She pushed her glasses up her nose and shot him a sheepishly adorable smile. "Clearly, I haven't had my coffee yet."

"A problem with an easy solution," he said. "Let me find you the book and then I'll get you some coffee fresh from the kitchen."

"Oh, you don't have to do that," she said. "It's not like I'm going to leave you a bad review on Yelp at this point."

He chuckled. "Well, that's a relief. What would your review say?"

She tapped her finger against her mouth as they walked into the lounge, and he realized that he'd woven his fingers with hers. He hadn't even noticed himself doing it. Maybe because it felt like the most natural thing in the world.

"Hmm. Beautiful inn. Possibly haunted, but in a fun, quirky way. If cozy was a place, the Shephard Inn would be it. Owner is..." She turned to look at him, her eyes flaring with heat. "Very professional."

"That's not what I thought you were going to say."

The same glint of mischief he'd seen last night was back, flashing in her eyes. "What did you think I was going to say?" She inched closer. "Owner is very hot? Owner is a fantastic kisser? Owner is—"

Before he even realized he was doing it, he was in motion, tugging her against him and brushing his lips against hers. Heat and need exploded through him, and he let out a shuddery breath. God, she was going to be his undoing.

"Owner is very welcoming," she murmured against his lips, and he kissed her softly before pulling away with a chuckle.

"Please know that not every guest gets this treatment," he said. It was suddenly important for him to make sure she knew. "In fact, I have a strict no dating guests rule for myself."

"You broke your rule for me?"

He nodded.

"Why?"

He slid his arms around her, pulling her back against him. Right where it felt like she belonged. "It started with a white robe. A very wet, very transparent white robe," he said, his voice low. He brushed his lips over hers, teasing his tongue along the seam of her mouth. "There was flirting, if I'm not mistaken. Innuendoes. Something about making you wet." She whimpered softly and he kissed her again, slow and lingering. "Then there was a riveting discussion about writing and the horrors of publishing." He kissed her again, deeper this time, his tongue sweeping against hers. She swayed into him, and it was all he could do to hold them both upright because his knees were on the verge of giving out, too. "And then that glowing Yelp review…well. That just sealed the deal for me."

"I'll post it as soon as I'm back at my computer," she panted, fisting her hands in his sweater and pulling him down for another kiss. His skin was on fire, his stomach swirling and dipping with need. He was normally so in control of himself. But with Hazel, he felt as though he could drown in the feeling of her mouth on his and not give one shit. His hands were shaking on her hips, his heart slamming against his ribs.

Somehow, he managed to break the kiss, even though he didn't want to. No, what he wanted to do was take Hazel back up to her room and spread her out like a feast on her bed. But for now, he had work to do, and she had a book to write. Or, at the very least, a screen to stare at.

She unfurled her palms from his sweater, and he captured her wrist, lifting it to his mouth and kissing her palm.

"Let me find that book for you," he said, turning and adjusting himself as discreetly as possible. The last thing he needed was for his employees to see the imprint of his rock hard dick pressing against the front of his jeans.

She made a soft humming sound and followed along half a step behind him. That buzzing from somewhere deep inside him was back, and he had a feeling it would always be there when Hazel was around and he wasn't touching her. Wasn't kissing her.

He skimmed the shelves and pulled out the slightly worn copy of *The Wicked Season* and handed it to her, their fingers brushing as she took it. "I guess it's only fair, since I started reading yours last night," he admitted.

"You did?" she asked, her eyes meeting his.

He nodded. "Yeah. I downloaded it onto my Kindle...I hope you don't mind."

She shook her head. "Of course not. Not at all. I...thank you. That's really sweet."

"You're an amazingly talented writer, Hazel. The lushly constructed world, the complex, fascinating characters, the heartbreakingly poetic prose..." He let out a breath and then tapped the cover of his own book in her hands. "Don't judge me too harshly."

She blushed furiously and laughed. "Clearly you didn't get to the part about his cock kissing her cervix."

His eyebrows inched up his forehead. "I didn't, but now I'm wishing I'd brought my Kindle to work with me." He stepped closer, slipping his fingers under her chin to draw her eyes upward. She didn't quite reach his chin, so she had to tilt her head up several inches. "I knew there was a heavy romantic element in your books, but...Hazel, is your book dirty?"

She bit her lip, doing nothing to help the situation in his jeans. "In parts, yes. Very dirty."

"Fuck, that's hot," he groaned and then they were kissing again. "Have dinner with me tonight," he said, his teeth scraping against her lips. "I'll cook for you."

"At your house?" she asked, pulling back slightly. Little lines dug in between her eyebrows.

"Or we can go to a restaurant," he amended quickly. "Whatever you're comfortable with."

"Your house," she answered quickly. "Definitely your house."

His heart thundered in his chest. "Okay. I usually leave

for the day around five or five-thirty...does that work for you?"

"I'll have to check my agenda," she said with a little smirk that made him want to kiss her again.

So he did. Her lips moved against his eagerly, sweetly, her arms winding around his neck, fingers snaking into his hair. He explored her mouth with long, gentle sweeps of his tongue, and he felt as though he'd taken a hit of the world's sweetest drug. He could easily become addicted to kissing Hazel. Fuck, he probably already was. Hazel seemed to melt into him.

God, her mouth was soft. Sweet. Open and giving. Lust rocketed through him as she nipped at his lower lip, and he broke the kiss again, pulling away before he started mauling her like a horny teenager.

"I promised you coffee," he said, his voice coming out rusty around the edges. She smiled and touched the tips of her fingers to her lips, which made him wonder if they were tingling as fiercely as his were.

"Right. Coffee. You know, I'm going to add that to my Yelp review. Owner has a mouth that makes me forget about caffeine. Which, I have to say, is *quite* the accomplishment."

A smile spread across his face. "Fucking adorable," he said, pressing a kiss to her temple before disappearing into the kitchen.

FOURTEEN

AFTER HER MUCH NEEDED CUP OF coffee, a second donut, and a few more kisses, Hazel headed back to her room to shower, dress, and video chat her bestie.

She'd sent her an email last night after her date with Adam. It was a very sophisticated worldly email that read "SOS I don't know what the fuck I'm doing and I'm so happy please can we chat in the morning."

Sarah had emailed back right away, and they'd agreed to chat at nine the next morning.

A sense of happiness and excitement filled Hazel when Sarah's pretty face filled the screen. Her red hair was up in a high ponytail, and her purple shirt emphasized her green eyes. They spent a few minutes catching up, and then Sarah sipped her ever-present mug of tea, one eyebrow arched.

"So. Are you gonna tell me what's going on, or what?"

Hazel laughed, her heart fluttering in her chest. "I went on a date last night."

Sarah screamed, her eyes wide. "What? Oh my God, tell me everything."

"His name's Adam Shephard, and he runs the hotel where I'm staying for the next couple of weeks." She told her about the shower incident, how he'd asked her out, and the amazing date they'd had, with flowing conversation, flirty banter, and how kind he'd been. She told Sarah about how hot Adam was, how funny and smart.

"And did this hot, funny, smart man kiss you at the end of this fabulous date?" she asked, hanging on Hazel's every word.

"Oh, yeah. He kissed the absolute shit out of me."

Sarah screamed again, the screen shaking a little. "I'm so happy and excited for you! How are you feeling?"

"Well, I'm...confused."

"Okay. About what?"

"Okay, so I like him. A lot. We're having dinner at his place tonight and I'm telling myself that we're not going to have sex, but we're probably totally going to have sex and I'm super nervous about that. I'm scared to let myself like him too much because I live like two hours away and I don't know about trying to do some long distance thing. I'm nervous about getting naked with someone for the first time since the divorce. And I can't stop thinking about how great he is. Like, all I can think about is him."

Sarah blinked rapidly, processing Hazel's word vomit. "I get being nervous about it. You haven't been with anyone since Seth, so it's kind of a big deal."

"Yeah, it is."

"But you want to, right?"

Butterflies erupted in her stomach at the thought of sleeping with Adam. "I'm scared, but yeah. I want it. I want him."

"I have to admit, I'm happy for you, but a little surprised."

"What do you mean?" she asked, pulling a pillow across her lap.

"Well, when you were dating, before you met Seth, you were always so cautious and guarded and this feels like the opposite of that. I don't mean that in a bad way. It's just an observation."

"I know. That's why I'm kinda freaking out. Because I'm ready to jump in with both feet and I probably shouldn't."

"Why not?"

"The distance. The fact that it's so new. That I'm not sure what I want."

Sarah scoffed. "I don't know. It sounds like you're pretty clear on what you want. You want Adam."

"Yeah," Hazel admitted. "I do." She traced her fingers in a whirling pattern over the pillow in her lap. "I think..." She scrunched her nose up and shook her head, cutting off what she'd been about to say.

"You think what?" asked Sarah.

"Okay, you're going to laugh at me. But, I think there might be something more going on."

"I promise I won't laugh. What do you mean?"

She told Sarah about the legend of the falls and her moonlit visit, and how Adam had been in her room the very next morning, fixing her mysteriously broken shower.

"So...what? You think you're like...meant to fall in love with him because you visited a waterfall?" asked Sarah, brow furrowed.

Hazel sighed. "See? I told you you'd laugh at me."

"I'm not laughing! I'm just trying to understand. I

mean...yeah, it's probably just a legend meant to get tourists to visit. But on the other hand...maybe...maybe it would explain why you're so head over heels for this guy already, which definitely isn't like you."

"Right?" She tossed the pillow aside. "I'm scared and confused and I'm so into him and yeah, there are reasons why I should probably hit the brakes, but you know what? I don't want to. And for once, I'm just going to go with it. Please tell me I'm not crazy."

"You're not crazy! If anyone deserves some fun with a hot man, it's you, Hazel. I don't know about the legend and all of that, but if you're into him, go for it."

She smiled. "Thanks, Sarah. I think I needed to hear that."

"Of course! You know I'm always here for you."

They chatted for a few more minutes, and then said their goodbyes. Hazel felt more settled than she had before talking to Sarah. She didn't know if there was some kind of crazy magic happening. All she knew was that she felt something for Adam, and it was strong enough that she wasn't going to ignore it.

As if she could.

Knowing she needed to get to work, she opened her manuscript and her notes file, dread settling over her. She proceeded to stare at the expectantly blinking cursor for over an hour, only taking breaks to scroll Facebook, read the news, decide if several people were or were not the asshole on Reddit, and look up her horoscope for the day. And that was when she wasn't daydreaming about Adam. Adam with his dark, soft curls and warm hazel eyes. Adam, with his full mouth and cleft chin. Adam, with his broad shoulders and muscled arms. Adam, with his deep, soothing voice and a laugh that felt like hot chocolate on a cold day.

She couldn't stop replaying it all in her mind. The kiss last night. The kisses this morning. The flirting and obvious mutual interest. The shared passion for writing and books.

How freaking hot he was without even trying.

It almost seemed too good to be true, but for once in her life, she wasn't going to rationalize something away. She'd spent far too much of her life talking herself *into* things that weren't what she wanted, deep down. Doing a sociology major when all she'd wanted was to study English lit. Signing up for three months of hot yoga because Leah had wanted to, even though being hot and sweaty made her feel nauseous.

Marrying Seth, if she was honest. Her mind flashed back to the almost panic attack she'd had the day before, wondering if she was making a huge mistake. The little voice inside her—the one she'd learned to ignore over the years in order to make others happy—had told her she was. That he wasn't the one for her. Her parents and Leah had talked her out of becoming a runaway bride. But sometimes she wondered if they'd talked her into marrying Seth because calling off the wedding the day before would've been so terribly inconvenient for all of them. No one had asked her why she was having doubts. Only told her she was wrong for having them in the first place.

God, no wonder she sucked at trusting her own instincts. She'd been made to question them by all of the key people in her life, over and over again. She wasn't going to let that happen this time. Whatever was happening between her and

Adam felt good. Natural, and easy, and happy. For once, she wasn't going to question it.

Her eyes flicked back to the computer screen, where her outline was open. She'd decided to try starting in a different place today. Normally, she was a linear writer, writing each scene in order. She'd hoped that shaking that up would tap into some secret well of inspiration.

Tension crept across her shoulders and up her neck, all the way into her jaw. She sighed and opened her web browser. She'd spend five minutes finding out which pop culture witch was her personality match, and then she'd get back to work.

If procrastination was an art, she'd be freaking Da Vinci by this point.

After learning she was most like Bonnie Bennett from *The Vampire Diaries*, she decided a change of scenery was in order. So, she gathered up her laptop, her notebook and a handful of pens, slipped her shoes on, and headed down to write in the sunroom, as Adam had suggested.

And yes, her decision to write there was partially—mostly—motivated by the hope that she'd catch glimpses of him as she worked. She hurried down the wide staircase, her footsteps muffled by the thick carpet, only to be met with a sagging disappointment when Adam was nowhere to be seen. The front desk was quiet, and she could hear the chatter of a few other hotel guests in the lounge.

As she passed the front desk on her way to the sunroom, she saw that the small door marked "management" was slightly ajar, and her heart doubled its tempo when she heard the deep timbre of Adam's voice coming through the door.

"...as much time as you need," he was saying, his tone kind. "We can find someone to fill in temporarily. Family comes first, always."

The corner of her mouth pulled up and her eyes actually stung a little. God, he was sweet. Kind and warm and so genuine. She'd never met anyone like him before. She wasn't sure if that said more about him, or the company she kept.

She reached the sunroom, which was empty, warm sunlight streaming in through the glass ceiling. The view through the French doors was breathtaking, all open fields and the edge of the woods, aflame with autumn. She picked a spot at a round table and sank down into the wicker chair, setting her things down. Just then, Adam emerged from the office, and her heart leapt into her throat and then dropped back down into her stomach, like she was on a wild carnival ride.

He saw her immediately and winked at her before stepping behind the front desk, his strong fingers moving quickly over the keyboard. She swallowed thickly, openly staring. Thinking about the feel of his mouth on hers again. The way he'd rasped out "*fuck, that's hot,*" when he'd learned that her books had some steamy bits.

She opened her laptop and then immediately opened a new document. He was right. Forget the outline. Forget anything Seth had had his hands on. What did *she* most want to write? What kind of story did she want to tell?

She glanced over in Adam's direction again to find his eyes on her. When their gazes met, he lifted his eyebrows slightly and made a typing motion with his hands, followed by a thumbs up. The message was clear.

Just write. You've got this.

A wave of happiness so intense it made her want to bounce out of her seat washed over her. Acting purely on instinct, she reached for her phone, wanting to text Leah to tell her all about Adam and Gossamer Falls. But she couldn't text Leah, because they weren't friends anymore, and it was moments like this, moments she wanted to share her life, when she felt the loss most acutely.

She set the phone down and returned her focus to the fresh, new document in front of her. She glanced out the windows, at the Hudson Highlands, around the gorgeous sunroom, and then finally back at Adam.

And she knew. She knew exactly what she wanted to write. The idea came to her in a flash, fully formed and tangible. Obvious but still exciting. Her fingers started to fly across the keys. Within minutes, she was in that flow state, where the story poured out of her, faster than her fingers could move.

She wasn't aware of time passing until Adam quietly set down a steaming mug full of coffee beside her. He pressed a kiss to her temple and then disappeared as quickly as he'd arrived, but that didn't stop her from taking a second to appreciate the hell out of his rounded, muscular ass in his jeans.

She cradled the mug in her hands, blowing steam away from the rim as her eyes skimmed over what she'd just written. A smile pulled at her lips as relief poured over her like warm sunshine.

Even if what she had on the page didn't end up being *The Book*, it felt good to know that she could still write. That she could still make something out of nothing. Put words and emotions on a page.

The main character was Mary Elizabeth Axton, the author of the beloved Gossamer Falls legend that she'd read a few times over now. Except that Mary Elizabeth Axton didn't live in the 1890s. She lived in present day Massachusetts and was a professor at Wellesley. She was also grieving for her husband, who'd died from a rare form of brain cancer just over a year ago. Her life felt stagnant. Sad, and lonely. And so, she decided on a whim to visit the picturesque town of Gossamer Falls.

Hazel had written two chapters—one introducing Mary Elizabeth, her world, and her grief, and a second, where she traveled to Gossamer Falls and visited the landmark under the light of the full moon. The chapter ended with something wholly unexpected happening, however—she slipped on a rock and tumbled into the creek, hitting her head. She nearly drowned, but was eventually rescued.

By a man in period clothing. Because unbeknownst to her, she's traveled back in time to 1864.

Hazel had never written about time travel before, despite the fascination she had for the concept. But whenever she'd tried to make the concept actually work, her brain started to hurt, and she couldn't keep the converging timelines straight. But for this story, it felt like a natural choice. The obvious choice.

She stretched and picked up her empty coffee cup, glancing at the front desk. Autumn was there, and she gave Hazel a little wave as she spoke on the phone. Needing to get up and get her blood flowing, she walked into the lounge, depositing her coffee cup on a little tray reserved for used cups and dishes. She wandered to the window, but she looked out at the front of the hotel's grounds without really seeing anything; her mind was still back in 1864 with Mary Elizabeth. She couldn't remember the last time she'd lost herself to the fog of a story like this. Where it seemed to envelop her and take over her brain.

She wandered across the room and started perusing the bookshelves, trailing her fingers over the spines of the books, some worn, some fairly new. A cold but gentle breeze brushed past her, carrying the scent of roses and hot chocolate, and Hazel's fingers started to tingle. She glanced at where they'd landed on a lime green book.

It was called *Time Travel in Einstein's Universe: The Physical Possibilities of Travel Through Time* by J. Richard Gott.

"No way," she whispered, yanking the book off the shelf. She skimmed the description on the back, snippets of phrases making her pulse race and the hairs on the back of her neck stand at attention.

"...Building on theories posited by Einstein and advanced by scientists such as Stephen Hawking and Kip Thorne, Gott explains how time travel can actually occur..." she read out loud, and then let out a small laugh. "Unbelievable. I can't..."

The scent of roses and hot chocolate washed over her again, and she smiled, clutching the book to her chest. "Thank you," she whispered, and hurried back to the sunroom with her treasure.

"You're not going to believe what just happened," she said to Autumn as she passed the front desk.

Autumn shrugged. "I probably will," she said with a little smile.

Hazel laughed again. God, she'd laughed more in the

past forty-eight hours than she had in the past year. "I've decided to write a book with a heavy time travel element. Something I've always been interested in, but always too intimidated to touch. I went into the lounge to stretch my legs, and I felt like something—or someone—was practically handing me this book." She held it up for Autumn to see, and a wide smile spread across the younger woman's face.

"Good job, Grams. That's exactly what she was looking for."

"Thanks, Grams," added Hazel, and she could've sworn she caught the faint scent of roses one last time.

"So," said Autumn, leaning on her elbows, her chin in her hands. "I hear you're having dinner with Adam tonight. I take it the cider tasting went well?" She grinned expectantly at Hazel, and she felt that spark of connection, of friendship towards Autumn. The warmth, the trust, the desire to share.

Hazel blushed slightly and zipped her thumb through the book's pages, relishing the scent of paper and the soft burr. "Very well. Best first date I've ever had, honestly. We talked for hours, and then...well, I don't want to get TMI with you."

"Please tell me that idiot kissed you."

Hazel laughed. "He did. Last night, and then again this morning."

Autumn's eyebrows practically flew into her hairline. "This morning? Does that mean—"

"Oh, no! I'm realizing how that sounded. He was a complete gentleman. He kissed me last night and saw me safely inside the hotel before going home. I ran into him this morning and we started talking and…" Her blush deepened. "We might've made out a little in the lounge."

Autumn's eyes lit up and she clapped her hands together. "I knew it! As soon as I saw you, I knew you were meant for him."

"I like him. A lot. And while I'm not really looking for anything serious, I do want to see where this goes, because I have the feeling that men like Adam aren't a dime a dozen."

"There are only five Shephard brothers, so you'd be right."

They both laughed. "Speaking of, I met your brother Jack this morning."

"Did he behave?"

"Mostly. Although he did blast his siren at me and Adam last night when he was about to kiss me by the front doors."

"Honestly, sometimes I think Jack is short for Jackass."

Hazel laughed. "He was just having a little fun."

"That's Jack. He's all about fun. Ever since his divorce, he's been all about it, sometimes to the point of obsession."

Hazel let out a breath. "Divorce is hard. It sucks. We all cope differently."

Autumn nodded sympathetically. "I get that. So," she said, changing the subject. "What are you going to wear on your date tonight?"

FIFTEEN

NERVES AND EXCITEMENT shot through Hazel as Adam drove through the small town, wending his way through the main streets before taking the same turn Autumn had when she'd visited the falls. Music played softly from the car's radio, a Harry Styles song from a local Top 40 station. As soon as she'd fastened her seatbelt, Adam had woven the fingers of his right hand through those of her left, leaving their fingers intertwined over the center console separating the seats. She wondered if he could feel her pulse thrumming in her wrist. She wondered if he needed to touch her as badly as she needed his hands on her.

"Be warned, I wasn't expecting guests," he said, glancing sideways at her as he steered confidently with one large hand draped over the wheel.

She grinned. "Are there dirty socks on the floor? Rotten milk in the fridge?"

He made a face. "God, no. I *am* an adult."

She gave his hand a squeeze. "Adam, I'm sure it's fine."

He was nervous about taking her to his place. And God,

it was endearing. Had Seth ever been nervous about anything when it came to her? He'd always seemed so confident. Overconfident, as though he knew he could get Hazel to do anything he wanted. He knew he'd had the upper hand —after all, he was older, more successful, with more money and more life experience.

He cleared his throat softly. "Also," he said, turning away from the center of town and towards the road that went to the falls, "I want you to know that I have no expectations. Physically, I mean," he said, the tips of his ears turning red.

Adam Shephard was endearing as hell.

"I just don't want you to feel any pressure because we're alone at my house."

She squeezed his hand again, nerves fluttering in her belly. Was she ready to have sex with someone new? She wasn't sure. The idea was exciting, but also more than a little intimidating. Did she *want* Adam? Well, duh. Obviously.

"I don't feel pressured," she assured him. "Let's just see where the evening takes us, no expectations. Because Adam?"

"Yeah?"

She sucked in a deep breath, feeling as though she were peering over the ledge of a cliff. A very steep, very rocky cliff with churning waves below. "I really like you, and getting to know you has been the best thing that's happened to me this year. Seriously."

He lifted their joined hands and placed a kiss on her knuckles, leaving her skin tingling. "I really like you, too, Hazel." Something flashed across his face, darkening his features for a second, but then it was gone as quickly as it had come.

The cabin she'd seen from the road the night she'd visited the falls grew closer, and then closer still as Adam turned off of the main road, navigating his Subaru down a gravel one. Stones pinged softly against the car.

"Wait," she said as Adam rolled the car to a smooth stop in front of the cabin, which was larger than she would've guessed from the road. "*This* is your house?" It felt too coincidental that the cabin she'd been drawn to was Adam's.

"Yep. I had it built about ten years ago."

He let go of her hand so they could step out of the car. The sky above was quickly darkening, the sunset painting the sky with streaks of burnt orange and dusky blue. To the right of the gravel drive, she could just make out a pond ringed with large rocks. Past the pond was a rock garden, with hardy evergreen shrubs, pine needle ground cover, and moss-covered rocks. All around them, pine trees stretched up to the sky, as though the cabin were half in the forest, filling the air with their scent. The cabin itself was a gabled A-frame with a steeply sloped roof and a wraparound porch. A log façade made it look rustic and cozy, as though it were much older than it was. Porch lights glowed warmly, illuminating their way to the front door.

Hazel couldn't explain how she was feeling in that moment. Despite her excited, happy nerves at being alone with Adam, her muscles felt relaxed. Her heart wasn't racing anymore, but beating slow and steady. The sound of the forest enveloped her, and it sounded like home. Which was crazy, because she'd lived her entire life in one of the world's biggest cities. But she'd never felt so instantly connected to a place in the city as she did to Adam's cabin on the edge of the Hudson Highlands. She hadn't even been inside, and somehow it felt as though it was where she belonged.

Goosebumps danced along her arms as Adam took her hand and led her up the three steps onto the porch. A jingle of keys and then the front door was open. It was dark inside, but Adam quickly turned on a light.

"Oh, wow, Adam," she said softly, looking around. The main floor was open concept, with a small entryway that opened onto a large living room to the left and an equally large kitchen on the right. Her eyes danced over the hand scraped wooden plank flooring, the stone fireplace that arched all the way to the ceiling, the rustic stone covering the back wall of the kitchen. "This is incredible. I've never..." She was almost overcome with the sensation that she'd found something she hadn't even known she'd been looking for.

He set his keys down on a small table by the front door and shrugged out of his jacket, hanging it on a mounted hook on the wall opposite the table. After slipping off her shoes and leaving her stuff by the front door, she followed him farther inside.

"This is what your place looks like when you're not expecting guests?" she asked, shaking her head and making a tsking sound. It was lived in, with a basket of folded laundry sitting at the bottom of the stairs, a discarded coffee cup on the coffee table in the living room, a few dishes in the kitchen sink, a rumpled blanket on the large gray sofa.

He laughed. "You were warned."

"I was. But I wasn't prepared for the horrors of bachelorhood," she teased.

He laughed even harder and then took her hand again. "Come on, I'll give you the tour."

The main floor felt like something out of a movie, all wood floors and stone accents, with humongous windows that looked out onto the pond and the forest. She walked through the living room, taking in the fireplace, where Adam was busy making a neat pyramid of kindling and logs, and then into the kitchen, which was just as cozy as the rest of the house. A large breakfast nook was nestled into the windowed alcove, with a built-in bench and a round table. Beside it, there was a window seat beneath one of the large windows, looking out onto the darkening forest. Twilight glowed softly through the trees, illuminating the forest with shades of silvery purple.With a sigh, she sat down on the window seat and pulled her knees up to her chest, feeling something settle inside her. She never would've thought she was someone who preferred a quiet cabin on the edge of the woods to a condo in a bustling city. Then again, she was starting to realize that maybe she hadn't actually known herself that well at all.

Adam stepped into the kitchen, brushing a stray wood-chip off his jeans. The scent of a newly kindled fire filled the air, and Hazel let out another contented sigh. She turned and found Adam staring at her, an unreadable, almost wistful expression on his face.

"What?" she asked, ducking her head slightly.

"You look good here." He shoved his hands in his pockets, rocking back on his heels, something she was coming to know was a nervous gesture from him. "I mean, you always look good, but you look good *here*."

She stood from the window seat and crossed the kitchen

to where he stood. "I feel good here. Like…" She trailed off and bit her lip. She couldn't say it out loud. It was too sappy. And it was too soon.

"Like you belong," he said, his voice low, his eyes hopeful and bright.

"Like I belong," she whispered, and then his mouth was on hers, kissing her gently. Before the kiss could turn into anything more, he pulled away and retrieved a bottle of wine from a cabinet. He held it up and met her eyes, a wordless question, and she nodded. He popped the cork with a deftness that was very sexy, and then handed her a glass.

"There's more to see upstairs," he said, and she took her glass with her as she followed him up the stairs to the second floor. "This is my office and library," he said, pushing open a door to reveal walls filled with bookshelves, a worn but comfortable looking sectional, and a desk facing the windows with a laptop and papers scattered across it.

Her footsteps were quiet as she padded across the large area rug to the desk. The window looked out onto the forest. "This would be an amazing place to write," she said, her eyes moving to his laptop.

"It was. It's mostly just a library now," he said, and again, something flashed across his face. She set her wineglass down on the desk and crossed the room to him, sliding her hands around his waist. God, he was so warm and solid. She wanted to curl into him and never let go.

"It still could be," she said softly. "You have a lot of talent. I was almost late coming downstairs to meet you because I got sucked into your book."

His face lit up. "Really? How far did you get?"

"The police have asked Brady to come help investigate

the disappearance of the young woman, they found her body in the woods, and now he's at the prison, interviewing her ex-boyfriend. I like Robert Brady, a lot. He's sharp and witty, but still human." She hugged him a bit tighter. "It's really good, Adam. Like, should've been on the bestseller list good. Publishing is a brutal industry, and I understand why you stepped away. But I hope someday you come back to it."

"Hazel," he said, his voice low and rough, and then he was kissing her again, his free arm banding around her waist and holding her against him. Unlike the kiss downstairs, this one was hungry and demanding. Like a dirty, tantalizing promise she very much wanted him to keep. She let out a moan, and he deepened the kiss, his tongue licking into her mouth and caressing. He tasted like the single sip of wine he'd had, sweet and heady. It was enough to make her feel a little drunk.

She lost track of time as he explored her mouth, making her knees go weak and her pussy flutter in anticipation. If Adam Shephard could kiss like that, she had a feeling he'd also be good at other *things*. Especially ones involving his mouth.

Her stomach rumbled, and he laughed softly against her mouth, breaking the kiss. "I did promise you dinner, didn't I?"

"Mmm," she said. "And we never finished the tour."

He let out a shaky breath. "Maybe we should go back downstairs. If I take you into my bedroom..." He let the unfinished thought dangle in the air.

"We might never eat. Well, food, anyway."

.   .   .

Who was this woman who dropped innuendos like they were nothing? New York City Hazel would've never said something so brash and bold.

She was starting to like Gossamer Falls Hazel better.

He laughed softly. "If you had any idea what you saying those things did to me…" He huffed out a breath, clearly reaching for some reserve of control, and stepped away from her. "Come on," he said after she'd retrieved her wine and her hand was firmly tucked in his again. "You can tell me about how writing went today while I cook."

They headed back down to the kitchen, and Hazel settled in at the island in the center of the kitchen while Adam rummaged in the fridge, examining ingredients with an ease and confidence that was very, very sexy.

"I would offer to help, but I'm pretty useless in the kitchen."

"You don't need to do anything but enjoy your wine and tell me about your day." He opened the fridge again, bracing his palms against the top while he peered inside. Every single thing he did was like an electrical shock to her system, making her feel overly warm and squirmy. "Do you like Italian? I could make pasta alfredo."

"From scratch?" she asked, and there was another one of those little shocks.

"Sure. It's easy."

"Sounds delicious."

He laid the ingredients out on the counter – a block of parmesan cheese, butter, fresh linguine. Then he turned on the small BlueTooth speaker on the counter and connected his phone to it. Soft, mellow jazz floated through the air, and Hazel never wanted this night to end.

He moved to the sink and washed his hands. "I saw you typing away for a good chunk of the day," he said, drying his hands on a kitchen towel and then tossing it over his shoulder. He rolled up his sleeves and retrieved a cheese grater from one of the cabinets. "Looked like you were making good progress on something."

Hazel sipped her wine. "I took your advice and started writing something totally new. Something that intrigued me and got my creative juices flowing. And, most importantly, I think, something Seth hasn't had his hands or eyes on. Because you're right. Writing for him, with him, whatever, is totally stifling my creativity. I can't get out of my head long enough to get into the flow, you know?"

He nodded, listening intently as he set a pot of water to boil and then returned to the island, where he started grating the parmesan into a bowl with practised ease. She sipped her wine and stared at him as he worked, his corded forearms flexing. After a moment, he glanced up at her, one of his curls falling across his forehead. Their eyes met and a blast of heat poured through Hazel.

Ha, and she'd thought she might not sleep with him tonight. *Obviously* she was going to. The truth was, she wanted Adam more than she'd wanted anything in a long time. Wanted his mouth on her, his hands on her, his body moving inside hers.

"What are you thinking about?" he asked, a heated look on his face that indicated he knew exactly what she was thinking about.

"You."

A sexy grin spread across his face. "Tell me about what you wrote today."

She gave him a detailed rundown of the story she'd started, with Mary Elizabeth Axton, the time travel element, and her rescue by a soldier in 1864.

"I have no idea where I'm going with it," she said, almost a little breathlessly. Adam dumped the linguine into the now boiling water, still listening intently. "But for the first time in a long time, I'm actually enjoying writing again."

She watched as he took a soup ladle and spooned a small amount of the pasta water into a large skillet, then tossed in a mouthwatering amount of butter, letting it melt and mixing it with the water.

"Can I read it?" he asked, stirring the pasta, and then removing it from the boiling water with a set of tongs. She loved watching him move. Adam Shephard was thick in all the right places. Massive arms, broad chest, muscular ass, tree trunk thighs. Even his hands were huge, with thick, strong fingers that she—

"Hazel?" he asked, his voice bringing her out of her drool-inducing staring. She blinked rapidly and took a long sip of her wine.

"Sorry, what?" she asked, feeling her cheeks warm. She'd totally been caught ogling him, and she didn't care. She wanted him to know that she wanted him.

"Can I read the chapters you wrote today?"

She sat up a little straighter. "You want to?"

He nodded. "Definitely. The story sounds fascinating. I already know I'd read that book."

"Sure. I'll email them to you." She headed back to the front hall, pulled her phone out of her purse and quickly pulled up the document she'd been working on earlier that day. "What's your email address?" she called down the hallway.

"A.Shephard83@gmail.com," he called back, and she entered it quickly and hit send, her heart throbbing in her chest. She didn't normally share her work with someone else while it was still in such an early stage, but with Adam everything was different, in a good way.

With Adam, *she* was different. It was as though he brought out a version of herself she hadn't known existed. One she liked. A lot.

SIXTEEN

HAZEL RETURNED TO THE KITCHEN, sipping her wine and watching as Adam stirred the cooked noodles into the water and butter, then removed the pan from the heat and started sprinkling the parmesan on. Once it was all mixed together, he gave it a couple of casual tosses that had Hazel squirming in her seat.

"There's no rush," she managed, her eyes glued to his capable hands. "To read the chapters, I mean."

"I want to read them," he said earnestly. As he plated the pasta, topping both of their portions with more grated parmesan cheese and then a bit of freshly ground pepper, the conversation shifted and they talked about travel bucket lists (England was at the top of his, while New Zealand was at the top of hers) and places they'd traveled in the past. They settled in at the round table nestled into the alcove of windows, sitting almost hip-to-hip on the built-in bench.

Hazel lifted her wine glass and clinked it softly against Adam's. "To new beginnings," she said quietly, and his gaze dropped to her mouth for a moment before he smiled and took a sip of his wine.

"To new beginnings," he echoed, and then set his glass down. "Dig in," he said, not picking up his own fork but watching her intently.

Obliging, she twirled several strands of pasta around her fork and raised them to her mouth. Buttery deliciousness exploded across her tongue, mingling with the saltiness of the parmesan. She pressed her fingers to her lips, letting out a little moan.

"Sweet Jesus, that's good," she said, savoring the mouthful of food. Not only could she not remember the last time someone had cooked for her, but she couldn't remember the last time she'd had something this simple yet delicious.

She glanced at Adam, and his gorgeous hazel eyes were dark and glittering as he stared at her mouth. She smirked slightly, enjoying the fact that she wasn't the only one doing the ogling tonight.

"What are you thinking about?" she asked innocently, echoing his earlier question.

He swallowed thickly and then shifted closer, brushing her hair away from her neck before whispering in her ear, "What I can do to make you say that again, in a much different context."

She moaned softly, tilting her head to the side as he dragged his lips down the side of her neck. He worked his way back up and then scraped his teeth over her earlobe. She whimpered, heat and lust swirling through her in a dizzying mix.

"If you keep doing that, this delicious meal you made

will go to waste," she said. Then she turned and pressed a kiss to the corner of his mouth. "And I have a feeling I'm going to need my energy tonight." Their eyes met, heat and need passing between them, pulsing like a heartbeat. He exhaled heavily and nodded.

"If that's what you want," he said, toying with a lock of her hair. "You're in control tonight. No pressure, no expectations."

"What do *you* want?" she asked quietly, and she could see his heart shining out at her through his eyes.

"You, Hazel. In as many ways as you'll let me have you." The words were simple and plain. Honest and real. "I think you're beautiful," he murmured, kissing along her neck again. "And smart." More kisses. "And fun." More kisses. "And sexy as hell. I can't stop thinking about you. Ever since that morning in your hotel room, you're all I think about."

"Oh, God," she whispered, and then they were kissing, slow and languorous, tongues sliding, lips melding, teeth nipping. She was already addicted to the way he kissed. As though she was the most delicious thing he'd ever tasted and he couldn't get enough.

After a moment, he pulled away, leaving her lips tingling and her nipples poking insistently against her bra. "But you're right. We should eat. We have all night."

A hot shiver coursed through her, and she took another bite of her pasta. The conversation shifted back to less spicy ground, and they talked easily as they ate, about hobbies (crochet for her, building furniture for him, because *of course* he had a sexy hobby), childhood memories, pet peeves (other people's messes for him, people who talked on speakerphone in public spaces for her), her job as a librarian before she'd become a full-time writer, his love for the hotel.

"I still love it, but it's different now," he said, finishing his wine and setting the glass down. His plate was already empty. She could see the sadness flickering in his eyes, pulling at his handsome features.

She laid a hand over his. "Autumn mentioned that your dad died not that long ago."

Adam nodded, slowly twirling the empty wine glass. "I ran the hotel with him, and while I'd always planned to take over for him someday, I hadn't thought that someday would come so soon."

"I'm sorry. I can't even imagine."

He curled his hand around hers, as though he was seeking out her comfort. Comfort she was more than happy to give. "I miss him every day. We were really close, and his death was so sudden...I think a part of me still isn't over it."

She nodded and leaned into him. "I'm sorry, Adam. I've never lost someone like that, but I don't know that you just get over it, you know? I think you learn to live with it, but that doesn't make it any less shitty that he's gone and you wish more than anything that he wasn't."

Their eyes met, and he nodded slowly. "Yeah. I think you're right." He sighed. "It's not the remembering him that's hard. The memories are comforting and happy. It's the missing him that kills me."

She moved closer and slid her arms around him. His grief was palpable, and she wanted to do anything she could to make it more bearable for him.

For a moment, she just held him, feeling the solid weight of him against her, and it amazed her that she'd only known

Adam for a couple of days, and yet it felt as though she'd known him for a couple of years. All of this was so, so easy.

Her mind flashed back to the falls, the experience she'd had, and the wish she'd made.

What if it was true? What if the magic of the falls was real, and Adam was her true love? What if everything Fiona had read on her palm and in her tarot cards was true?

The thought sent her heart galloping in her chest, beating so hard it was jostling her insides.

He pulled away slowly. "Thanks. I needed that."

She lifted a hand and traced her fingers over his jaw, the underside of his lips, the slight cleft in his chin. Learning his contours. "Anytime," she answered softly. He leaned forward, kissing her forehead with so much tenderness that it made an ache flare to life right in the center of her chest.

After another moment, they slid apart and he stood from the table, taking their plates with him, the sadness gone from his expression.

"Can I help you with the dishes?" she asked, bringing their empty wine glasses over to the counter and setting them down.

He shook his head, leaning back against the counter, his arms braced behind him. "Absolutely not." She noticed that he had a white knuckled grip on the counter, and she realized she could see the outline of his cock pressing against his jeans. He followed her gaze and shifted his weight. "We could watch a movie," he said, his voice a little rough, and she laughed. She couldn't help it. He was so freaking charming.

"What?" he asked.

"You're trying so hard to be a gentleman," she said, stepping closer and walking her fingers up his chest.

He swallowed thickly. "I am trying not to maul you, quite honestly."

She arched up onto her tiptoes and dragged her mouth along his razor-sharp jaw. "Maybe I don't want you to be a gentleman."

"Fuck, Hazel," he groaned, his mouth claiming hers in a kiss that had her stomach dipping and swirling and her toes curling inside her socks. "I've been thinking about you all day," he breathed, nipping at her lips hungrily.

"What have you been thinking?"

He buried his face in her neck, his mouth scorching a path from her collarbone to her jaw, the drag of his lips against her sensitive skin exquisite.

"That I want your eyes on me. Your hands on me. That I want all of you."

"Oh, God," she moaned, melting into him. He kissed her again, his tongue sweeping against hers in a way that made her pussy ache with arousal. Her panties were wet, and she was rubbing her thighs together, trying to get some relief for her throbbing clit. He pulled her tighter against him, and his hard cock was like a brand against her, even through the layers of clothing separating them. She rocked into him, and he groaned gruffly against her mouth.

"I want all of you, too," she whispered, sucking his bottom lip into her mouth. "I want to watch you come undone."

"Tell me you're sure," he moaned, his hands dropping to her ass, his lips moving over her throat.

"I'm sure," she breathed. She couldn't remember the last

time she'd been more sure of something. "I want you, Adam. I think you're the sexiest man I've ever met." Her fingers tangled in his hair as he slid a hand up under her sweater, his fingers teasing along the underside of her breast. Hot tingles followed in the wake of his touch, making her feel fizzy and alive. "Make me yours."

"Mine," he groaned, his mouth crashing into hers again. "Hazel." He broke the kiss with a low, anguished sound and then took her hand. "We'd better go upstairs before I fuck you on the kitchen counter."

"I mean, I wouldn't complain," she said, hurrying to keep up with his long strides.

"Not for the first time. I need you in a bed. Naked and spread out."

Her stomach dropped to somewhere around her ankles. Seth had never talked to her like that, with dirty-edged words tinged with need. It made her feel like she could soar. Like she was sexy and desirable and ready to combust.

"Yes, please," she murmured as they mounted the stairs and then turned to enter Adam's bedroom. It was dark save for the moonlight shining in through the large window, and she could see the silhouetted trees of the forest outside. The walls were paneled in wood, and a soft, worn area rug covered the floor beneath her feet. Against the wall to the right was a king-sized bed, neatly made, with a large stack of books on the nightstand.

"I came home and fantasized about you," he said, pulling her close and kissing her. She felt as though her bones were dissolving. She was too hot. Stepping back, she tugged her sweater up over her head, tossing it onto the floor. Adam's eyes flared at the sight of her lacy pink bra.

"What did you fantasize about? Specifically?" she asked, wanting the words. She slid her arms around his waist. His cock pressed against her, and he stifled a groan as she rubbed against him.

"Making you come with my tongue," he rasped, and she let out a shuddery moan, molten heat pouring through her.

"Adam Shephard, you have a dirty mouth."

He pulled back slightly, one eyebrow arched in such a sexy way that she wanted to shove him onto the bed and have her way with him, patience be damned. "I do. Is that a problem? Because I can…" He seemed to lose his train of thought when she reached between them and stroked him over top of his jeans.

"Most definitely *not* a problem," she said. He groaned and pressed into her touch.

He kissed her and snapped open the button of her jeans, and she shimmied out of them haphazardly, not wanting to break the kiss. Not wanting to lose the connection.

"I want to fuck you so bad, Hazel. Want to fuck you so hard and so deep that you feel me for days."

She gasped out a moan and arched into him. "I'm adding dirty talker to my list of things I like very much about you."

"Yeah?"

She nodded, and only then did she realize that for the first time since her divorce, she was in her bra and panties in front of a new man. A wave of nervousness suddenly pushed through her, and as though he could sense what she needed, he kissed her again, guiding her slowly toward the bed. The back of her legs hit the mattress and she pulled Adam down, springs creaking softly under their weight.

He cupped her breast, thumbing her nipple through the delicate lace, making her arch up into his touch.

"God, Hazel. You're so fucking beautiful. I look at you and I feel like I can't breathe. You make me feel like I'm going to lose control," he said, the sandpapery edge to his voice ramping up her own arousal.

"So lose it," she said. "I'm yours."

"Oh, God," he ground out, pulling down the cups of her bra and letting her breasts spill free. He lowered his head and sucked one nipple into his mouth, making her back arch off of the bed as gentle flames licked at her skin.

"Yes," she hissed, threading her fingers into his hair and holding him exactly where she wanted him. She wrapped her legs around his waist, working herself against the ridge of his cock. He groaned, the vibrations hot on her hard nipple. Sliding her hands up under his sweater, she traced the tips of her fingers over his warm skin, across his flat, hard stomach, up to his pecs.

"Off," she said impatiently, tugging at the hem of his sweater. "I want to see you."

He rose to his knees, reached over his head, and yanked the sweater off, tossing it to the floor.

"Oh my God," she whispered, her hands tracing over him again. He was even better than she'd imagined. All hard muscle and taut skin, thick arms and the hint of abs. A dusting of dark brown chest hair covered his pecs, and a line of the same arrowed down from his navel and into his jeans.

She felt as though she were magnetized to him, and any distance between them was painful. She reached forward and undid the button on his jeans, then slid her hand inside, palming him over top of his boxer briefs.

"Oh, fuck, Hazel," he groaned as she stroked him, his eyes shuddering closed. "That's it, sweetheart. Stroke my cock. So fucking hard for you."

His words thrilled her, emboldened her, so she stroked him with more confidence, quickly learning the length and shape of him, which, like the rest of him, was perfect. Long and thick and so incredibly hard.

She was ruining her panties at this point, but she didn't care. She wanted this, all of this—Adam's dirty words and her out of control arousal and the feeling that she was on the precipice of something monumental.

He lowered himself down with her hand still in his pants and kissed her again, then rolled onto his side, his hands in her hair, her breasts pressed against his bare chest as they kissed, slow and deep. She liked the way his chest hair teased her nipples. The way she was aware of his hard body pressed against hers. The scent of his skin.

"Tell me what you like, Hazel," he said, kissing along her jaw. "I want to make you feel so fucking good."

Her cheeks went hot, and she felt suddenly shy. Unable to form the words she needed. Lifting up onto his elbow, Adam rested his head in his hand, his curls a mess from her fingers.

"Well, um...I like..." She sucked in a breath. "I like you. And I want you."

"I have an idea," he said, a sexy smile on his full lips as he trailed his fingers between her breasts, down her stomach, and then stopping just shy of the waistband of her panties. "Why don't I make suggestions?" he said, his fingers skimming just beneath her panties, teasing her with a tantalizing graze. Her legs fell open in invitation. "And we'll use your reactions as a barometer."

"A barometer?" she asked, not quite following. But then her brain stopped working as he removed his hand from her panties only to push them to the side, his thumb tracing gently over her clit. Her eyes fluttered closed and she moaned, heat and pleasure curling through her.

"Mmmhmm," he said huskily, trailing his fingers up and down her slit, toying with her clit in slow circles, then doing the same to her dripping entrance. "Like this." He slid a finger inside her, working her open, and she moaned loudly and clenched around him. He fucked her slowly, stretching her, thumb working her clit as her entire existence went fuzzy around the edges.

"You're so wet, Hazel. So hot and tight around my fingers. I'm going to fucking die when I get inside you," he said, his voice taking on a throaty quality.

"Wet for you," she whispered, and he stroked her clit in approval.

"You look so goddamn beautiful, all open and spread. You look like a fucking feast." He lowered his head to her breasts again and licked and sucked at her nipples until she was panting, her breasts feeling so heavy and full.

After a minute or five or ten—time had ceased to have any meaning at all—he slid another finger inside her, making her feel deliciously full.

He nipped at her shoulder. "Good. Now we can talk."

"What? I..." Her head lolled back and forth as she fought to be coherent. "Talk?"

"Mmm. For example..." He nipped at her ear, her jaw, his

thumb slow and steady on her clit. "I think you like having my fingers inside you."

"I do," she nodded, clenching around him. "It feels so good."

He stroked her clit slowly. "Would you like me to eat your pussy, Hazel?" She sighed, stomach twisting in anticipation at the thought, and clamped around him. He let out a low chuckle that she felt through her entire body. "That would be a yes." He stroked in and out of her once, and she wasn't even embarrassed at the wet sound it made. She was beyond that at this point, just a bundle of nerve endings and lust and adrenaline. "Tell me what you want me to do with my mouth once I'm between your pretty thighs."

"Oh, God," she whispered, her hips writhing of their own accord. "Kiss me. Lick me all over, slow, at first. No fingers. And then faster. I like it when…I want you to suck on my clit." The thought of his mouth on her was making her lose her mind.

He flicked his thumb over her clit and hummed his approval. "And then, after you come on my tongue…when I'm inside you…" She could tell he was starting to lose control too, which made what he was doing that much hotter. "Should I fuck you slow and sweet?" he asked, stroking in and out of her again, almost lazily.

"At first," she moaned, pleasure sparking low in her stomach. She was already riding the edge of what was promising to be a brain-melting orgasm.

"And then?"

"I like…Passion. To know that the person I'm with is as into me as I am them." She'd always struggled to find that assurance in relationships, but maybe it was partly because she'd been so closed off. She felt vulnerable and open with Adam, but safe, too.

He dropped his forehead to her shoulder, his fingers moving faster. "You never have to doubt that with me, Hazel. God, you make me feel..." He exhaled shakily. "Like this could be everything."

He lifted his head and their eyes met. "I know," she answered.

"Oh, God, I need to taste you," he said, slipping his fingers free of her body.

SEVENTEEN

HAZEL FELT bereft at the temporary loss of Adam as he moved away, but he quickly settled himself between her legs, hooking his fingers into her panties and slowly working them down over her hips, then sliding them down her legs and tossing them onto the floor. He kissed a path across her stomach, down her thighs.

"Fuck, sweetheart, you smell so good. And you look so pretty spread out on my bed. So fucking pretty," he growled, nipping at the seam of her thigh. "My Hazel."

His words seared through her, the warmth of them almost obliterated by the feel of his tongue sweeping over her entire pussy.

"Oh, shit!" she moaned, weaving her hands into his hair. "Yes, oh God, yes."

He nipped at her lips and then kissed her, slow and deep, his tongue working in heady circles. He licked and kissed and sucked, over and over again, working her so expertly with his mouth that she wondered if she'd died and this was heaven. He was moaning as much as she was, and he sucked her clit into his mouth, working it with his lips and tongue. His soft curls tickled the insides of her thighs, his broad shoulders spreading her wide.

"You make me feel like I've been starving my entire life," he said between licks and sucks. "Like I've been waiting for exactly this."

Her pussy clenched almost painfully, and she pushed up onto her elbows, a shaky, breathless smile spreading across her face. "You make me feel like I've been starving, too." Starving without fully realizing it, but now that she was here, in Adam's bed, she couldn't imagine being anywhere else. Their eyes locked and held as he slowly licked her clit. It was the hunger, the lust, the adoration in his eyes that ignited the storm inside her. She felt as though she couldn't catch her breath as pleasure spiraled through her.

"Oh, my God!" she cried out, her hips writhing as she started to come. "Adam, oh my God! Don't stop. I'm coming so fucking hard. Don't stop." And he didn't, licking and sucking and swirling until she was limp and breathless, utterly wrung out.

"You're so beautiful when you come," he said, kissing her clit gently. She whimpered, her hips jerking up as she slowly started to come back down to earth. He kissed his way back up her body, over her trembling thighs, her stomach, lingering over her breasts, kissing pathways up and down her neck, across her collarbone until she felt like she was glowing from the inside out.

"That was so good," she panted, wrapping herself around him and pulling his face down to hers for a long, deep kiss. She could taste herself on his tongue, which only made her want him more. "I want to make you feel good, too." She pushed at his shoulders, and he let her roll him onto his back.

"Oh, God, Hazel," he said, his voice low and shaky. "The thought of your lips around me...fuck." They worked as a team to undress him, tossing his jeans and boxer briefs onto the growing pile of clothing. She reached behind her back and undid her dishevelled bra. Once they were both fully naked, he pulled her against him, kissing her deeply. Slowly, she slid a hand down his chest, over his stomach and into the dark thatch of curls at the base of his cock. He let out a shaky breath, and she could feel his heart pounding in his chest.

"Adam," she whispered, stroking him slowly. The tip of his hard cock was weeping, a fresh bead of moisture quickly replacing the one she'd just swiped away with her thumb. His breathing was ragged, his cheeks flushed. She loved seeing him like this, all breathless and barely in control because of how much he wanted her. His eyes were glued to where her fingers were wrapped around him, as though he couldn't quite believe this was happening.

He was so hard beneath her fingers, the skin warm and impossibly soft. So thick she could barely get her fingers all the way around him. Anticipation made her heart kick in her chest. She smoothed her thumb over the tip again, then lifted it to her lips, sucking his taste into her mouth. Needing a part of him inside her.

"Oh God, Hazel," he said, almost reverently, his eyes molten, his stomach muscles trembling. "Fuck, sweetheart." The last words came out deeper, more growly, and she felt as though her skin were burning, imaginary flames licking at her.

It had never been like this with Seth. Or with anyone. Ever.

She urged him onto his back, an excited tremor working its way through her. Tension radiated through his body, in the taut lines of his muscles, the flexing of his jaw.

"Can I?" she asked, settling herself between his legs and stroking his impressive cock. "I want you in my mouth."

He let out a low, rumbling chuckle. "Perfect, because I want to *be* in your mouth."

She laughed and then pressed a kiss to the tip of his cock, swiping her tongue through the pre-come gathered there. Adam reached down and gathered Hazel's hair in his hands, holding it in a loose fist.

"I need to see," he said, and when she looked up and their eyes met, she could tell he was just as gone for her as she was for him. Like they were falling together into a beautiful unknown. Still holding his gaze, Hazel licked up the length of him, his skin warm and soft against her tongue. She swirled her tongue around the head of his cock, then sucked just the tip of it into her mouth. Teasing. Tasting. Savoring.

She settled further between his legs and cupped his balls with one hand while stroking him with the other.

"Yes," he hissed out, his hips shifting restlessly on the bed. "Suck my cock, sweetheart. Wanna see those gorgeous lips wrapped around me."

Hazel moaned, loving his filthy words, knowing that they were just for her. Her body felt warm, her pussy already wet and aching again after the killer orgasm he'd given her. She licked him once more, and then smiled just before taking the entire head of his cock into her mouth.

"Oh, Jesus," he groaned, his eyes glued to her as she started to move up and down, taking a little bit more of him with every sweep of her mouth. "Your mouth feels so good, sweetheart." His hand tightened in her hair. She could feel it shaking slightly. "I'm not..." he panted, his head moving back and forth. "Fuck, you're beautiful. God," he ground out, his voice thick with tension and need.

He reached down and stroked her face, and she pressed the head of his cock against her cheek, letting him feel himself in her mouth. He made a sound almost like he was in pain, but then he urged her farther down his cock with gentle pressure. Hazel moaned, turned on by how turned on he was. Everything was shared. His arousal was her arousal. His sadness was her sadness. His laughter was her laughter. As though parts of them were already inextricably twined together by some kind of magic.

She sucked and licked, learning every contour, every ridged vein with the tip of her tongue. Her clit was throbbing, and she swung her leg over one of his so she could grind against his thigh as she sucked him.

"So fucking hot," he growled. "Does it make you wet, having my cock in your mouth?" he asked, and she moaned in response, rubbing herself on his leg like a cat in heat. He dropped his hand from where he'd been tugging on his own hair to her breast, rolling her nipple between his skilled fingers. Pleasure arrowed through her, and she sucked him deeper. "I can feel how fucking wet you are," he breathed, moving his hand to her other breast. "You're dripping all over me, sweetheart. So ready for my cock inside you."

She moaned around him again, taking him deeper and deeper with every sweep of her mouth up and down his length. His hips thrust up to meet her, his breathing jagged, his groans warming her like sunshine. Their eyes met again, and he heaved a sigh and then eased back, dropping his hand from her hair.

"I'm gonna come all over your tongue if we keep that up," he said with a sexy smirk before hauling her up his body and settling her on top of him. Her legs fell to either side of his body, the head of his cock resting teasingly against her pussy. She moaned and kissed him, tongues and lips melding as his hands smoothed up and down her back.

"Fuck," he said, but it wasn't in the aroused tone of a moment ago.

"What?" she asked, lifting her head slightly. Her heart jolted at the sight of him. It felt almost surreal that she was in bed with this gorgeous, sweet man.

"I don't have any condoms. I mean, I might, somewhere, but I haven't dated in a long time, so they're probably long expired."

"Oh," she said, frowning slightly. All of this was so new to her—not just Adam, but dating in general—that condoms hadn't even crossed her mind. "I mean...I have an IUD. And I got tested after Seth..." She shook her head, not wanting to think about him right now.

"If I swear to you I'm good, you trust me?" he asked, eyes luminous in the dark.

"I trust you, Adam. I want you. And if I'm honest, I don't want anything between us. I just want you."

"Hazel," he said, in that reverent way that made her name feel like a prayer. He kissed her, slow and deep. "Tell me you're sure."

"I've never been more sure." And it was true. He grinned

as he rolled her beneath him, her arms and legs twining around him effortlessly, as though they'd done this a hundred times before. He dropped his head and kissed her neck, her throat, her breasts. He swirled his tongue over her nipples until they were stiff, aching points.

"I can't get enough of the taste of your skin," he murmured, nuzzling between her breasts. His cock lay hot and heavy on her thigh, making her squirm and want. He skimmed his lips over her jaw, nibbled on her earlobe, licked along the outer ridge of her ear, making her shudder. She reached between them and stroked his cock, rubbing it against her pussy. They moaned in unison, her hips rising up to meet his. The tip of his cock caught on her entrance and he stilled, his eyes meeting hers. The question in them was obvious. She nodded, weaving her fingers into his hair.

"I want you, Adam. More than I've ever wanted anyone," she whispered.

"God, Hazel," he groaned, and let himself slip inside of her, just a tiny bit. She fought back the urge to arch her hips up and take more of him, wanting the slow tease. She skimmed her hands up his muscled back and he sank inside another inch. The stretch was intense but good. So, so good. He let out a low groan and kissed her, sinking inside a bit deeper. She gasped against his mouth, trying to relax against the stretch, wanting more of him. Wanting all of him. "Mine," he whispered against her lips as he pushed in farther, starting to work himself in and out of her clenching pussy.

Their chests rose and fell in unison, eyes locked on each other as he sank all the way home. The room suddenly lit up with a flash of lightning followed by a deafening crack of thunder. Rain started to fall in a sheet, pounding against the roof and windows, the storm outside matching the storm of emotion Hazel was experiencing inside.

She felt as though her entire life had been leading up to this moment.

"Adam, oh God," she whispered shakily, tracing her fingers over his cheekbone. "Yes. Oh fuck, yes."

He started to move, and she clung to him, every single thrust of his thick cock sending her higher and higher, winding her tighter and tighter. One of his hands tangled in her hair, holding her tight as he kissed her. Kissed her and fucked her, hard and deep, just like he'd promised.

She was never going to get enough of this. Ever.

Her hips arched up to meet his, seeking out more of him, even though he was buried deep inside her. Even though she was so full, stretched around him. "Adam," she gasped out, clinging to him. Sighing and pulling his scent into her lungs.

"You feel so fucking good, Hazel. This is heaven. Here, in this bed, with you. Fucking heaven," he groaned, swiveling his hips in a way that had her eyes rolling back in her head. The movement made the base of his cock grind against her clit and she gasped out a string of incoherent words. Adam's lips traced along her jaw, her neck, and he slowed his movements, thrusting in deep and then pulling out so slowly she felt him over and over and over again, pleasure sparking along her nerve endings. "Tell me you feel this too," he rasped. "How fucking perfect this is."

"I do," she said, her voice coming out as a shaky, breathy moan. "I feel it. I feel it, Adam." She tightened her legs around him as it felt like thunderclouds identical to the ones outside gathered inside her. "How could I not?"

He lifted his head, their eyes meeting just as a flash of lightning lit up the room for one glorious second before slowly fading. Hazel felt as though her heart was trying to leap out of her chest and into Adam's body.

As though her heart was trying to go home.

Adam kissed her and slipped a hand under her ass, lifting her slightly off the mattress so he could fuck her even deeper.

"Can you come like this?" he asked, his voice raw. "I want to feel you come around me, sweetheart."

"I need more," she gasped, and suddenly she was on top of him, impaled on his thick cock.

"Ride me and take what you need, Hazel." He pushed up onto his elbows, smoothing her messy hair away from her face. She rocked her hips, moaning at the decadent slide of his body inside her. He grinned and reached between them, stroking her clit with his thumb in a sure, steady rhythm. "Like this?" he asked, his gaze hooded and intent on her, his chest heaving. She could tell he was holding back, wanting to get her there.

"Just like that," she managed, moving faster. "It's perfect."

"The sight of you stretched around me is fucking obscene," he rasped, beads of sweat dotting his hairline. A thrill charged through her, and she rode him harder, moans and breathy sighs falling from her lips. Adam's hips rose up to meet hers, the sound of heated skin meeting heated skin filling the room and tangling with their moans and sighs. Hazel felt the first spark of her second orgasm down in her toes, the muscles contracting almost to the point of cramping.

"Fuck, I'm so close. You feel so fucking good." He worked her clit between his thumb and forefinger while thrusting up into her. "You're the most beautiful thing I've ever seen, Hazel."

"Adam!" she screamed his name as a crushing orgasm rushed through her, and she clamped around his cock. She fell forward, her muscles locked as she struggled to breathe through the most intense orgasm of her life. Adam caught her, wrapping his arms around her and holding her close. Her eyes fluttered closed, her pussy convulsing wildly around him.

"Oh fuck, Hazel," he moaned loudly, and he stilled inside her. He was buried so deep that she felt every single pulse of his cock as he emptied himself inside her. An impossibly loud crash of thunder shook the cabin, rattling the windows in their panes, vibrating Hazel's bones.

Their mouths met, seeking, craving, tongues sliding lazily as they both came down. Adam's hands stroked up and down Hazel's back.

In that moment, something that had been lost for a long time settled within Hazel. As though she'd found what she hadn't even known she'd been looking for.

She didn't know what the future held. Didn't know what would happen with the book or her writing career. Didn't know what her next five years looked like. But one thing she did know with absolute certainty was that she was never letting Adam Shephard go.

IT WAS STILL dark outside when Adam opened his eyes. Hazel was curled against him, her back pressed against his chest, her feet twined with his. Her breathing was slow and even, her skin warm and sweet.

A bolt of sheer panic shot through him, and he carefully disentangled himself from Hazel and the twisted sheets, threw on a sweatshirt, jogging pants, and socks, and slipped out of the room.

He'd known Hazel for, what? A few days? He couldn't be falling in love with her. It wasn't possible. It couldn't be. And yet after one night he wanted to ask her to stay. With him, in Gossamer Falls. He wanted a future with her. He wanted it so bad he could see it with startling clarity, and it scared the shit out of him.

He shoved his feet into his worn running shoes and stepped out onto the porch. The rain had stopped, but there was still the occasional patter of water falling from leaf to leaf. And then he took off down the gravel path, trying to outrun his swirling thoughts. The ground crunched beneath his feet as his body settled into a familiar rhythm. The sky was lightening to a soft gray, birds chirping with increasing intensity as he jogged a well-worn path into the forest.

The pull he felt toward Hazel was like a swirling vortex, and it was as though every time he thought about distancing himself, something happened to suck him right back in. Something as simple as hearing her laugh, or watching the way she chewed on her bottom lip when she was lost in thought.

As he thought about her, as his blood pumped through his veins and his breath came in harsh, staccato pants, he found himself smiling. Not just smiling, but grinning like an idiot. Like a crazy person.

Like a fool on the cusp of love, which is exactly what he was. He was falling for Hazel. If he was honest, a part of him had always known he was going to fall for Hazel. Like the Universe had made the decision without consulting him, and now he was powerless to do anything but go along with it.

Maybe this time things will be different.

The voice was so clear and close that he stopped in his tracks, hands on his hips as he looked around, trying to catch his breath. Of course, there was no one. He was alone in the forest, surrounded only by trees and animals. A squirrel darted across the path in front of him, cheeks full to bursting with his haul. Shaking his head, Adam resumed his jog, trying to sort out his thoughts.

The panic wouldn't be there if Hazel didn't mean something to him, and he didn't want to pretend that what they had wasn't special. Because it was. He was forty. He'd dated enough, had enough long-term relationships to know that the connection he felt with Hazel was a once in a lifetime thing. And he was sure she felt that connection, too. That spark of awareness whenever they were around each other. That magnetism that seemed to take over.

So then what happened when her time in Gossamer Falls was up? He couldn't move to the city. He had a life he loved here, with friends and family and a business he was proud of. Plus, he hated the city. It was too noisy and busy. It was too lonely while simultaneously being too crowded. The truth was, he wanted her here. Two dates, and he was all in. All. The. Way. In.

He turned, taking the same loop he usually did as he jogged back towards his cabin. The loop was just under four miles, and he aimed to jog it three mornings a week. He knew it like the back of his hand, so even in the faint glow of dawn, he knew exactly where he was going.

He stepped back into the quiet house, shutting the door carefully behind him. The run had done him some good, the exercise and the cool, fresh air clearing away the panic at his feelings for Hazel.

He flicked a light on in the kitchen and toed off his damp running shoes with bits of mulch and leaves stuck to them. He made himself a cup of coffee, pacing the kitchen, feeling a bit at loose ends. He took a sip of his coffee and then had the sudden urge to head up to his office. So he did, taking his coffee with him.

He settled in at his computer, trying to remember the last time he'd sat down at this desk as the sun rose. Probably while he'd been working on the last book. He'd always been a morning writer, preferring to get his words in before the business of the day took hold.

But he wasn't writing anything right now. He hadn't in a long time. Sure, he'd tinkered here and there, writing a few short stories, jotting down ideas in a file as they came to him, but he hadn't tried to write a book ever since the spectacular failure of the Robert Brady series. The series that had sold so poorly that his publisher had dropped him and his agent had told him his only course of action was to completely start over.

So, instead, he opened his email and started reading the two chapters Hazel had sent him. Hazel, who was still asleep, naked in his bed. Hazel, who was leaving soon. Hazel, who could so easily and effortlessly become the center of his entire world.

He quickly lost himself in the chapters, making a couple of small notes—questions, really—in the margins. The story was riveting right from the start, and he found himself frowning in disappointment when the two chapters were over. He wanted more, especially because it was obvious to him what was going to happen next.

It started out innocently enough, with a few notes about the next couple of scenes. Questions to be answered, new ones to be asked. Research to be done about the time period. But then, before he fully understood what was happening, his fingers were moving over the keys with increasing speed as he lost himself in the scene.

He was writing. The scene poured out of him effortlessly, words filling the page. He only lifted his fingers from the keyboard for an occasional sip of his coffee or to gaze out the window at the forest as he searched his brain for just the right word. He didn't notice the passing of time. His entire focus was on the scene he was writing, picking up where Hazel had left off by telling the story from the soldier's perspective.

"Adam?" Hazel's voice came from the doorway of his office, and he hastily closed the laptop. Shit. Mild embarrassment swirled through him. He'd been writing a scene in *her* book. She was going to think he was a weirdo. At best.

He spun in his chair, and the second his eyes landed on her, all of the earlier panic he'd been feeling felt laughable. It didn't matter that she was leaving. It didn't matter that the future was uncertain. She was a flame, and he was a moth. His wings were probably going to get singed, and he couldn't bring himself to give a fuck. Not when he was looking at Hazel all adorably sleep rumpled with his robe wrapped around her body. His blood heated at the sight of her as he remembered the weight of her perfectly full breasts in his hands, the softness of her skin against his, the way she'd come so hard around his dick.

A sleepy grin stretched across her pretty face, and she tucked a strand of her golden brown hair behind her ear. "Are you writing?" she asked, eyes shining brightly despite the fact she'd just woken up.

"I, um. Well," he said, rubbing a hand over the back of his neck. "I was reading your chapters, which are amazing, and then I guess I was writing, but it's stupid and I shouldn't have done it."

She stepped closer, frowning in a way that had those little lines digging in between her eyes. "What do you mean?"

Adam had never been a man who made excuses or tried to avoid the consequences. He winced slightly and opened the laptop back up. "I was just playing around after reading your chapters. I...I wrote what could be the next scene," he said, his chest feeling tight, his blood pounding in his ears as he waited for Hazel to tell him that he was a creep.

Instead, she took another few steps closer, her eyebrows raised. "You did?" Her expression was unreadable, but she didn't seem to be mad. "Can I see?"

He closed his eyes for a second before disconnecting the laptop from its power source and handing it to her. She took it from him, their fingers brushing, and leaned her hip against the edge of the desk, facing him as she read.

He was staring, drinking up her reactions like a man dying of thirst. It had been a long time since he'd watched anyone read something he'd written. Especially someone who meant something to him, like Hazel did, as much as it scared him. She frowned slightly and his stomach dropped. Then the corner of her mouth pulled up in a smile and his heart thumped against his chest. As though there were some invisible bond between them because she was reading his words. Words about a character she'd come up with.

The room was silent as she read, her eyes skimming across the screen. Outside, the sun was climbing slowly into the sky, poking its way through the pine trees. Birds chirped happily. Needing something to do, Adam picked up his coffee and drank the last of it.

After several minutes, Hazel carefully set the laptop down. She leaned against his desk, facing him.

"Adam," she said, and he actually held his breath. "It's *so* good."

It was as though she'd doused him in sunshine. "Yeah?"

he asked. "I didn't mean to overstep. I just got caught up reading and I just had the urge—"

She cut him off by pressing her index finger to his lips. "I have a crazy idea."

His eyebrows rose. "What?" he asked, speaking the words against her finger, which was still pressed against his lips. She removed her finger, blinking rapidly. Was she...nervous?

"What if...what if we wrote this book together? Like, co-writers?"

He blinked slowly. "Write the book together?"

She bit her lip, nodding. "Yeah. We can plot it out together, and then I'll write the scenes from Mary's point of view, and you write the scenes from Samuel's. Which, I mean, great name, by the way," she said quickly, her cheeks going pink.

He swallowed thickly. "You want to write a book with me?" His body was still, but his mind was flying. Did he want to jump back into writing? What about her contract? Her ex-husband/editor? But if they were writing a book, which would take months, it would tie them together... maybe she'd stay. Maybe...

Maybe it was the perfect solution. Maybe it was every-thing Adam hadn't realized he'd needed.

"Yeah, Adam. I want to write a book with you."

Their eyes met, and a wave of heat so intense it nearly stole his breath washed over Adam. He could tell Hazel felt it too from the way her eyes both widened and darkened.

He rose from the chair, tugging open the sash of his robe, revealing her naked body to him, all creamy skin and soft curves. He slid an arm around her waist, pressing her breasts against his chest and lifting her onto the desk.

"Adam," she whispered just before his mouth crashed into hers. She moaned against his mouth as he slid his tongue against hers. She wound her arms around his neck, her legs around his waist, pulling him closer.

He kissed her deeply, thoroughly, losing track of time until they were both moaning and gasping for air.

"Hell yes, I want to write a book with you," he said, kissing along her jaw and down her neck. "But that means you have to stay. You have to stay with me."

Maybe it wasn't fair for him to ask that of her, but he wanted her to choose him. To choose to stay. To choose this book, whatever it might turn into. To choose the future he could see shimmering in front of them.

"Of course I'll stay," she breathed, her head tipped back to allow him better access to all of her sensitive skin. He licked a path up her neck, making her shudder in his arms.

"Thank God," he whispered, kissing her again. He slid his arm from around her waist and between her eagerly parted thighs, teasing along the seam of her pussy. In some distant part of his brain, he knew he should ask her if she was sore, if this was okay.

But then his fingers slid over her slit, and he groaned at how slick and hot she was.

"Fuck, Hazel. Sweetheart, you're soaked. Is this all for me?" he asked, nipping at her ear.

"It's all for you, Adam," she said shakily, and he pushed the robe off of her. Needing her naked like he needed his next breath. He lowered his head and sucked her nipple into his mouth, swirling his tongue around it, teasing it with his teeth until she was panting, her hands making a mess of his already dishevelled hair. He kissed a path across her chest and gave her other nipple the same treatment, teasing and tormenting it until it was a hard peak.

She ground against him, her pussy pressing against the erection tenting his jogging pants. She was eager and needy, just as much as he was. It didn't matter that he'd been inside her less than twelve hours ago. He needed her again.

He had the feeling that he'd always need her.

"Tell me what you need," he said, trailing his knuckles over the very tip of her nipple. Her head fell back, her eyes closed.

"You. Your cock. Inside me. Please," she moaned, writhing around him, her nails scoring down his neck.

"Since you asked so nicely," he said, and her eyes opened, a smile playing across her kiss-swollen lips. They both let out a little laugh as he pushed his pants and boxer briefs down, letting them fall around his ankles. She reached between them, closing her slender fingers around his cock, stroking him as she lined him up.

"You're not too sore?" he asked, gentlemanly instinct managing to surface.

"No," she said, then moaned as he notched the tip of his cock at her entrance. "I want you, Adam. I want to write a book with you and have sex with you and laugh with you and—" Her words dissolved into a loud moan as he slowly thrust all the way in, not stopping until she'd taken all of him. He clenched his jaw at how wet and hot she was around him. How fucking perfect.

He held her close, eyes glued to where his cock disappeared inside her. Eyes glued to where her gorgeous pink pussy was stretched around him. "Fucking hell," he ground out. "I didn't think anything could top yesterday, but this..." He kissed her, holding perfectly still inside her. "You feel like home, sweetheart."

Hazel moaned, clinging to him, clenching around him. Her cheeks and neck were flushed, and Adam didn't think he'd ever seen a more beautiful sight in all of his life. He dropped his hands to her hips and slid slowly out of her before thrusting back in.

She sought out his mouth, pulling him down for a kiss as he started to fuck her, establishing a slow, deep rhythm that was making his blood boil and his legs shake. The kiss was messy, uncoordinated as they moved, her hips meeting his. The pens in the metal pencil cup rattled with every thrust, the rhythm matching the slap of skin on skin.

He broke the kiss and dropped his head to her neck, sucking on the sensitive spot just below her ear that he'd discovered last night. He nipped at it before licking away any sting he'd made.

"Adam," she moaned, and he didn't think he'd ever get enough of hearing his name on her lips. "Of course I'll stay," she murmured again, and this time he could hear the relief in her voice. Relief that he'd asked her. Relief that she had a reason.

He was more than happy to be her reason.

He started to move faster, taking her harder and deeper. Her pussy fluttered around him, as though trying to pull him deeper, and he slipped a hand between them, working her clit in rhythmic circles until he felt her tighten around him, her moans filling the room.

"I told myself I wasn't gonna fall for you," he rasped, heat gathering in his balls and at the base of his spine. "But I was wrong. I was fucking wrong."

"Oh my God," she moaned. "Fall, Adam. We'll fall together." Her lips brushed across his jaw, his chin.

"We'll fall together," he echoed, and then she was coming, her pussy squeezing the life out of him and setting off his own orgasm. "Hazel," he groaned, thrusting deep and coming inside her.

OVER THE NEXT FEW DAYS, Hazel lost track of time, in the best possible way. She spent her days working on scenes for the book, sometimes at the hotel, sometimes at Deja Brew. She spent her nights with Adam, brainstorming, reading over his scenes, and having endless orgasms. She wasn't even sure if it was fair to think of herself as a guest at the hotel anymore, given how much time she spent at his cabin. She liked to drink her morning coffee sitting in the cozy window seat in the kitchen while Adam went for a jog. (He'd invited her to join him and she'd laughed. She wasn't a jogger. At all. She was more of a Sunday morning yoga and long walks kind of exerciser.)

When they weren't in bed, she still spent most of her time with Adam. They watched movies, hiked in the colorful Hudson Highlands, strolled hand in hand down Main Street. Being in Gossamer Falls felt like stepping into a different world, not only because it was a far cry from her life in New York City, but because *she* felt different.

For the first time in a long time, she felt like she could

actually breathe. Like she could actually hear her own thoughts.

She also spent time with Autumn and Autumn's friends, Sienna and Laurel. Who, in truth, were starting to feel like her friends.

And while people knew that she and Adam were dating—which felt like a pale, hollow word to describe what she and Adam were doing—they hadn't told anyone that they were writing together. They emailed chapters to each other, passing the growing manuscript back and forth like a flask at a boring family function. A secret that was just theirs.

But Hazel knew that soon, they'd have to let the outside world in on their secret. Something she was loath to do because she knew from experience that once her agent knew about the project—once Seth knew—there was the chance that the creative spark would dim. It was a funny thing about writing. Hoarding the story, keeping it to herself fed it, like oxygen to a fire. Showing it to others could smother it with just a few well-placed, cutting sentences.

Her fingers hovered over the keys, gmail open on her browser screen in front of her. She'd been trying to figure out exactly how to word this email to her agent, Alex. Fear sat like a boulder in her stomach, and her mind flashed back to the conversation she'd had with Adam in bed that morning.

"Are you going to email Alex today?" he'd asked, fingers trailing a path between her breasts. "We have five solid chapters now, just over forty pages."

She'd let out a shaky breath. "I know I should. But...I don't know. This kind of feels like one of those 'it's better to do what we want and ask for forgiveness rather than ask up front and be told no' kind of situations."

He'd arched an eyebrow at her, a gesture that always made her melt. "I think we should be upfront about what we want to do. Better to know that the answer's no forty pages in rather than four hundred."

"But if it's no..." she'd trailed off, the fear and anxiety she'd managed to keep at bay over the past few days popping back up to the surface.

"Then we'll figure it out," he'd said, a slow, sweet smile spreading across his face.

She sighed, leaning back against her wicker chair in the sunroom at the inn. It creaked softly beneath her shifting weight. Outside, a V-formation of geese flew by, heading south for the winter. The colors on the trees were even more intense, and after a few days of gloomy weather, the sun was shining brightly, making everything look golden and soft. A gentle, sepia-toned world.

Adam stepped into the room, and her heart did its usual gymnastics at the sight of him. He held two steaming mugs of coffee in his hands, and he set one down beside her before dropping into the wicker seat across from her. His chair protested louder than hers had, and her entire body warmed at the memory of his weight above her, so solid and warm and—

"Why, Miss Woodward, are you mentally undressing me right now?" he asked, and she laughed, her cheeks warming.

"I admit nothing."

He leaned forward, arms braced on the table. He was wearing an emerald-hued sweater that made his eyes look more green than hazel. A curled lock of hair fell forward onto his forehead and she felt her heart give a happy, wondrous sigh. "Have you written the email yet?"

She bit her lip and shook her head. "No. I'm still agonizing over what to say."

"Dear Alex," he said, taking a sip of his coffee. "I've met the world's most talented writer, and between screaming his name and coming on various parts of his body, we've decided to co-write a book."

Hazel almost choked on her coffee, pressing a hand to her mouth. "Yes. That's exactly what I should write. How could anyone say no to a request like that?"

"Tell me what you're worried about," he said easily, taking another sip of his coffee.

She sighed. "That I tell Alex and he says no. That Alex says maybe and Seth says no. That Seth says maybe and the legal department says that my contract says no." She pushed her glasses up onto her head and rubbed at her eyes. "I'm tired of everyone making decisions for me. I'm tired of jumping through hoops, having big success, and then still being told it's not enough."

"What happens if they do say no?"

"Then I'm right back where I started, struggling to write, which will be even harder now that I know exactly what I want to write and who I want to write it with."

He pursed his lips, his brow furrowing. It was a look that she already knew meant he was writing in his head.

He crooked his fingers at her, gesturing for her to pass him the laptop. She did, spinning it around and sliding it carefully across the table to him. He started typing, his fingers moving across the keys in smooth, practiced movements.

God, even the way he typed turned her on.

"Does…does the fact that we'd have to work with Seth bother you?" she asked.

He stopped typing and took a breath, his chest rising and falling. "It's not my favorite thing in the world, but I can handle it." He said it easily, and she knew it was the simple, honest truth. "But I'm not jealous if that's what you're asking. He's your ex for a reason, and you woke up in my bed this morning. The only reason I'm wary is that from everything you told me, he sounds like a massive asshole, and I've had my share of publishing assholes."

"Ha, that makes two of us. Maybe Seth won't like the fact that I'm writing with someone that I'm in—" She caught herself. It was too soon to think about giving voice to the bubbling joy inside her. Too soon to bring it into the light and really examine it, because that would make it real, and real was still a little scary. "That I'm involved with," she finished. "Maybe he'll actually let someone else edit this book."

Adam tilted his head, considering. "That's a definite possibility." His eyes dropped back down to the laptop and he resumed typing. While he drafted an email that might change everything, her gaze drifted out the windows again. A gust of wind rushed through the trees, sending yellow and orange leaves soaring through the sky, scattering them across the field. A fast-moving cloud blocked the sun for a moment, shifting everything into a darker shade of gold for a moment before everything burst back into vibrant color.

"Here," he said, passing the laptop back toward her. "Tell me what you think."

She started to read, cradling her warm coffee mug in her hands. The phone at the front desk rang, and Adam leapt up out of his seat to answer it. Autumn was off-site, picking up a vanload of fall mums to decorate the hotel with. She'd asked Hazel if she wanted to come with her, and when Hazel had declined, saying she had work to do, Autumn had sent her a knowing smile.

She could hear Adam's deep voice in the background as he spoke on the phone and she returned her attention to the email.

Hello Alex,

I hope this email finds you well. I have some unexpected news for you, but I promise that it's not bad. I have about forty pages of the book drafted, and it's taken a different turn. I've decided to write a different story, inspired by my recent stay in Gossamer Falls, NY. I've also started working on it with another author, and we would like to co-write the book. Let's set up a phone call to discuss.

Best,

Hazel

"Here goes nothing," she whispered, and then hit send on the email. Not even three minutes later, her cell phone started ringing from where it lay facedown on the table. The noise was so loud in the peaceful quiet of the sunroom that she jumped, then fumbled to answer it. Alex's name flashed on the screen. "That was fast," she muttered.

"Hi Alex," she answered, her mouth suddenly dry.

"You're co-writing a different book? I don't understand," he said by way of greeting. She could hear the noise of the city around him, but instead of giving her a pang of homesickness, she had an overwhelming sense of gratitude at being here instead of there.

"I am."

"Tell me what's going on," he said, his tone completely neutral.

"The outline I submitted wasn't working. I tried, Alex. I really did. It was just flat on the page. So I started writing a new story, based on some of the local history here. It's still on brand with my modern fantasy stuff—it's got a time travel element this time, sort of like *A Discovery of Witches* meets *Outlander* because of the heavy romantic element."

"Hmm. Well, sounds intriguing. Who's, uh, who's the co-writer."

"His name is Adam Shephard. He wrote a mystery trilogy for Penman a few years ago."

"Penman, eh? Okay. Strong sales?"

"Well, uh...I don't really know. But I can absolutely vouch for his writing. And Alex, this book is flowing. We've only been working on it for a few days and we've already got five chapters." Just then, Adam stepped back into the room. "He's actually here if you'd like to talk to him."

"Sure, what the hell."

"I'll put you on speaker." She pressed the button and set the phone down on the table. "Adam, this is Alex Goldblatt, my agent."

"Hi Alex, nice to speak with you," he said affably, easing himself back down into the chair. He looked up, meeting Hazel's eyes across the table.

"Uh, yeah, yeah, likewise. Hazel tells me you wrote a mystery trilogy?"

"I did, yeah. And now I'm co-writing this time travel romance with her."

"How did this come about?" he asked, and Hazel could practically picture Alex scratching his head.

"She's a guest at the hotel I run. We got to talking about writing and books and one thing led to another."

"Uh huh. Well, uh, this is very interesting, but I'm not sure where we go with this. Not only is this not the outline the editorial directors signed off on, but the contract is for, uh, just for you, Hazel. So I'll have to look and see what kind of amendments can possibly be, uh, be made at this late stage."

"Right. So where do we go from here?" asked Hazel. "Because I'm firm in that this is what I'd like to do."

"I'm having lunch with Seth tomorrow. I'll talk to him then. In the meantime, send me a synopsis and those five chapters, I'll take a look and see where, uh, where we're at. This is complicated because the advance they paid you, Hazel, was for a different book, and not a co-written one, and I don't think they'd be paying any kind of advance to uh, to Adam...Anyway, I'll let you know what he says after tomorrow."

Hazel inhaled a shaky breath. "Okay, great. Thanks, Alex."

"Thank you," Adam echoed. "And nice speaking with you."

"Yeah, you too. I gotta go. Email me the pages."

The call disconnected, and Adam and Hazel met eyes over the table. "Well, it wasn't a no," she said after a minute.

"It wasn't a no," he agreed, nodding.

"But now we have to write a synopsis. Like, today."

Adam groaned, a loud "ugh" sound that conveyed exactly how she felt. They met eyes again and both laughed.

TWENTY

LATER THAT EVENING, **Adam** sauteed mushrooms to go over the pork chops that were currently in the oven while Hazel grated parmesan cheese for their Caesar salads and poured them each a glass of wine. She'd eaten dinner at his place every night this week, and had slept in his bed every night.

It was an arrangement he could damn well get used to. It surprised him how at ease he was with having her in his space. He'd lived alone off and on for most of his adult life, and in past relationships, he'd always felt a little put out at having to share what was his. But not with Hazel. No, he wanted her here. The cabin felt lifeless and empty without her.

But, unlike their first date, this was a working dinner, and so they each had their laptops open on the island, a synced Google doc with notes open on both screens. They hadn't plotted much beyond the five chapters they'd written, but now that things were real, they needed a proper plot and a proper synopsis.

And while writing synopses were one of his least favorite things on the planet, Adam had to admit that he was enjoying the writing. It felt as though he were stretching long-unused muscles, the muscle memory of fingers moving across a keyboard making him feel more like himself than he had in a long time. He didn't think he'd realized just how much he'd missed writing until he'd started again.

He glanced over at Hazel, who'd finished with the grated parmesan and was now staring intently at the screen of her laptop. She pushed her hair over one shoulder, winding a lock of it around her finger, a gesture he already knew meant she was deep in thought. Truth be told, he'd spent much of the day deep in thought, too. Not about the book, but about if he was really ready to jump back into publishing again, if all of this worked out. On the one hand, this was a different situation with a different set of circumstances. To go into it assuming the same outcome would likely create a self-fulfilling prophecy. But on the other hand, if this went badly, he didn't know if he'd ever write again. And after having just rediscovered that piece of himself, he wasn't sure if he was willing to risk it.

"Right?" asked Hazel, pulling him out of his thoughts. As usual, he'd lost himself in them.

"I'm sorry, what?" he asked, lowering the heat on the mushrooms and turning his full attention to Hazel.

"We're going to end it on a cliffhanger, right? She figures out how to get back to her own time just as he's captured?"

He nodded. "I think that's the way we should end it, yes." The story was moving and complicated, about Mary Elizabeth Axton who'd accidentally traveled back in time to a Gossamer Falls stand-in town in 1864. She's desperate to figure out how to get back to her own time, but is also falling in love with the handsome soldier who saved her. While in the past, Mary Elizabeth discovers that she's actually a witch with a tie to the soldier—he's immortal, and has been searching for her because she's the reincarnation of his love, and he's the one who summoned her to the past. They'd borrowed that idea from Hazel's vampire story. Towards the end of the story, Mary Elizabeth has the chance to return to her own time, where she feels she belongs. She feels she's been tricked by the soldier, despite having fallen for him.

There was a chime from Hazel's phone and she picked it up. "Shit," she sighed, setting it back down. "We have more work to do."

"What?" he asked, plating their pork chops, spooning the sauteed mushrooms over top, and then adding a generous helping of salad to each of their plates. They settled in at the table.

"That was Alex. He wants a sample of a sex scene so he can see 'how spicy we're talking here'," she said, making air quotes around the word and imitating her agent's staccato style of speaking.

"So we need to write a sex scene tonight, too?" he asked, sipping his wine, his mind already flipping through all of the dirty possibilities. "How steamy do *you* want the book to be?"

She shrugged. "I don't shy away from including sex in my books, so I think readers will be expecting it."

"True," he agreed. "Okay, so when in the book do they first fuck?"

He didn't miss the way her eyes widened a little, and she

set her fork down. "The wedding night. After he has to marry her to keep her safe from the other soldiers."

"Not until then?" he asked, his eyebrows raising. The wedding was going to take place about fifty percent of the way through the book.

She chewed thoughtfully on her pork chop. "I don't think she'd give in until then. She's stubborn and headstrong and not wanting to admit that she wants him as much as she does because of how complicated it all is."

"Okay, so the wedding night," he said, nodding his head in agreement. "Is she nervous? Excited?"

"A little of both, I think. He takes charge."

"So it's from his perspective, then? We can see how much he loves her, how much he wants this, what it means to him, which I think we need."

"I agree, yeah."

They ate in thoughtful silence for a moment, the tension between them growing, pulsing like a heartbeat.

With a soft growl, Adam set his fork down, grabbed Hazel's hand, and pulled her to her feet. "I'm not going to be able to eat until we figure out this scene," he said, savoring the little squeak she made as her body came flush against his.

"Okay," she said, a little breathlessly, and Adam grinned, especially because he could tell she didn't know exactly what he had in mind.

She let out a surprised squeal when he tossed her over his shoulder and started toward the stairs, carrying her like a caveman up to his bedroom. He tossed her down on his bed, his heart constricting at the sight of her, hair a little mussed, eyes bright, chest heaving.

"Spread your legs," he said and she did, easing back on the bed and spreading her legs for him. She was wearing jeans, so there was nothing to see, but the fact that she'd obeyed his dirty command turned him on.

"Samuel stared down at his bride," he narrated. "Nervous anticipation filled the room, making them both feel a little drunk. For once, he couldn't quite read her emotions, leaving him feeling confused. But that confusion did nothing to abate the throbbing urgency in his stiff cock."

Hazel's mouth opened and her eyes grew heavy lidded as he narrated. Adam grinned, stepping closer, taking inspiration from the woman in front of him.

"Mary Elizabeth's mouth parted, drawing his attention to her full lips, swollen from the kisses he'd stolen earlier. Samuel grinned darkly, his mind racing with exactly what he wanted to do with that mouth."

Hazel hummed in approval, and he moved onto the bed, his knees on either side of her hips.

"He eased her down to the bed, following her with practiced grace. She wasn't the first woman he'd had in this bed. But goddammit, she would be the last."

"Don't stop," she whispered, fisting her hands into his shirt.

"He wanted every part of her so badly. He wanted to taste and claim and devour. But he knew that patience and a slow, gentle touch were what she needed."

He leaned over her and kissed her, nipping at her lips.

"His wife deserved more than a quick fuck. She deserved pleasure, and he intended to give it to her, over and over again."

"Yes," she breathed, hips starting to writhe beneath him.

He slipped a hand up under her sweater, tracing his fingers across her ribs, toying with the fabric of her bra. Their eyes met, and she looked so beautiful that he forgot to breathe. Everything he'd been about to say about the scene and their characters flew out of his mind because now, all there was was Hazel.

"His fingers glide over her skin," she whispers, "raising goosebumps on the delicate swath on her stomach."

Adam sucked in a shaky breath. Holy fuck, this was hot.

He did as she'd suggested, moving his hand from her ribs to her stomach, playing along the waistband of her jeans. God, she was so fucking warm. So fucking soft. He'd never get enough of touching her. Ever.

"He swallows thickly, gathering his restraint," he said. "He wants to ravage her."

"But he knows to go slow."

He flicked open the button of her jeans. "He starts undressing her, making swift work of petticoats and corsets." He cupped her through her jeans, resting his hand over top of her pussy. He could feel the heat of her even through the fabric separating them. "With one fleeting touch, he can feel that she's drenched for him."

Still on his knees, with one hand in her pants, he used the other to push her sweater up, tracing circles over her hard nipples through the lacy fabric of her bra. He loved how his big hands swallowed her up, making her cheeks go pink and her nipples harden even more. He slipped his hand out of her pants and pressed against her, letting her feel him.

She let out a shuddery gasp, eyes only half open. He leaned down, his lips brushing against her ear as he spoke.

"He presses his hard cock against the core of her,

wanting to assure her that he wants this as much as she does. That her desire is welcome. Encouraged. Something to bask in. Because he can barely contain himself at this point. Already, he's thinking of the hot clench of her around him, of filling her with his come."

He pressed into her again, working his cock against her, and they both let out a shuddery moan. Adam's eyes fell closed, a groan bursting out of him as Hazel rubbed herself against him.

"He trails his lips down her neck," she whispered, and he did as she asked, kissing and licking and biting down the length of her delicate neck. She tasted warm and sweet, like sunshine and home. She moaned as he sucked on the spot just beneath her ear that always made her a little wild, and sure enough, she tangled her hands in his hair and pulled him to her for a kiss. His dick pulsed between them, getting harder and harder, and he rocked into her, the teasing friction only making his blood pump harder and hotter.

Hazel tugged on his hair and deepened the kiss, and he could taste the wine on her tongue. It was the kind of kiss that he wanted to drink forever. That he wanted to drown in. Desperate and needy and full of passion. Her tongue tangled with his, and Adam knew that Hazel was the only one he ever wanted to kiss like this. The only one.

"The kiss is intense," he pants against her lips. "And Samuel wants nothing more than to devour his wife. He can sense her passion, and he wants to let it loose, like a summer storm. He wants to ravage her. He wants her to scream his name and forget her own. He wants to make it so good that she begs for more.

Hazel writhed beneath him, her hips pushing up to his. Seeking friction. Seeking relief.

He pulled the cup of her bra down, exposing her sweet pink nipple. He tugged it between his fingers, making her gasp and arch up into him.

"You're so fucking hot, Hazel," he said, breaking the spell for a moment. But he could see how close she was to unraveling, and he wanted her to know he was right there with her. That beneath the façade he was putting up, he was feeling just as desperate for her. "If I come in my pants while we're figuring out this scene, that is *not* going in the book."

She let out a musical laugh, twining her arms around him. "Well, Samuel's immortal and has had over a thousand years of practice when it comes to restraint. You're a mere forty. It's not fair to compare."

He toyed with her nipple and she stopped laughing. "'Do you like that, darling,' he'd ask as he touched her for the first time."

"Yes," she said breathlessly, and he didn't know if that was Hazel's answer or Mary Elizabeth's, but he didn't care.

And just like that, his patience evaporated. He pulled her sweater off over her head, made quick work of her bra, and then pulled his own shirt off, tossing the garments to the floor, one by one. Then he undid the zipper of her jeans and tugged them down over her hips.

"Fuck me," he growled. "Have you been walking around without underwear all day?"

She grinned at him, mischief sparkling in her eyes. "Surprise."

He wrestled her jeans off, his hands trembling slightly. "The idea that you've been bare all day..." He exhaled heavily as he brushed his fingers against the cleft of her pussy. "Fuck."

The last of his restraint evaporated, and he pinned her wrists above her head. "Spread your legs. Show me how wet you are," he said, his voice taking on a rough edge that he barely recognized. She did, spreading herself wide for him and showing him the glistening pink between her legs.

He dragged his fingers slowly and deliberately over her clit, making her gasp and buck up into his touch.

"Soft as silk, wet as water," he said. "That's what Samuel would say."

"And what would you say?" she asked. His eyes roved over her body, from her pinned wrists to her breasts, and down to her spread legs where she was eager for him to play with her wet pussy.

"That you're fucking perfect."

He moved his fingers in a circle over her clit, over and over, feeling the nub harden against his touch, seeing the wetness seep out of her. She moaned, her head moving back and forth against the mattress, and he circled faster, adding pressure. Releasing her wrists, he tugged her to the edge of the bed and dropped to his knees, licking up the honey dripping from her wet pussy.

He parted her lips with his fingers, opening her up wider for him as he gorged himself on her, sucking and licking her clit before fucking his tongue inside of her, making her cry out and flood his face with fresh arousal. He captured her clit between his fingers and traced his tongue around it. Then, still working her clit with his fingers, sliding up and down, around and around, he slid his tongue back inside her, wanting to taste the exact moment she shattered.

"You taste so fucking good, Hazel," he growled, his mouth popping off of her wetly. "So fucking soaked for me." And she was. She was dripping, making an absolute mess, and he loved every single second of it.

He felt her thighs start to shake, trembling against his shoulders, her muscles tensing and tensing, her pussy squeezing his tongue in a way that had his balls throbbing painfully.

"Adam!" she screamed, her hands fisted in the duvet as she came hard against his mouth. He waited until her spasms and tremors subsided before he kissed his way back up her body, lingering over her thighs, her stomach, her breasts. When he reached her mouth, he kissed her, letting her taste her orgasm on his tongue.

"I'll never forget the way you squeezed my tongue as you came," he whispered, dragging his teeth over her neck. "You fucking milked me, and my cock is jealous."

She reached between them and managed to open his jeans, stroking him. He was a mess too, his cock dripping pre-come, over and over again. "Tell me what Mary Elizabeth would say to Samuel," he said, pushing into her touch.

"'You're so hard and thick', she'd whisper. She'd touch him, learning every ridge, every vein."

"Gonna stretch your sweet pussy with this. Make you so full you don't know where you stop and I begin." He didn't know if he was speaking on behalf of Samuel or was just being himself. He couldn't think straight anymore. Not with the taste of Hazel lingering on his tongue and her fingers curled around him.

He backed away just enough to shuck his jeans and urge

Hazel onto all fours. Quickly, he lined himself up at her entrance, his knees braced on either side of her spread legs. But instead of fucking into her, the way he wanted, he slid forward, teasing his cock against her wet pussy, the head bumping against her swollen clit. She let out a hiss and he backed off, returning to her entrance.

"Please," she whispered, and he slowly pushed in. His chest heaved as he tried to catch his breath. She pushed back against him slightly, and he eased in another inch, and then another, and then another, her pussy impossibly tight from her orgasm.

"Hazel," he whispered, taking another inch. "How does it get better every single fucking time?"

"I don't know," she moaned as he slid in to the hilt, the sound tangling with his low groan. "You're so deep, Adam. So fucking deep."

His balls were nestled snugly against her ass, his eyes glued to where her pussy swallowed him up, stretched around him.

"It's okay?" he asked, forcing his hips to stay still.

"It's so much better than okay," she said. "It's *so* good."

"How good?" he asked, sliding almost all the way out and teasing the head of his cock against her entrance. She slammed back into him, making him groan loudly.

"This good," she moaned, pulling away and sliding back, fucking herself on his dick.

It was the hottest thing he'd ever seen.

"This good?" he asked, hands coming to her hips as he took over, fucking her slow and deep.

"Oh my god, yes," she said, dropping down onto her elbows and pressing her ass higher in the air. "Don't stop."

"Don't think I could if the fucking house was on fire," he ground out, dropping over her and trailing kisses across her shoulders. He let the rhythm of his hips take over, losing himself in the feel of Hazel. The scent of her. The taste of her. The sound of her. Every single nerve ending in his body felt like a bowstring, pulled taut and ready to fire. A thousand flaming arrows, ready to be unleashed. "God, Hazel, you feel so damn good. Being inside you is...it's fucking beautiful," he said, his voice coming out strained.

The need to feel her come again, to come around him, seared through him, and he slipped one of his hands between her legs, petting her clit with gentle strokes that matched the rhythm of his much harder ones.

"Don't...don't stop," she begged. "I'm so close. I'm gonna...Oh, God," she moaned, her hips moving back to meet his thrusts. "Adam...coming," she screamed, her arms giving out as her pussy fluttered wildly around him, pulling his cock deeper inside her.

Adam felt as though the pleasure building inside him was going to split him in two, and a guttural sound he didn't even recognize ripped out of him. His hips slammed against her, her pussy milking his dick in such an exquisite way that he couldn't hold back. He thrust into her one last time, so hard that the slap of skin on skin echoed through the room, and spilled inside her.

Taking everything inside of him, including his heart. It was hers now, and he was never getting it back.

TWENTY-ONE

"I'M SO glad I was able to tear you away from Adam long enough for this," said Autumn, her cheeks glowing as she hooked her arm through Hazel's. She'd been in Gossamer Falls for almost ten days, and it was astounding how much had changed in the span of less than two weeks. She'd met and started to fall for Adam, started working on a new book, and had begun questioning just about everything about the way she'd been living her life up to that point. She would've thought that by now, she'd be going crazy with missing the city, but she didn't. She wanted to stay here and drink hot chocolate and browse All Booked Up, the cute little bookstore, and watch movies by the fire with Adam. She wanted to have girls' nights with Autumn and Sienna and Laurel— like she was doing tonight—and spend her weekends learning to cook and hiking and falling asleep with Adam's huge, warm body pressed against hers.

It was as though her entire life had shifted. And it had all started with that night at the falls. Something had felt different since then. Before being "kissed by the mist," before having her tarot cards read with startling accuracy, she'd felt certain that she wasn't ready for dating or love. But now, just a week into her relationship with Adam, she had to admit that being with him felt obvious, in the best possible way.

"Me too," she said, giving Autumn's arm a squeeze as they walked down Main Street. Autumn had picked her up at the hotel and parked in her usual spot at Hemlock Square. It was after dark, but the street was cheerily lit with glowing streetlamps, illuminating the receding puddles from the rain they'd had that morning. A cool gust of wind blew, swirling the leaves around their feet as they walked, the rustling sound soothing.

Pour Decisions, the town's pub, was located at the corner of Main and Balsam, in an old stone building. The front was all trimmed in thick beams of wood, just like a proper English pub, the hand-lettered sign crowned with a row of red and orange mums in overflowing pots. The front doors were solid wood with enormous polished brass handles, and warm light glowed from the front window that looked out onto the street.

"I think Laurel and Sienna are already here at our usual table," Autumn said, yanking open the door and holding it for Hazel.

Hazel gasped when she stepped inside. It wasn't anything like she'd been expecting. The exterior was all British pub, but the interior was pure Gossamer Falls. Brightly colored tapestries hung on the wood paneled walls, and the dark parquet floor beneath their feet was polished and waxed to a high shine. In the center of the room, a large, modern fireplace rose up to the ceiling, open so that it was visible on both sides. A built in nook rose up beside it, filled with neatly stacked firewood. The mantel was decorated with a mix of plants and historical photographs of the area.

An eccentric mix of wood tables and chairs were dotted throughout the space, with large booths in the corners. Near the fireplace was a long couch in a striking burnt orange color, with a few colorful ottomans scattered around it. To the right, a long bar took up the back corner, bottles lining the backlit shelves, with old-timey alcohol advertisements framed and hanging above the highest shelf.

The fire crackled warmly and soft jazz floated through the speakers, mingling with the low hum of conversation and the clinking of glasses. Hazel could smell the woodsmoke, the ale, and something delicious that smelled like butter and garlic.

Autumn led her to a booth in the far left corner, where Sienna and Laurel were both already sipping glasses of wine and deep in conversation. They sat, and Autumn lifted her hand in a wave to an attractive blond man working the bar. He waved back, winking.

"I take it that's Beckett," she said, tipping her head in the bartender's direction. Several young women flanked the bar, openly vying for his attention.

"Yep," said Autumn. "In all his glory. I'll go order us a round. What would you like?"

Hazel gestured at Sienna and Laurel's glasses. "White wine sounds good."

"Perfect. Be right back." She rose and made her way to the bar.

"How's everything going?" asked Sienna warmly, turning her attention to Hazel. "With the book and *everything*." Hazel didn't miss the emphasis she put on the last word.

Clearly, the fact that she was dating Adam was now common knowledge among the residents of Gossamer Falls.

"Honestly, things are great," she said with a little shrug. "The book is great, Adam is great." She and Adam hadn't yet told anyone that they were writing a book together, deciding to keep that quiet until they knew for sure if the book was something that could actually come to fruition. Hazel didn't mind sharing, but Adam had dealt with publishing failure in the past, and he didn't want to publicly broadcast what might be another failed venture, which she understood. The other factor was Seth. Hazel knew that Alex had had lunch with him today, and Alex had sent her a quick email saying that Seth was going to call sometime within the next few days. It felt like everything was hanging in the balance.

"Okay, quick, before Autumn gets back," said Laurel, glancing around conspiratorially. "On a scale of one to ten, how does Adam rate in the bedroom department? Because between you and me, that looks like a man who can get it."

Sienna smacked her twin's arm. "Gross. I dated his brother for like, forever. I don't want to think about Adam that way."

"Then plug your ears, because I want details."

Hazel hesitated. Memories of everything she'd shared with Leah pushed up to the surface, making her want to close in on herself and not let anyone in. She'd shared everything with her, and when the shit had hit the fan, Hazel had been left feeling humiliated. But then she looked around, looked at Laurel and Sienna, who'd been nothing but welcoming and open with her, and realized that this wasn't the same situation. And if she treated it as such, then she'd never move past the hurt that Leah caused.

And she wanted to move past it. For a long time, she'd clung to it, to the point where being the "woman wronged" had become how she'd seen herself. How she'd identified and defined herself. When, in truth, she was so much more than that, if she'd step out of the cocoon she'd forced herself into for survival.

But she'd survived. Now she needed to thrive, and that meant stepping out of that little cocoon and spreading her wings.

"He's a solid twelve and a half," she said to Laurel, grinning. "At least."

Laurel pumped her fist. "I knew it! I always had such a crush on him, but he was never interested. I think he just saw me as his kid sister's friend."

"Do not let her make you feel bad," said Sienna, shaking her head. "Laurel was boy crazy as a teen and she's had a crush on just about every man between the ages of twenty-five and fifty in this town."

"Hey!" said Laurel, frowning indignantly. "How dare you describe me accurately?" Her frown morphed into a smile, and they all laughed. Just then, Autumn returned with two glasses of wine, setting them down on the table.

"How much do I owe you?" asked Hazel, reaching for her wallet, but Autumn waved her away.

"First round's on me." She took a sip of her wine and then leaned on her elbows, practically batting her eyelashes at Hazel. "So..." she said, the single syllable heavy with expectation.

Hazel rolled her eyes good naturedly and then laughed. "Okay, okay. You were right about me and Adam being a good match."

"Damn right I was." She sipped her wine. "So things are going well?"

Hazel nodded. "Really well. He's..." She let out a dreamy sigh and everyone laughed. The thing was, she hadn't done it for comedic effect. He really made her feel that way. "It's the real deal," she said with a little shrug. "We're talking butterflies and that giddy feeling when he walks into the room and thinking about him constantly."

Autumn pointed at her. "That's some falls magic right there if I ever saw any, because not that long ago you were pretty uncertain about men and dating and now look at you, mooning over the local innkeeper."

Hazel laughed. "I know, I know. It sounds like something out of a movie or a book. But I'm starting to think that there's more to the Gossamer Falls legend than just a good story."

"Really?" asked Sienna, eyebrows raising. "You believe in the whole 'kissed by the mist' thing?"

"I'm starting to think I might. I don't know," she added hastily, then took a big gulp of wine. It warmed a path down the center of her chest, and she eased back into the seat.

"And how's the book going?" asked Autumn. "You seem to be working away every time I see you in the sunroom at the inn."

"It's going," she said. "I might have some news to share soon. It's gone in a...a different direction than I'd planned, but a good direction."

"You're writing with Adam, aren't you?" asked Autumn, eyes narrowed at Hazel as she seemed to scrutinize her for evidence of co-writing. "That's why the book's going well and you're with him all the time and he finally seems like himself again."

"What do you mean, he seems like himself?" Hazel asked, stepping around Autumn's question.

"Well," she said, tracing her finger up and down the stem of her wine glass, "After he wrote the trilogy and then stepped away from publishing and writing, it was like he'd lost a piece of himself. He was still Adam, but we could all tell that something was missing. That something is back, and at first I thought it was because he was dating you, but there's more to it than just dating someone." Her eyes met Hazel's. "You gave him back a part of himself that he'd probably thought he'd lost forever."

Hazel bit her lip, not wanting to betray Adam's trust. "I can neither confirm nor deny that we're co-writing, but I'm glad to hear that he seems happy. That makes me happy."

They all sipped their drinks, and then Autumn leaned in closer to Hazel. "So then...what happens when your stay here is up? Aren't you technically supposed to go back to the city in a few days?"

Something cold and hard took root in the center of Hazel's chest at the thought of leaving, not just Adam, but the town and the people in it, behind.

"I'm extending my stay for another couple of weeks," she said. She'd promised Adam that she'd stay to work on the book, and she meant to keep that promise.

"And after those couple of weeks are up? Adam's life is here." Autumn eyed her with a hint of wariness, and Hazel knew she was worried about her brother getting hurt.

"Then maybe my life will be here, too," she said, and as

soon as she spoke the words out loud, the cold, hard knot in her chest dissolved into something warm and soothing.

"That would be amazing if you moved here!" said Laurel. "Like, seriously. Amazing."

"It would," said Autumn. "It kinda feels like you belong here, you know?"

Hazel grinned, watching the way the firelight reflected off of her wine glass. "I know what you mean," she admitted, even though a part of her still felt like all of this was crazy. But maybe crazy was what she needed. After all, it felt as though her life had spiraled out of control over the past couple of years. Hell, she was still stuck working for Seth because she'd felt powerless to do anything about it. "Question for you," she said to Autumn, who cocked her head. "Not to change the subject, but do you know if Fiona might have anything for taking your power back?"

A slow smile spread across Autumn's face. "I bet she does, if you believe in..." Her eyebrows went up. "You know, magic and witchcraft and new agey stuff."

"You know, Autumn, I'm starting to think I might."

The next morning, Hazel walked the four blocks from the inn to The Mystic Muse, getting there just after it opened at eleven. A windchime tinkled softly above the door as she entered, and it appeared that she was the first customer of the day.

"Good morning," she called out to the empty shop, her voice seemingly dampened by the sheer number of items in the shop. As though they absorbed all sounds from the outside world, shutting it out completely.

"Be with you in a minute," came Fiona's voice from behind a door that was slightly ajar. Hazel could hear the rustle of papers, the scrape of a cardboard box over the floor. Fiona popped her head out after a moment and smiled instantly.

"Hazel," she said warmly. "What brings you by on this crisp fall morning?"

She twisted her fingers together in front of her, feeling suddenly self-conscious. "Um, well, I was hoping you could help me with something."

"Of course. What did you need?" She blinked at her through her thick glasses, studying her. "A spell, I think. Yes. But about what? Hmm."

"I want to reclaim my power," said Hazel, her voice coming out stronger than she'd anticipated. As though the simple act of speaking the words was already getting her closer to her goal.

Fiona's eyebrows inched up over her glasses, but she nodded, her frizzy curls bouncing around her shoulders. "Yes. That's it, of course. That's it. Come. I can help." She waved her toward the back, to the same table where she'd had her cards read not that long ago. "Tell me about the power you wish to reclaim," she said once Hazel was seated at the table. She lit a large candle in the middle and placed several pointed crystal towers around it. They were beautiful, catching the glimmers of light from the flickering candle. One was a silky white with jagged ledges, pointing upward in a gentle circle. Another was smaller and almost perfectly clear, save one small imperfection near the base. Another was white with whorls of a soft peach color.

"I'm tired of feeling like a bystander in my own life and having everyone else make decisions for me. My agent, my editor, even my former friends. Somewhere in the mess of my collapsing marriage, I seemed to have lost my voice."

"Just because something is buried doesn't mean it's forgotten. Just because something has been hidden doesn't mean it's not still there." She turned and walked toward an ancient looking wooden cabinet, opening one of the doors with a low creak. Then she turned and scrutinized Hazel over her shoulder. "Sometimes what we most need is a little sacred medicine. Something to connect us to the past and the present while allowing us to step into the future with power and confidence."

"Yes," said Hazel, calm settling over her as she watched Fiona take out several small bottles and bring them over to the table. They contained things like salt, dried rose petals, chili pepper flakes, and fragments of dried bay leaves. She set them all in the middle of the table, and then brought out a small empty glass vial, a bundle of sage, and an unused stick of incense. Finally, she set out a small piece of plain white paper and a black Sharpie.

It was fascinating and new, and yet somehow familiar, too.

"First, we cleanse ourselves," said Fiona, retrieving a lighter from her pocket and then lighting the bundle of sage, blowing on it until it was smoldering. She waved the fragrant smoke over herself, over the table, and then over Hazel. It stung her eyes a little, making her blink rapidly. She set the still smoldering sage down in a plain black bowl and then lit the stick of incense, shoving it into the small empty vial and leaving it there until it was full of smoke. "More cleansing," she said when she caught Hazel's curious gaze. She removed the stick and then set it in an incense holder near the cash register.

She sat down at the table and picked up the marker, then wrote what to Hazel looked like a strangely sloped letter n. "This is the rune for power," explained Fiona. She rolled up the small piece of paper and then handed it to Hazel. "Hold this in your right hand while I prepare the spell jar."

Hazel leaned forward eagerly, drinking in every single thing Fiona did. She'd never been into magic or witchcraft or anything remotely new agey beyond reading her horoscope from time to time, but something about this practice resonated with her in a way nothing ever had before.

Fiona poured salt into the base of the small vial, followed by some dried rose petals and the chili flakes until it was three quarters full. "The rune," she said simply, and Hazel handed it back to her. She placed it in the center of the vial, pushing it into the chili flakes and rose petals until only a small bit of it was visible. She filled the rest of the jar with the flakes of bay leaves and then inserted a cork stopper.

"Oh, the candle. I almost forgot." Fiona jumped from her seat and returned to the cabinet, where she retrieved a slim red candle. She lit it and then dripped red wax all over the vial's stopper until it was covered with a thick layer.

"Does this really work?" asked Hazel in a quiet voice. It seemed too easy. Too simple to really be magical. And yet she was buzzing. Like she'd swallowed a hive of bees.

"It does if you believe in it. It's not the ingredients that are magical. Not by themselves. The real magic comes from you."

The wax dried quickly and Fiona pressed the jar into Hazel's hand. The wax was warm but the glass was cool and smooth to the touch. "Keep this with you at all times as your power returns. Believe that your power is returning. Believe that you've asked the Universe for this, and it is already so."

"Thank you, Fiona," she said, slipping the small jar into her bag. "How much do I owe you?"

Fiona waved her off. "Nothing. I'm always happy to help, if I can. I've done my part. Now you do yours and believe in yourself, Hazel. You can do anything, have anything, if you're brave enough to ask for it." She patted her on the arm and then returned to her supply closet, humming cheerfully.

Hazel stepped out of the shop and walked back to the inn, feeling taller with every step.

TWENTY-TWO

ADAM SAT behind his small desk in his closet-sized office at the inn, the brown leather of his worn chair creaking softly beneath his shifting weight. Hazel sat on the other side of the desk, across from him, her thumbnail caught between her teeth as she stared at her phone. It sat in the middle of desk, the screen dark. There was a tension in the room, thick and palpable. He felt like a student who knew a fire drill was imminent.

Hazel pulled her thumb out of her mouth and picked up her mug of tea, cradling it without sipping. She was nervous, and truth be told, so was Adam.

Seth Collins, Hazel's editor, had sent an email yesterday saying that he was going to "squeeze them in" to his schedule for a phone call at one o'clock today. There was no question about if that time worked for them, just an edict that the phone call would take place today. It made Adam think back to his own publishing experience, when his editor would sometimes go weeks without answering email, treating Adam like a second class citizen because if he didn't write a book that sold, there were a hundred others waiting for the chance. He'd been treated as a disposable commodity, not a human being with emotions and hopes.

But, according to Hazel's agent Alex, the lunch had gone well, Seth was intrigued, and willing to work with them on this.

Did he want to write a book for Hazel's ex-husband? Fuck, no. He did not. But he wanted to write with Hazel. And, honestly, he would've done anything Hazel asked. He'd do anything for her. Even work with her ex-husband.

"God, he's such an ass," she muttered, glancing at the time on her phone screen. 1:07. "He always pulls this crap. No one's time is more valuable than his," she said, rolling her eyes. Adam's chest tightened, not out of jealousy, but because he could see how much pain Seth had caused her, and seeing that pain in the tense line of her mouth, the tension in her jaw, made him hurt, too.

The phone started to ring, seeming too loud in the small, quiet room, and Hazel reached for it. He bit back a smile when he noticed that when Seth's name popped up on the screen, so did the poop and red flag emojis, right beside it.

"Seth, hi," she said, putting the call on speaker. "I'm here with Adam."

"Great," he said brusquely, and Adam had the distinct impression that he was annoyed by the phone call. "So, as you know, I had lunch with Alex the other day, and he pitched this whole new book co-writing thing to me."

"And?" said Hazel, leaning forward in her seat. Adam's pulse pounded dully in his temples. God, he didn't know if he could get back on the publishing roller coaster, even if it was with Hazel.

"And I have my reservations," he said wearily, sounding as though he were talking to a petulant child and not a *New York Times* bestselling author. Then again, maybe he did sound very much like a man talking to his ex-wife.

"Did you read the pages?" she asked. They'd sent Alex everything they'd had, including the love scene they'd stayed up late drafting after finally untangling themselves from each other.

"A few, yeah. Obviously I didn't have time to read them all."

"Okay, so..." said Hazel, rolling her eyes. "The pages are good. Alex wouldn't have shown them to you if he didn't agree. So what's the issue?" She sat up a little bit straighter, eyes narrowed at the phone.

Seth sighed heavily. "Well, for starters, you're deviating from the approved outline, which is a concern."

"Why? The old outline wasn't working. This new story is so much stronger."

"Right, but now I have to go back to the editorial team and get them to approve this new one."

"Okay, so meet with them. We gave you a synopsis."

"There's also the issue of your co-writer," he said, and Adam swore he could hear the sneer in Seth's voice. Did he know that Adam and Hazel were a hell of a lot more than just co-writers?

"What issue?" Hazel asked, her tone sharp as shattered glass.

"Well, his sales record for one. I looked up his numbers in BookScan and...I mean, no offense, but they're not good."

Adam felt tension gather along his shoulders, radiating up his neck. This was exactly what he'd been afraid of. This was exactly why he'd left publishing in the first place. It didn't matter how good the book was, how many glowing reviews it received. If it didn't make money for the publisher, it was a complete and utter failure.

"It was one three-book series several years ago. This is a different genre, and we're co-writing. Surely this is a different enough situation that those old numbers don't matter."

Seth laughed, and the sound was cold. "Surely you know that's not how any of this works. This is a business, not a charity, and if I can't convince the directors this is a sure thing, I don't see how they'll green light it."

"But Hazel's sales are excellent," said Adam, clearing his throat. "Isn't that more important? She's the recognizable name, not me. So my track record is irrelevant, right?"

"Then why put your name on the book at all?" asked Seth, and Adam sat back in his chair, feeling as though he'd just had a knife slip right between his ribs.

Hazel's eyes flared. "Because he's writing half of it, that's why," she said, and he could tell she was fighting back her anger in the way her fists were clenched at her sides, a muscle in her jaw jumping.

There was an awkward pause. "How did this all come about, anyway? What are you doing in some Podunk town?"

"Adam and I met a couple of weeks ago and it happened very organically. This wasn't something I sought out, but now that we've started drafting the book, it's absolutely what I want to pursue," she said, gaze intent on the phone.

"Well, it might not be what I want to pursue," said Seth. "I mean, we haven't even talked about the legal side of this. We don't have a contract with Adam, and that massive advance we paid you was for a different book, not a co-written one with a completely different plot. If this is an angle to get more money as an advance for him, you're barking up the wrong tree."

Adam's lip curled at the way Seth spoke to Hazel, his tone dripping with condescension. He wasn't a violent guy, but the way he spoke made him want to punch the guy in the face.

"Listen, if you don't want to edit this book, that's fine, Seth. I know how busy you are. Pass us to another editor and we'll go from there."

"No."

Hazel scoffed. "No? Why on Earth wouldn't you at this point? You've made it clear that you have zero enthusiasm for the project, that you don't want me to co-write. Fine, so this project isn't your cup of tea. There are other editors who would be a better fit. Ones who might be able to see past Adam's sales numbers and really look at his writing, which is excellent. I wouldn't be writing with him if he wasn't incredibly talented." Their eyes met and his chest flooded with warmth.

"I think you're misunderstanding me," he said after a moment, and Hazel shook her head, her golden brown hair swishing around her shoulders.

"No, I don't think I am. You want me to do what you want. That's always the way it's been. You want control over everything, including me. But this is the direction I'm going. So either get on board, or pass us to someone else, because this is the book I'm writing."

"We have a contract," he said and Hazel smirked. It was

so sexy that his arms practically vibrated with the urge to haul her across the desk and kiss the hell out of her.

"I have a contract with the publishing house, yes. Not with you. You seem to be under the impression that you have more control here than you do. Because it sounds like what's happening is that you're passing on the option material. If you do that, I'm free to shop the book elsewhere, and I don't have to pay back the advance."

"No, that's not what I'm doing here," said Seth, and even through the phone, Adam could tell he was starting to feel a little frayed. Good. He deserved that, and much, much worse for everything he'd put Hazel through. "This is a discussion, that's all. I'm not saying yes or no to anything."

"Sounds a lot like a no to me," she said. Pride filled him up, expanding his lungs. It was as though he was watching her blossom right in front of him.

"Well, it's not," he said almost sulkily, and Adam grinned. "Obviously I need to talk to the editorial team and to legal."

"And consider passing us to another editor," she added, her bottom lip caught between her teeth.

"No." Seth's response was quick and flat.

"Why?"

"I don't really want to get into the complicated politics of publishing houses right now," he said, and Adam narrowed his eyes. That was a brush off if he'd ever heard one. Seth heaved another sigh. "Are you coming to the gala next weekend?"

"I wasn't planning to," she said, making a little face, her nose wrinkling in distaste.

"You should come," he said. "We can discuss this further, and I can meet this co-writer of yours."

Hazel met Adam's gaze across the desk and blew out a breath. "I'll think about it."

"Good. I have to go, but we'll talk soon once I have more information."

"Okay," said Hazel, and then the line went dead without so much as a goodbye.

"I don't understand why it didn't work out with Prince Charming," deadpanned Adam, and Hazel laughed, the sound breaking the tension in the room.

"Such a prince, I know."

"I can't fathom how you're expected to work with him like everything is normal and he didn't have an affair and treat you horribly."

"Seth likes to be in control. If he lets me work with someone else, he has to give up that control, and I honestly don't think he knows how to do that."

"What gala was he talking about?" asked Adam. His mouth felt dry, so he picked up Hazel's mug of tea and took a sip. A soft smile spread across her face, and he knew she was thinking the same thing as him, marveling over this easy intimacy that had bloomed seemingly overnight.

"Every fall, the publishing house puts on a fancy cocktail reception for authors, agents, editors, etcetera. I've skipped it last year, not wanting to try to make small talk and eat tiny canapes while my ex swans around with his new woman."

"Maybe we should go," he suggested, tilting his head.

"Why would you want to?" she asked, eyebrows climbing upward.

"Well, all the editors are there, right? If Seth won't pass

us along, maybe it's an opportunity to talk to some of the other editors about our book."

"Hmm," she said, sipping her tea thoughtfully. "That's not a bad idea."

He leaned forward, lacing his fingers with hers. "And don't you want to see the look on Seth's face when you walk in on my arm? I clean up real nice," he said, wiggling his eyebrows at her.

She laughed. "I bet you do. And yes. As immature as it is, I do kinda want to shove my hot, talented, amazing new boyfriend in his face."

"Amazing, eh?" he asked, rubbing his thumb over the smooth back of her hand.

"Among other things," she answered, her eyes sparkling.

"We could make a weekend of it. I'd love to see all your regular haunts. Walk through Central Park. Maybe take in a show."

She bit her lip and then nodded. "Okay. You've convinced me. We'll go to the gala and have a weekend in the city. We can stay at my place."

"Perfect. Speaking of weekend plans, my mom would like you to come to Sunday dinner this weekend," he said, his heart starting to beat a little faster. It had been a long time since he'd brought anyone to Sunday dinner, and never this early in a relationship. But he knew that what he had with Hazel was special and rare, and he wanted her to meet his family.

"Oh," she said. "Sure. I'd love to. Can I...can I bring anything?"

"We'll pick something up from You Little Tart before we head over."

"Okay. Wow. I..." She trailed off, shaking her head.

"You can say no, if you think it's too soon. I won't be offended," he said, studying her reactions.

"No, I want to come. I was just thinking that if someone had told me a few weeks ago what my life would look like today, I wouldn't have believed them."

"Me neither, sweetheart." He lifted her hand to his mouth and kissed her knuckles. "Me neither." He stilled, blinking once, twice, as an idea took root. "If I asked you to come to the cemetery with me, would you go?"

TWENTY-THREE

ADAM WOVE his fingers through Hazel's, leaves crunching beneath his booted feet as they walked through the cemetery. It was a glorious fall day, with a brilliantly clear, azure sky, and a crisp breeze in the air. The gravel path was wide and well maintained, dappled with shade from the towering oaks above. There was no one else around, and the only sounds were the birds chirping softly from above, the gentle breeze ruffling the leaves, and his measured footsteps. Adam scratched at his cheek as they walked, anxiety churning his stomach in a sickly swirl.

"It's this way," he said quietly, pulling Hazel down a narrower path toward an area beneath a tall, skinny birch. He hadn't been back here since the day of the funeral, but he still remembered exactly where his father's grave was.

Over the past few days, he'd had a growing sense of unrest. Not over Hazel, and not over the book, which was still going well despite Seth's reservations. He was writing again, and no matter what ended up happening with the book, if it ever saw the light of day or not, he'd always be grateful for the project that brought him back to himself, and for the woman behind it.

But now, feeling more settled in himself than he had in a long time, he knew there was something he needed to do. A loss he needed to face. To accept, as hard as that was.

The leaves above the area where John Shephard lay were a vibrant orange, rippling softly in the breeze. He found the stone easily, large and a dove gray color with a photograph of John in a round frame at the top. Adam's breath stuck in his lungs as he took it in. The last time he'd been here, everything had been unsettled, with piles of dirt and disturbed lawn. Today, everything looked orderly and peaceful, and it hit him just how long his father had been gone. Two years had gone by slowly and all at once, it seemed.

He cleared his throat around the lump of emotion lodged there. "Here he is," he said, gesturing at the headstone that read "John Shephard, 1959-2021. Beloved husband, adored father, and a pillar of the community. Remembered with love and never forgotten."

He inhaled a shaky breath, eyes stinging as he stared at the epitaph, simple and true. A sense of loss washed over him, so intense it nearly knocked him over, and as though she could sense what he needed, Hazel slipped her arm around his waist, holding him tight.

"He was the best," he said, voice thick with emotion. "He taught me everything. How to ride a bike. How to chop wood. How to be a useful part of the community. How to be a man, and not in any macho bullshit sense. How to love and be loved and look after the people around you. He always looked after everyone." His voice wobbled on the last word, and he cleared his throat. "And no one supported me more in my writing than he did. When the first Robert Brady book came out, he kept an entire box of them in the trunk of his car so he could pass them out to anyone he happened to meet."

"He sounds amazing," Hazel said, squeezing him tight. "I wish I could've met him."

"Me too, sweetheart. He would've loved you."

The word hung in the air, bright and shimmering, and she snuggled into him. "He was handsome, like you," she said.

"And he was funny. He had this loud, deep voice that you swore you could hear from halfway across town. He was a maniac for holidays, like Halloween and Christmas. Always went all out decorating the house. No one loved a turkey dinner like he did. When he—" He cleared his throat again. Grief and loss were pulling at him, but the words were flowing out of him like water. "When he died, we did a turkey dinner for his wake."

"It was sudden, right?" she asked, and he nodded.

"He was on the porch, drinking his morning coffee, like always. He had a massive heart attack and he was gone. Mom found him less than ten minutes later." He shook his head. "I hope he wasn't scared or in pain, not that anything ever seemed to scare him. John Shephard was a man who faced life head on, no matter what. He was the life of the party and a shoulder to lean on for anyone who needed it. And he was smart. God, was he smart. He always knew what to do or what to say. When he died, I felt like I'd lost my North Star."

"He's still with you," Hazel whispered, sniffling and

wiping at her eyes. "You just have to look for him in different places."

He sighed. "Maybe. Yeah." For a long time, Adam had been certain that there was no such thing as ghosts or legends or magic. That it was all the stuff of fairy tales and Disney movies. But now, knowing Hazel had gone to the falls and wished for her true love only for him to literally be smacked in the head with awareness of her the very next day...Hazel felt like magic. Writing again felt like magic, too. And if those were real, maybe the other things were real, too.

They stood in silence for a moment, and then Hazel rubbed his arm affectionately. "How about I give you some time? I'll go for a little walk and meet you back at the car when you're ready."

He nodded, and she rose up onto her tiptoes to kiss his cheek. As she walked away the wind whipped up, swirling orange and yellow leaves around her legs, and Adam almost jumped out of his skin at the deep, familiar voice that seemed to speak right into his ear.

Oh, I like her. You keep her around.

Another gust of wind kicked up, bringing with it the scent of evergreen and woodsmoke. The scents he associated most with his father, and Adam smiled, fighting back tears. Slowly, he sat down on the cold grass, leaning back against a huge pine that sat across from his father's grave. He picked up a pinecone that lay near his leg, rolling it around in his hand, and a sense of peace came over him. It felt almost tangible, like someone laying a blanket over him. Warm and comforting.

"I'm sorry it's taken me so long to come here," he said, bracing his arms on his bent knees, the pinecone dangling from his fingers. "I know almost everyone else has been to visit except me. I just couldn't...I didn't want to face it." He sighed. "I know, I know. I can hear you telling me that I have to feel it to heal it. I think you got that from Oprah. So, I guess I'm feeling it now, because fuck, do I miss you." His voice came out raw and he didn't fight back the tears that wanted to fall. "A part of me was so damn angry. Angry at you for leaving, angry that it happened so suddenly, angry that I had to figure out everything without you. I'm not angry anymore. But I don't think I'll ever stop missing you."

He took a minute to catch his breath and stem the tears. "Mom's good. Autumn's a pain in the ass, as usual, but I couldn't run the inn without her. Jack's...figuring stuff out. You'd be proud of the father he is. Oliver's still teaching, and people are starting to notice his art. He works really hard at it. If you see Drew wherever you are, tell him we all say hi." Drew was Oliver's best friend who'd died from colon cancer about a year ago. God, he'd lost his best friend and his father within a twelve-month span, Adam realized. He'd always known that, but the magnitude of Oliver's losses was hitting him in that moment. He'd been so stuck in his own grief, in his own head, that he probably hadn't been there for Oliver the way he should've been. He'd have to make up for that.

"Beckett's working at Pour Decisions, having fun. And Finn...you probably know this, but after you died, Finn left. He took off with his computer and his cameras and he hasn't been home since. He left us behind, and he left Sienna behind. We keep up with him through his YouTube channel, but...I don't think he's okay. We're all just giving him space for now, but I think Mom's going to lose her patience with it soon."

The words flowed out of him as he talked about the few changes he'd made at the inn, like the new furniture for the terrace off of the sunroom, the revamped menu in the restaurant, Autumn's monthly tours to the falls, the interesting guests they'd had. "But I haven't changed much, because not much needs changing. It was perfect the way you had it, minus that horrible, glitchy software you insisted on using. That's long gone and good riddance." He chuckled softly, feeling lighter as he spoke. Wishing he'd done this a year ago, all the while knowing he hadn't been ready.

"As for me, I'm writing again, which I think would make you happy, but that's not why I'm doing it. I'm doing it because it makes me happy. I feel most like myself when I'm writing. But no matter what happens, I'm not giving up the inn. Being there makes me feel close to you. I see reminders of you everywhere, and that was really painful for a long time. But now I'm glad they're there. The inn was a part of you, and it's a part of me."

The wind picked up again, gusting in the trees, shaking the branches and showering leaves down onto the cemetery below. It felt like being in a snow globe made of leaves, all swirling beauty. And then he heard the voice again.

Tell me about her.

Adam inhaled in surprise and the scent of evergreen was so strong it was almost astringent, filling his lungs with its sharp scent. A smile played across his lips.

"Her name's Hazel Woodward and she's a guest at the hotel. At least, she was. That's how we met. She's an author from the city, and we're co-writing a book. I'm pretty sure I'm in love with her, but I can't say anything yet because it's only been a couple of weeks, and we haven't talked about the future. But…" He tossed the pinecone up in the air, catching it easily. "I think she's it for me, Dad. I wish you could've met her. She's smart and funny and loves books and writing as much as I do. She's sweet and kind. And she's so beautiful it makes my heart stop every time she comes in the room. I've never felt like this before." He chuckled to himself. "Autumn took her to the falls her first night here. There was a full moon, so they did the whole 'kissed by the mist' thing, and now Autumn's convinced Hazel's my soulmate." The word was like honey on his tongue, sticky and unexpectedly sweet. "She might be right."

The wind blew, stripping leaves from trees, and Adam was sure he heard his father's laugh in the whistling air around him. His father had always believed in the magic of the falls, the ghosts at the inn, and that there was more to life beyond what a person could see with the naked eye.

Adam was starting to think he believed, too.

He sat in silence for a few more minutes, feeling about a hundred pounds lighter than he had when he'd first arrived, and he realized now that trying to pretend his grief wasn't there had only been feeding it. He hadn't wanted to feel it because grieving sucked. And because acknowledging that grief would've made his father's death more real. But it was real no matter how much he shoved down his feelings.

So now he was feeling his grief, and he was still standing. Still breathing and functioning. Maybe he always would've been able to face it this way because difficult emotions were still just emotions, fleeting and temporary. Or maybe it was because loving Hazel had strengthened his heart, making it stronger, the feelings within it more assured.

Hands in the pockets of his open coat, he walked slowly

back to the car, taking in everything around him. Grounding himself in the present moment with the colors of the leaves, the scent of the air, the sound of birds chirping, the feel of the weakening sun on his face. His heart kicked happily against his ribs when he saw Hazel leaning against the car, gazing off into the distance, lost in thought.

He paused, wanting a moment to observe her before she saw him. To appreciate the way the sun made her hair look like burnished bronze, the way her eyelashes cast shadows on her cheeks. The way her full lips were turned slightly upward, as though she was thinking about something pleasant.

A twig crunched beneath his boot as he started forward again, and she turned in his direction, a bright smile lighting up her face. She pushed off of the car and met him halfway, sliding her arms around his waist.

"You okay?" she asked, her fingers skating along the crease of his spine.

"Yeah. I am. I needed to do that." He dipped his head, pressing a kiss to her temple. "Thank you for coming with me."

"Of course," she said, snuggling into him. "Anything you need."

I need you to promise me you'll stay. Not just while we're working on the book. But stay.

The words seared through him, and he held her tighter, as though if he squeezed her hard enough now, he could change whatever might happen in the future. It was easy to picture a future with her, wrapped up in their little Gossamer Falls bubble. But what happened if the book was dead in the water? What happened if she went back to the city? He swallowed thickly, knowing he needed to talk to her about his feelings, but letting fear hold him back.

"I just need you," he said, the words muffled against her hair. It was the best he could do for now, until he found the words to explain to her that she was already the owner of his heart.

"You've got me," she answered.

And for now, her answer was enough.

TWENTY-FOUR

HAZEL HAD LEARNED from both Adam and Autumn that Sunday dinners at the Shephard house were kind of a big deal. Everyone was expected to attend if able, and it was almost always just the actual Shephards. So, the fact that Adam's mother had invited her was a big deal. A big deal because it meant she and Adam were headed somewhere serious—something she already knew, even if they'd only talked about it in abstract terms so far—and a big deal because making a good first impression mattered. These people were important to Adam, and therefore, she wanted them to like her, because Adam was important to her.

She was already friends with Autumn, so that was one Shephard down. They had coffee together at least once a week, texted all the time, sent memes on Instagram. She'd even run into her at the Mystic Muse the other day.

Truth be told, she loved the shape her life had taken in Gossamer Falls. Waking up in Adam's bed to the sound of him typing away in the next room, the scent of coffee wafting gently on the air. After breakfast, they'd head to the hotel together, where she still kept a room in case the common areas weren't conducive to creativity. She often joked about the size of the tab she must be racking up, but Adam assured her that no bill would be coming her way. She accepted that kindness, but only with the assurance that if the room was needed for a paying guest, he'd kick her out.

She'd spend the morning reading over Adam's pages, making some notes, and then writing her own pages, which she'd then add to their shared Google doc. They'd eat lunch together, and then she'd spend some time on her own during the afternoons while he worked, hiking, shopping, walking. She'd become a regular at both Deja Brew, and All Booked Up, the charming bookstore in the town's core. Afterward, she and Adam would head back to his place where they'd have dinner together and discuss that day's writing. Once the dishes were cleared, they'd cozy up on the couch together, reading, or watching a movie. It usually wasn't long before they were making out instead. Sometimes they didn't even make it up to the bedroom. In fact, just yesterday, he'd hauled her up onto the kitchen island and—

"What are you thinking about?" he asked, shooting her a grin. He drove confidently, with one wrist draped over the steering wheel as he navigated the streets through town from his cabin to his mother's house.

"When you ate my pussy on the kitchen island last night," she answered honestly. Her cheeks flamed, and her clit pulsed at the memory of his mouth on her, licking her slowly, over and over again, like she had the world's most delicious ice cream between her legs.

He groaned softly. "You can't say things like that when

we're about to have dinner with my family," he complained, but she knew he was teasing.

"Hey, you asked, I answered," she said with a little shrug, and he chuckled. A silence fell as they turned down Cedar Street, and she blinked rapidly, her earlier nerves returning with a vengeance. She smoothed her hands over her thighs, trying to wipe away the clamminess. But despite her nerves, she had no desire to bail. She wanted to meet his family. It was important. It mattered. She closed her eyes and inhaled slowly, trying to pull in some semblance of calm.

"Don't be nervous, sweetheart," said Adam, reaching over and laying a big hand on her thigh. "They're going to love you. Just be yourself. I know it's a lot, but I'll be with you the whole time, and I promise you, they're all excited that you're coming. It's gonna be fine."

She nodded, laying her hand over his on her leg, the heat of his touch seeping through her jeans. "I know. I just...I want them to like me. What if I make a bad first impression?"

"Then they'll tease you about it mercilessly in the future."

Her stomach dipped and swirled at the word future. More and more, she became certain that was what she wanted with Adam. A future. Which meant winning over his family, who meant the world to him, was important.

He squeezed her leg affectionately. "I'm glad you're here," he said. "Even though you're nervous."

"I'm nervous because it matters."

He pulled the car to a stop at the curb in front of a large colonial, lights glowing warmly from within. He cut the ignition and then he leaned across the center console, cupped her face, and kissed her, sweetly and softly. "You're gonna do great," he said, kissing her on the forehead and pulling away. The kiss settled the worst of her nerves, and she took one last deep breath as she undid her seatbelt and retrieved the two desserts they'd picked up at You Little Tart—an apple pie, and a chocolate cake with an orange glaze that looked like something out of a magazine. Adam grabbed the two bottles of wine they'd brought, and they headed up the steps to the wide front porch together.

He opened the front door without hesitation, and the sounds of classical music and warm voices greeted her as they stepped inside. A fire crackled in the fireplace in the living room to the right, but it seemed as though all of the voices were coming from the kitchen.

"Hello," Adam called, taking the desserts from Hazel so she could take off her coat and shoes.

A young girl came skidding around the corner, barrelling into Adam and throwing her arms around him. "Uncle Adam, Dad said you're bringing your new girlfriend. Is this her?" she asked, peering up at Hazel.

Adam nodded, ruffling the girl's hair. "Chloe, this is Hazel. Hazel, this is my niece Chloe. She's Jack's daughter."

Hazel's eyebrows rose at the unexpected news Jack had a daughter. She'd heard stories of his exploits from Autumn, Sienna and Laurel, but none of them had mentioned that he was also a single dad. Granted, it made sense that he'd keep a firm line between those to parts of his life.

An elegant woman with dark curls shot with silver came around the corner next, wiping her hands on the canvas apron tied around her slender waist.

"Hi, honey," she said, pressing a kiss to Adam's cheek.

"You must be Hazel," she said, turning to her and extending a hand. "I'm Julie, and we're so happy you could join us today. Please, come in, come in. Would you like a glass of wine?" she asked, waving for them to follow her into the kitchen.

"I'd love one," she answered honestly. She was feeling ten percent less nervous than she had in the car, but her stomach was still quivering with nerves.

"Hazel!" said Autumn as they stepped into the kitchen, wrapping her in a hug. "I'm so glad you're here! We could use some more estrogen in this place," she joked, and Julie laughed. Adam set the desserts down on the counter, watching his family greet her with a soft expression on his face.

"Here," she said, handing Hazel a glass of red wine. Hazel took a sip and then smiled. "Thank you. This is delicious."

"It's a Chianti from Italy, my favorite," said Julie. "You have good taste. Then again, you're dating Adam, so of course you have good taste."

Hazel laughed, feeling a little bit more of the tension ease out of her. No one was waiting to pounce on her, or trip her up, or humiliate her. She'd always hated doing anything with Seth's family. All they ever wanted to do was argue about politics, snark on whatever was popular at the time when it came to the arts, and try to one up each other.

"Well, I'd like to think so," she said, grinning up at him as he slipped an arm around her waist.

"You've met Jack," he said, who was leaning against the island and nursing a beer. She lifted her hand in a wave, and he nodded, smiling warmly. "And this is Beckett," he said, as his youngest brother walked over.

"Hey, yeah, I saw you the other night with the girls at Pour Decisions," he said, smiling affably. "But we didn't really get the chance to talk. It's nice to meet the woman who's got Adam swooning like—"

Adam elbowed him in the ribs. "Finish that sentence and I will end you."

"Swooning? Who said anything about swooning?" said Beckett with a goofy smile, swiping his hand through his hair.

Adam rolled his eyes and led her to the other side of the kitchen, where a man who looked the most like Adam out of all of his siblings stood in front of the stove, carefully frying what looked like breaded chicken cutlets.

"This is Oliver," he said, and Oliver turned, wiping his hands on the kitchen towel slung over his shoulder before shaking Hazel's. "This is Hazel."

"I've heard so much about you," said Oliver, a slight smirk to his smile. "Glad you could join us tonight."

"It's really nice to meet you, too," she said, leaning into Adam's side, taking comfort from his solid warmth. The music floated around them, the food smelled amazing, and everything felt warm and cozy. Safe and welcoming.

Being in that kitchen with the Shephards, Adam's arm around her as he joked with his siblings, felt more like home than anything had in a long time.

"So, Hazel," said Julie, approaching and then leaning a hip against the island. There were appetizers strewn around it—savory puff pastries, little bites of bruschetta, and roasted hazelnuts. Julie handed Hazel a small plate and then took one for herself, loading it up. "How are you enjoying your time in Gossamer Falls?"

A genuine smile spread across Hazel's face, and she helped herself to some bruschetta. "I love it here," she said with all sincerity. "It's quickly become my favorite place on the planet."

"I'm happy to hear that," said Julie, a hint of wariness in her eyes as her gaze flicked to Adam, who was talking to Oliver a few feet away. Autumn, Chloe and Jack were doing a puzzle in the living room as Beckett set the table. "We all love it here, too. I was born here, and so were my parents, and my late husband's parents. We go way back in this town."

"That's amazing," said Hazel. "My family's from the city, mostly. But we're not...close. Not like this, anyway." She gestured around them. "Everyone kinda does their own thing."

"How many siblings do you have?"

"Just one brother, and he lives in Australia, so we don't see much of each other."

"That's too bad."

"Very different than having a whole houseful, I can tell you that."

Julie laughed softly. "You know, I never imagined myself having six kids. I always thought I wanted two, maybe three. We had Adam, and then Jack came along two years later. I thought we were done, but John and I kept talking about trying for a girl. A few years later we had Oliver. We thought we'd try one more time, and we had Finn. At that point, I thought I was done, you know? I had four boys ranging from eight to a newborn. And that's how it stayed, for a while, but then a few years later, we got a surprise when we found out I was pregnant again. Along came Beckett, and I booked John an appointment for a vasectomy." She laughed, shaking her head, memories clearly playing behind her eyes. "It's a good thing he cancelled it at the last minute though, otherwise I wouldn't have had Autumn about eighteen months later. After she was born, I drove him to the clinic myself."

"I'm surprised your uterus didn't fall out," said Autumn with a little shudder as she passed through the kitchen, getting a soda for Chloe. "Six kids. You're nuts."

Julie hip checked Autumn as she passed. "Lucky for you, I most certainly am."

"What was Adam like when he was little?" asked Hazel, glancing over her shoulder at him, where he was still deep in conversation with Oliver, who she secretly suspected was his favorite brother.

Julie smiled wistfully. "He was smart and imaginative, and always so gentle and caring towards others. I often thought of him as my little teddy bear with the way he was so gentle and protective of his younger siblings. He was a good kid. Good grades, responsible, kind. We were always so proud of him. He's always been a sensitive soul with a big heart."

"Did he always know he wanted to be a writer?"

"He loved books from a young age. When the house was noisy and chaotic—I mean, with six kids, it pretty much always was—I'd sometimes find him in the large linen closet upstairs with a flashlight, a book, and a pair of earmuffs jammed on his head."

Hazel laughed, pressing her fingers to her lips. Her heart warmed at the mental picture.

"Are you telling stories about me?" asked Adam from the other side of the kitchen.

"Only nice ones, I promise," said Julie, who then winked at Hazel.

As Oliver, Beckett and Adam worked to get dinner on the table, Hazel and Julie chatted some more. She asked Hazel about her writing career, places she'd traveled, and hobbies. She appreciated that Julie was taking the time to get to know her without judgment or reserve. Again, it was the polar opposite of her experience with Seth's family, where she'd never felt like a member.

"Would you like a tour of the house?" asked Adam, weaving his fingers through Hazel's. "We have a few minutes before dinner's ready."

"I'd love that."

He led her out of the kitchen and up the stairs. She paused halfway to examine the pictures covering the wall there. A large framed photo that looked like it was from the late 90's hung in the middle, the entire family standing outside the Shephard Inn. Well, the entire family minus Autumn. But she was there, given Julie's enormously round belly in the picture. There were family pictures and individual pictures from all stages of life, as well as a few pictures of Chloe. At the top of the stairs, there was a small console table with a large, framed picture of John along with what Hazel assumed were a few personal mementos. A wedding ring, a watch, a hockey puck.

"I want to see the room where you grew up," said Hazel.

Adam nodded, leading her down the hallway to the left. "There are five bedrooms total, so I had my own room until Beckett was born, and then Jack and I started sharing." The bedroom was simple, with green plaid wallpaper, a queen sized bed, and antique looking furniture. "It's a guest room, now. Chloe stays here sometimes."

In a nod to the original inhabitants of the room, there were more pictures of Adam and Jack on the walls.

"Oh my God," said Hazel, moving towards one that caught her eye. "How old were you here?"

Adam peered at the picture, in which he was reading a book and looking very annoyed at having his picture taken. He was wearing a dark blue sweater, and his curly hair was long, flopping across his forehead and into his eyes.

"Seventeen or eighteen, I think."

"I would've had such a crush on you in high school. Curly haired boy who loves books was totally my jam."

"Please. Curly haired boy who loves books wasn't anyone's jam. Trust me."

Something sweet and sharp twisted in Hazel's chest. "Do you want kids?" she asked suddenly, and Adam's eyebrows rose.

"I'd always thought I'd have kids, yes," he said, a hint of wistfulness in his voice. "Not six. I'm not a lunatic. But one or two might be nice."

"I always thought one or two might be nice, too," she said. "For a long time, I'd thought I didn't want kids, but I think I just didn't want kids with Seth because deep down I knew it would be a bad idea."

"One or two," he said softly, eyes dreamy as he gazed at her. "Mmm."

"You'd have to build an addition onto that cabin of yours," she said, sliding her arms around his waist. He hauled her against him, holding her close.

"I think that's doable," he said. "Another bedroom on the main floor, maybe."

"We could build a treehouse in the woods."

"We?" he asked quietly, eyes intent on her.

"Yeah," she whispered, heart fluttering like a drunk hummingbird in her chest. "If that's what you want."

She felt as though her entire world had narrowed to the two of them, alone in the darkened room, the sounds of a family gathering wafting up from below. Like she was in a bubble made of hopes and dreams and things she'd thought she'd never have after her divorce.

"It's the only thing I want," he said hoarsely before claiming her mouth in a deep, lingering kiss.

"Dinner's ready!" Chloe called up the stairs, and they pulled apart with a rueful chuckle.

They headed back down the stairs hand in hand and took their seats at the table. Hazel's mouth watered at the scents that greeted her, and she piled her plate high with chicken schnitzel, salad with the most delicious lemon dressing she'd ever had, and homemade mac and cheese.

Everyone dug in, and for the first few minutes, the conversation died down as everyone savored their food. Throughout the meal, Adam's thigh was pressed to hers, anchoring her in the moment. It was a moment she didn't want to leave. Being with Adam and his lovely, welcoming, fun family was a kind of happiness she'd never really experienced. She'd never had that closeness with her family, or Seth's, so finding it with Adam's felt like a special gift.

"I can see why you do this every Sunday," she said. "Thank you again for including me."

"You're very welcome," said Julie, sipping her wine. "I

have a feeling this won't be your last Shephard Sunday dinner." Warmth bloomed across Hazel's chest at Julie's words. Hazel was very much hoping the same thing.

"So, Hazel," said Autumn, that mischievous twinkle in her eyes. "How's your book coming? Any *news* to share?" She shot Adam a pointed look. He cleared his throat and glanced at Hazel, and she nodded. If he wanted to tell his family about their project, she was on board.

"Actually, we have some news," said Adam, and the room went silent. "Hazel and I are co-writing a book."

"You're writing again?" asked Julie, clapping her hands together. "Really?"

He nodded. "Yeah. We've been working on it for a little while now, and we're hoping to have it published by Hazel's publisher. In fact, we're going to the city next weekend to talk about it some more."

A hundred questions exploded around the table about what the book was about, if it was related to Hazel's earlier book, how they were managing the co-writing, when it was going to be published, and more. Hazel laughed as they fielded the questions, feeling like she was at a press conference with very enthusiastic journalists. By the time Julie brought out the desserts she and Adam had brought, the questions had died down, but the excitement in the air was still palpable.

It was utterly heartwarming how much they all cared for each other, how badly they all wanted success and happiness for the others. Hazel had never experienced anything like it.

After dinner there was tea and second helpings of the chocolate cake, and a highly competitive game of Scrabble between her, Adam, Oliver, and Julie. An equally competitive MarioKart tournament was happening in the family room. By the time the evening was winding down and it was time to head home, Hazel felt completely sated in every single way.

Her heart was full, and she felt as though she'd been shown something she hadn't even known she wanted. But she did. She wanted this cozy, happy life filled with love and support. Who wouldn't?

They said their goodbyes, with Adam promising to bring Hazel again in two weeks—since they'd just be getting back from the city the next weekend—and he held the door open for her as she slipped into the passenger's seat of his car.

A moment later, he pulled smoothly away from the curb, and she reached across, laying her hand on his thigh. She let out a wistful sigh and he glanced at her, the question in his eyes not needing to be spoken out loud.

"I wish my family was like that."

He smiled softly. "I'm happy to share mine with you."

Her stomach swirled and her heart fluttered wildly as two words blazed through her mind.

Hazel Shephard.

She'd never taken Seth's last name. She'd never wanted to, because he'd never felt like hers. Not the way Adam already did. She replayed their conversation from earlier again, her stomach flapping with butterflies every single time she heard Adam saying "one or two might be nice" in her mind.

"I want to stay," she blurted out.

"Stay?" he asked, glancing back and forth between her and the road ahead.

"In Gossamer Falls. I think...I think I want to move here."

He pulled the car over to the side of the road, turned his four way flashers on, and leaned across, kissing her breathless.

"Then stay," he said.

TWENTY-FIVE

ADAM NORMALLY DIDN'T CONSIDER himself a lover of New York City. Having grown up only a hundred miles north, he'd been dozens of times, but he'd never really enjoyed it. He'd always found it too noisy, too crowded, too smelly, too chaotic. It usually made him long for his cabin and a cup of tea and a book.

But, Adam had never been to New York City with Hazel before, which changed pretty much *everything*. Then again, he was pretty sure he could visit a garbage dump with her and still have a good time.

They'd spent the preceding week working on the book (which was now over a hundred pages long, meaning Hazel would have no problem satisfying the deadline Seth had given her), drinking hot chocolate by the fire in his cabin, taking long walks in the forest, reading, and having sex. He was pretty sure there wasn't a surface in his cabin that hadn't seen some action. He'd made love to her in the shower, on the sofa, on the kitchen table, even on the stairs. He wasn't able to look at a single space in his cabin without thinking about being inside Hazel.

Which suited him fine, because he was going to ask her to move in with him. After she'd dropped the heart-bursting news that she wanted to move to Gossamer Falls, he'd been turning it over and over in his mind. Was it soon? Yeah, it was really soon. But it wasn't too soon. She was already practically living at his place, spending every night in his bed.

They'd taken the train to the city, and then a cab to Hazel's apartment, which was clean and modern, but without much personality. She'd confessed to him that she'd moved in shortly after leaving Seth and it had never really felt like home. More like a place to exist while she licked her wounds and tried to figure out how to put her life back together.

The first afternoon, they'd walked the High Line together, talking about the book, the original work by Mary Elizabeth Axton, and brainstorming dialogue for the scene they were currently working on. Afterward, they'd spent a couple of hours strolling the Met hand in hand. Once their feet were sore and their stomachs were rumbling, she'd taken him to her favorite restaurant, a cute little pub called Gallagher's Tavern. They'd spent the night at her place, and he'd felt like a goddamn king when she confessed to him that he was the only man she'd ever had in that bed.

If he asked her to move in with him and she said yes, he was going to buy a new bed, just so he could say the same thing.

They'd had a lazy Saturday morning, lounging in bed with coffee and bagels and the *Times* crossword. The weather was cool, but sunny, so they'd strolled Central Park and then she'd taken him to some of her favorite bookstores. They'd each bought several books, leaving the store with paper bags weighed down with paper treasures, and Adam was forced to admit that New York wasn't the worst place on the face of the Earth.

Now, as the sun started to set over the city, he sat on Hazel's bed, flipping through one of the books he'd bought, half dressed for the night in his suit pants and unbuttoned shirt. Hazel flitted about, spritzing on perfume and putting on jewelry while she hummed softly to herself.

"Are you just about ready?" she called from the bathroom, and he hastily tossed the book aside and started buttoning up his shirt.

"Almost," he said, which was mostly true. He'd already shaved and put most of his suit on. He was just reaching for his tie when Hazel stepped out of the bathroom, and his brain backfired. "Holy fuck," he said in a low, guttural voice.

"You like?" she asked, doing a little twirl. Her hair fell down around her shoulders in loose waves, and her make up was subtle but pretty. And the dress...Jesus, he was going to lose his mind trying to keep his hands to himself at the gala. It was a soft blue color that brought out the burnished gold undertones of her skin, with thin spaghetti straps and a deep V-neck. The slinky material clung to her, emphasizing her small waist and flared hips. A generous slit ran from where the fabric skimmed the tops of her feet to mid-thigh.

"You look ravishing," he said, closing the distance between them and hauling her against him. She whimpered softly and he knew that she could feel that he was already half-hard for her. "As in, I'm going to fucking ravish you later," he said, lips brushing against the shell of her ear.

She wound her arms around his neck. "Yes, please."

He wasn't sure who moved first, only that they were kissing and he'd backed her against the wall, his hand sliding up her bare thigh.

"Or you could just ravish me now," she said, reaching between them and palming him over his pants.

So he did, hard and fast against the wall of her bedroom, holding back until she screamed his name and flooded his cock, making him spill inside her.

"Oh my God," she whispered, eyes half-closed, arms limp. "I needed that."

"Happy to be of service," he said, carefully pulling out of her and then setting her down.

She laughed softly and swiped a hand across her mouth. "I think I need to redo my lipstick, given that you're wearing most of it."

The gala was being held at a swanky boutique hotel in Chelsea, the same location as always. And as the cab wove through traffic and the familiar hotel grew closer, Hazel could feel the glow from the fantastic weekend she'd had with Adam fading slightly.

She didn't want to be here. She didn't want to schmooze with people who saw her as nothing but a commodity, and she certainly didn't want to play nice with Seth, even though that was the whole point of them going. He'd apparently read everything they'd sent over and was negotiating everything with the editorial team. According to his last email update, things weren't looking good for all of the reasons he'd gone into on the phone.

God, she didn't want him to be right. She couldn't handle smug, self-satisfied Seth tonight. She'd probably do something colossally stupid, like throw a drink in his face.

"You good?" asked Adam, sliding his hand up her arm and to the base of her neck, where he massaged gently. She pressed back into his touch, letting it soothe her.

"Yeah. We have to do this, right?"

He tilted his head. "No. We're adults. We don't have to do anything. But, I think we should."

"Right. Because we're adults."

"Exactly."

The cab rolled to a stop, and Adam paid him, then jogged around to her side and opened the door for her, helping her out. She couldn't remember the last time she'd worn a gown and heels, and she felt a little unsteady on her feet.

Or maybe she felt unsteady because she knew what was riding on this. Not just her career, but Adam's dreams, too. She knew what writing meant to him, and if this project failed...She didn't want that for him. Her heart hurt just thinking about it, and she'd do anything to make it work. Even play nice with Seth tonight.

She slipped her arm through Adam's as they walked through the revolving door of the hotel. The lobby was as swanky as she remembered, with an overly large chandelier hanging in the center and a swooping staircase. She led Adam to the right and down a small hallway to a set of large double doors that were held open with massive white vases.

Her heart beat hard and fast in her chest as she stepped into the familiar ballroom, its shades of white and gold almost blinding. Noise bounced everywhere, voices and music and the clinking of glasses ricocheting off of the marble floors and filling her ears with an uncomfortable buzz. Adam laid his hand over hers and squeezed gently.

"Just breathe, Hazel. I've got you."

She glanced over at him and felt her heart slow almost instantly. Knowing he was here with her, that he had her back, was everything. Even when she'd been married to Seth, she'd always felt so lonely at events like this.

She blew out a steadying breath and nodded subtly. "It's just a party."

"Right." He dipped his head, his lips brushing against her ear and making her shiver. "In just a few hours, we can go back to your place and I can bury my face between your legs."

"Yes, please," she whispered.

"As long as you promise to leave the dress and heels on. This slit is driving me crazy."

Her nipples beaded beneath her dress and she blushed slightly. "Is it time to go yet?"

He laughed, the sound warm and sexy, and her heart melted at the sight of him. She liked Adam in his usual sweater and jeans, or in nothing but low-slung gray sweatpants, and obviously she liked him in nothing at all. But Adam in a suit...yes, please. The suite was dark gray, and he was wearing a white shirt and black tie. Simple, classic, and sexy as hell.

For a moment, she stood at the entrance to the gala, surveying everything. Clusters of people talked while servers circulated with trays of champagne and tiny canapés. On the left side of the room was a crescent-shaped bar, and a burbling fountain added to the cacophony from its recessed spot in the middle. A living wall took up space on the right, making the air smell like chlorine, dirt, and the faint astringent tinge of cleaning products.

Once upon a time, she'd thought events like this were fun and glamorous. Now, they felt different, and it wasn't just because of everything that had happened with Seth. They felt different because *she* was different. And walking in on Adam's arm, she knew she could handle whatever tonight threw at her.

"Oh, look. There's Alex," she said, tugging gently on Adam's arm. "Let's go say hi."

They wove their way through the little groups of people, and Hazel felt as though she was getting smacked in the face over and over again with the thick scents of cloying perfumes and the braying, fake laughter. Alex saw them as they approached, and he lifted his hand in a wave.

He was tall and wiry thin with black hair shot through with streaks of gray. His stylish glasses complimented his eggplant-hued suit and colorful skinny tie.

"Hazel," he said in his distinctive nasal voice and almost monotone inflection. "So glad you came. And, this, this must be, uh, Adam," he said, raising his eyebrows.

Hazel nodded. "Adam Shephard, this is my agent, Alex Goldblatt."

Adam extended his hand and offered Alex an affable smile. "Nice to meet you, Alex."

"And you. My goodness, you don't look like a writer. You look more like a lumberjack. Or like that British actor. You know the one. With the smile and the muscles," he said, pantomiming a flex. "Henry Cavill."

Adam laughed, his cheeks going slightly pink, which made Hazel want to maul him. "Uh, thank you, I think, but I can assure you, I'm definitely a writer. I have the terrible posture to prove it."

Alex laughed. "Funny, too. You know, Hazel, I'm starting to think there's something more than just co-writing going on here," he said, gesturing at where her hand lay on Adam's thick arm.

"You would be right," she said. "Adam's also my boyfriend. So, have you talked to Seth any more about the book?"

Alex shook his head. "Not really, uh, no. He's got the pages, the synopsis, everything, and he's supposed to be smoothing it all over with the editorial team and legal."

Hazel nodded slowly. "And if he can't?"

"Don't stress," he said emphatically. "We'll figure it out. Trust me. You're too big a name for them to not make this work."

They talked for a little while longer, Alex asking Adam about his Robert Brady mysteries, asking them about how co-writing was working out, before he was called away by someone Hazel didn't know.

"You sure you don't mind me riding your coattails?" asked Adam, a slight frown on his face.

She turned to him, cupping his cheek. "You're not. This book wouldn't be happening if we weren't riding it together. Yeah, I'm the one with the agent and the connections right now, but without you, this project wouldn't exist."

The corner of his mouth kicked up in a smile, and for a moment, it felt as though they were lost in their own little world, the party swirling around them.

"Hazel, I…" He stared at her, his heart in his warm, golden eyes.

"Oh, shit," she said, catching sight of a familiar head of black hair. "Here comes Seth."

Adam winked at her. "You've got this."

She stepped out from behind him, lacing her fingers with his, and caught Seth's eye.

She was going to replay the double take he did when he saw her over and over again, the way he looked almost past her, and then jerked his head back, eyes widening cartoonishly.

"Oh wow, Hazel," he said, dropping Grace's hand and striding toward her.

The next thing she was going to replay over and over was the way he nearly tripped over his own feet at the sight of Adam, and her hand linked with his.

"Uh, hi, hello," he said, catching himself, charming grin back in place. "Who's your date?"

She stared at him, waiting to see if the penny would drop.

It didn't.

Adam extended his hand. "Adam Shephard, nice to meet you," he said without a hint of malice. Seth stared at his hand for a second, not moving to shake it.

"You're Adam?" he asked, voice dripping with incredulity.

"Yes?" said Adam, glancing at Hazel, then slowly lowering his hand. She bit her lip, hiding the smile that wanted to burst across her face.

Seth openly gawked at Adam for a moment, and then gave his head a small shake. "Sorry, you're just not what I was picturing, and I don't think I got the memo that you two are an item."

A hundred snarky comments rose to the tip of Hazel's tongue, but instead of saying them, she took a breath, rubbed her thumb against Adam's hand and smiled as nicely as she could at Seth.

"So, how did the meeting with the editorial team go?" asked Hazel. "Do they still meet every Wednesday morning?"

"Uh, yeah. Wednesdays, yep." His eyes kept flicking down to where her hand was nestled in Adam's. "Hazel, do you think we could talk in private?"

"No thanks," she said breezily. "Anything you have to discuss with me, you can discuss in front of Adam. You know, since he's the co-writer on this project."

"Right," said Seth, his voice flat. She could tell he was struggling to put on his usual false charm because he was so completely thrown by not only how good-looking Adam was, but by the fact that he was more than just her co-writer. It was as though he was completely shocked she'd actually moved on from him. Not only moved on, but moved up. Big time.

An awkward silence hung between them and she sighed. "Did you talk to the editorial team?" she asked, prompting Seth out of whatever was swirling through his mind.

"I did," he said, "and I'm afraid it's not the best news."

"What do you mean?" she asked, tightening her grip on Adam's hand.

He shrugged, glancing around the room. "I don't know that I can convince them about the co-writing. They're not sold on the pages, and they want you to stick to the original idea. They don't like that we don't have a contract with Adam, who doesn't even have representation. And then, as I feared, there's considerable concern about his poor sales record."

Hazel's heart sank. They hadn't liked the pages. The only book she wanted to write was pretty much dead in the water and she was once again staring down the barrel of a financial gun. And Adam...God, she didn't want him to have to face this rejection, too.

"What didn't they like?" she asked. "It's just a draft."

"I...I don't think now's the time or place to get into it." He sighed and then leaned in closer, as though he were confiding some great secret. "I also don't think they're going to love that you're banging your co-writer. Little unprofessional," he said, holding his thumb and index finger about an inch apart.

Hazel laughed, the sound bitter. "I'm unprofessional? That's rich, coming from you."

"Excuse me?" he asked, having the absolute gall to look affronted. Grace started to approach with an uncertain look on her face, and Seth waved her off. Hazel watched the younger woman's shoulders droop, and she actually felt a little bad for her.

"You heard me." She let go of Adam's hand and took a step closer to him.

"Well, it is unprofessional. I shouldn't have to work with my ex-wife's new boyfriend."

"But I should have to work with my ex-husband? How is that any different?"

Adam was a bastion of calm beside her, watching the exchange with casual interest.

For several heartbeats, she and Seth stared, each waiting for the other to blink. "We'll discuss this another time," he said, turning and walking back to where he'd left Grace a few minutes earlier.

"What a charmer," said Adam easily. "A true prince among men."

Hazel laughed despite the heaviness sitting on her chest. Despite the fact that it seemed as though their book wasn't going anywhere, she wasn't willing to give up easily. This book was too special to let it die in Seth's hands.

"Come on, let's get a drink," she said, and he nodded, leading her through the crowd with a hand on the small of her back.

They each ordered a cocktail and then she sagged against the bar, feeling deflated.

"You okay?" he asked, eyes warm with sympathy. God, it was sexy that he didn't seem to have a jealous bone in his body.

"Yeah," she said, blowing out a breath. "I'm mostly just disappointed about the book, honestly. It sucks that they didn't like the pages."

Adam pressed his lips together, drumming his fingers on the bar. She could tell that he had something to say and was holding back.

"Just tell me, babe," she said, slipping an arm around his waist.

He licked his lips before he spoke, and God, she wished they were back at her apartment making out and watching British police procedurals instead of here. "You think he's being truthful?"

"Seth?" she asked, eyebrows inching up. "I...I assume so.

You don't?"

He shrugged and took a sip of his martini. "I don't know. I mean, obviously you know him and I don't, but the way he was looking around the room, not being forthcoming with details...it felt like bullshit to me." He chuckled into his drink. "Then again, maybe I'm too jaded and just think anything publishing related is bullshit."

"Hear hear," came a British-accented female voice from behind Adam, and he turned. The woman's face lit up when she spotted Hazel.

"Hazel Woodward!" She moved around Adam and pulled Hazel in for a hug.

"Daisy," said Hazel with equal warmth. "Daisy, this is my boyfriend Adam," she said, and Daisy briefly shook hands with him. "Daisy Bancroft is the editorial director of the publishing house."

"Very nice to meet you," he said.

Daisy turned her attention back to Hazel. "I wasn't expecting to see you here tonight given that you're not writing these days," she said, waving her glass of wine precariously through the air as she spoke.

Hazel frowned. "What do you mean? Of course I'm still writing. Seth just showed you pages from my new book."

Daisy laughed and then stopped when Hazel didn't join in. "What are you talking about?"

"I'm co-writing a book with Adam. Alex sent in the first hundred pages, plus a sample scene further into the book, along with a detailed synopsis. Seth said it would be an uphill battle since it was different than the book I'd originally proposed, but..." She trailed off at the look of pure confusion on Daisy's face.

"Darling, seriously, I haven't the faintest idea what you're on about. Seth told us you were on a sabbatical and he wasn't sure if you were still writing. We knew all you'd been through with the divorce, so we were happy to leave the option open."

Hazel could feel her pulse everywhere in her body. "He said *what*?" She shook her head quickly, the room spinning around her. "I was under the impression that I had to write a book or I was in financial trouble."

Daisy laughed. "Who told you that?"

"Seth."

Daisy's laughter died once again. "Well, that's a flat out lie. One of many he's told, I'm starting to suspect. You submitted pages? To him?"

Hazel nodded. "Yeah, about two weeks ago. When did he tell you I wasn't writing anymore?"

Daisy blinked slowly. "About two weeks ago."

Hazel gasped as realization dawned. "He's trying to kill the co-written book," she said. "This is all about control and getting me to do what he wants."

Daisy frowned, tapping the tips of her long nails on her wine glass. "Tell me about this book."

So Hazel did, with helpful interjections from Adam. She told her about Mary Elizabeth Axton, Gossamer Falls, and the time traveling love story they were writing together.

"Well, it sounds bloody brilliant," said Daisy, lips pursed. Then she turned to Adam. "Would this be a debut for you?"

"I've been published before," said Adam, and there was a hardness to the set of his jaw that made Hazel ache for him. She could see that he was bracing himself for rejection.

"He wrote a mystery trilogy for Penman," said Hazel.

"Critically acclaimed, but the sales weren't what they should've been, given the quality of the books."

He gave her hip a small squeeze.

"Penman have always had ridiculous expectations, especially given how little they spend on promotion. They don't care about author development. Usually what's their loss is someone else's gain." She turned, grabbed her clutch, and fished one of her cards out. "Email me the pages and everything you have directly. Something's fishy here, but you're a star, Hazel. We don't want to lose you."

"Well, you came close, I think, with Seth lying about pretty much everything." She paused, hesitating. "Can I ask you something?"

"Anything."

"Did he ever try to move me to another editor? Because after we split up, I asked multiple times."

Daisy frowned. "Not to my knowledge. Honestly, we all thought it was a bit weird that you still wanted to work with him given the whole Grace-gate situation."

"I didn't want to work with him. But he wouldn't..." She stopped. "He's been lying to you, and to me."

"That little shit," whispered Daisy. "I've never liked him. Listen, send me the pages. I'll take care of everything." She tossed back the rest of her drink. "So glad I ran into you, darling. Can't wait to read." She pulled Hazel in for another hug and then disappeared into the crowd, a purposeful set to her shoulders.

"Uh oh, I think someone's in trouble," said Adam in a teasing singsong, a sexy grin on his face.

Hazel laughed, sipping her drink. "I think someone's about to get exactly what he deserves."

TWENTY-SIX

WITH THE REVELATION that Seth had been lying, trying to control Hazel and quite possibly sink her career, Adam had expected her to be angry. But instead, she'd seemed serenely satisfied, enjoying the rest of the gala, introducing him to a few people, and even posing for a few pictures. Seth seemed to disappear not long after her conversation with Daisy, and Adam had a feeling that wasn't a coincidence.

Watching Hazel at the gala had been a special kind of treat. Watching her stand up to Seth, advocate for Adam, fight for their book. Watching her laugh and talk and soak up the evening the way she deserved, given her success.

And God, that dress. That fucking dress. He was a dirty bastard who'd been doing his best not to stare at her breasts all night. But he'd failed. Miserably. He wanted to rip that dress off her. He'd been fantasizing about it for the better part of the night.

He'd also almost told her what he needed to tell her. Words that were burning a hole in his chest with how badly they needed to be spoken.

Now, she was tucked against him in the back of a cab, her head on his shoulder, her hand resting on his stomach. She glanced up at the cab driver, who was in his own world, and slid her hand lower, cupping him through his pants. He sucked in a sharp breath.

"Tell me what you're going to do to me once we're back at the apartment," she whispered. She shifted closer, her breath tickling his ear. "I'm so horny right now." Her voice was low, pleading. "Tell me. In detail."

"I'm going to unzip this dress so that I don't tear it off of you, spread you out on your bed, and bury my face in your pussy until you're dripping for me."

She let out a ragged breath. "And then?"

"And then I'm going to haul you onto your desk and fuck you, hard and deep." He trailed his fingers down her arm, and she shivered. "Fill your pretty pussy with my come."

"Oh my God, I love your dirty words so much."

"I'm not done, sweetheart. Then, we're going to take a shower together. I'm gonna fill my hands with your gorgeous ass, your legs wrapped around my waist. Back against the tile. I'll fuck you slow at first, and then faster, working your clit until you come all over my cock. And then, when you're coming, I'll slip my finger inside your cute little ass so you can feel me everywhere as you come."

"And then?"

He laughed. "And then we go to sleep because I'm not twenty-five."

She laughed too, the tips of her fingers, running up and down the ridge of his cock, making his balls throb. It didn't seem to matter how many times he had her; it was never enough.

He dipped his head, whispering in her ear, lust and love and need all pouring through him and making his skin feel tight. "And then in the morning, I'll feed you my cock for breakfast while I eat your pussy again. I want you on top, dripping on me as I come down your throat."

Hazel leaned forward and rapped her knuckles on the plexiglass divider. "There's a forty dollar tip for you if you step on it."

Three hours, two orgasms and one steamy shower later, they lay in Hazel's bed, arms and legs entwined lazily. Adam felt as though he was glowing from the inside out. As though he'd swallowed the sun. He didn't know that this kind of happiness—whole and consuming and life-giving—was possible.

But it was.

"I've been thinking about something," he said, stroking a hand lazily up and down her bare back.

She trailed her fingers down his chest, smiling sleepily. "That breakfast you promised me?"

He laughed. "Obviously, yes. But no, that's not what I'm talking about right at this moment."

"Are you sure?" she asked, sliding her hand between them and cupping him. He was totally spent, but he still grew half-hard under her touch.

He laughed, and then tipped her chin up, meeting her eyes. "I've been thinking about how utterly and completely I love you."

Her eyes sparkled at him as a soft smile spread across her face. "Funny, I've been thinking the same thing." She leaned forward and kissed him gently. "I love you, Adam Shephard.

"I love waking up to you in my bed. I love writing with

you. I love telling you every insane thought that crosses my mind. I love being inside you and watching you think and the sound of your laugh. I love your beautiful smile and your ridiculously gorgeous body. I am totally addicted to you, Hazel Woodward."

She scraped her fingers through his hair. "I love being with you in your cabin. I love your family. I love the story we're creating. I love your dirty mouth and your curls and your muscles. I love that you see me for me. I love laughing with you and falling asleep in your arms every night. If you're an addict, so am I, Adam Shephard."

"So, what I was thinking was…" He trailed off, gauging her reaction. "That you should move in with me. Since you're moving to Gossamer Falls, you should move in with me."

Her expression went soft, but her arms and legs tightened around him. "Are you sure?"

"Completely."

"Then, yes. Absolutely, unequivocally, yes."

Fireworks burst inside him as he kissed her, and she flung her leg over his hip. He'd thought he was spent, but knowing that Hazel loved him, that she was staying, moving in, that she was his and he was hers made him want her all over again. He slid a hand between her legs, finding her slick and hot.

"Are you sore?" he asked, and she shook her head.

"I need you right now. I love you and I need you."

"I will never get enough of hearing you say that," he said, stroking his fingers gently over her clit.

"I love you, I love you, I love you," she said, opening her

legs wider for him. His mouth crashed into hers, a tangle of tongues and lips, hungry and eager, but also so, so sweet. With a sudden movement, she was straddling him and sinking down onto his cock, engulfing him in wet heat that had his eyes rolling back in his head. She slid all the way down, taking him deep, and he trailed his fingers over her breasts, her nipples, her arms, her neck.

"I love you," he said. It was as though he'd undammed a river of emotion, and now that he'd said it, that he loved her, he couldn't stop. He didn't want to stop. Ever.

She inhaled a shaky breath, her eyes bright. "I love you," she echoed. She leaned forward, her breasts pressing deliciously against his chest as she started to move her hips in a slow, sensuous circle. She kissed him, sweet and thorough. When she lifted her head, their eyes met, and it was like a bolt of lightning passed through him.

Hazel was his. Forever, if he had anything to say about it.

He gripped her hips, working her up and down his cock. The strokes started out slow, almost lazy, but then grew rougher as need spiraled between them. When she came, moaning his name, pussy fluttering around him, he held her tight against him, following her over the edge.

After a lazy Sunday morning in the city, Hazel and Adam had taken the train back to Gossamer Falls, and Hazel felt like she could breathe again. Away from the city, away from Seth, she felt more like herself than she ever had in Manhattan. Once they'd unpacked, they'd headed over to

Adam's mom's house for the tail end of Sunday dinner, and then fallen into bed, where Adam had made love to her slowly and sweetly while whispering gorgeously filthy words in her ear.

On Monday morning, she woke up in Adam's bed. She could hear the sound of him typing away in the office next door, and she smiled into her pillow. Outside, the sun was just creeping into the sky, and the first frost of the season clung to the evergreens. A sense of joy filled her at the thought of spending Christmas in Gossamer Falls with Adam and his family.

As usual, once they were showered and dressed and had eaten, they headed over to the hotel together, and Hazel was eager to read the pages Adam had written that morning. Every time she read his words, she felt like she fell a little deeper in love with him, just as Mary Elizabeth fell deeper in love with Samuel. But unlike Mary Elizabeth, who had an anguishing decision ahead of her, Hazel didn't. She was moving here, moving in with Adam. It felt as though she were grabbing handfuls of happiness and feasting on it.

She was at her usual spot in the sunroom, making notes for an upcoming scene, when her phone buzzed with an incoming email. When she saw that Daisy Bancroft was the sender, she opened it immediately, her eyes skimming quickly over the words.

Hazel,

I hope this email finds you well. Thank you for sending over the manuscript pages along with the synopsis. I devoured them yesterday and was so disappointed there wasn't more! Needless to say, we want this book.

In light of Seth's behavior, the board of directors has

decided to let him go. He'll no longer be working here, and I'll be the editor for you and Adam. On behalf of the company, I want to apologize for his dishonesty and what he put you through. I'm ashamed that we didn't realize what was going on.

I'm meeting with Alex later this week to discuss everything. He's going to offer to represent Adam as well, and we'll make sure he gets a fair offer.

Very excited to be working with you!

Best,

Daisy

She rose to her feet as she read the last few sentences, picking up her phone and jogging into Adam's office. He was on the phone, so she waited impatiently, bouncing on her toes. She was going to burst. As soon as he hung up the phone, she thrust it at him.

"Read this," she said breathlessly, watching as he read the email. Watching the play of emotions across his face as his slight frown morphed into a wide smile.

"They're going to publish the book and Seth is fired," he said, looking up and meeting her eyes. "Oh my God, Hazel. You did it. You did this."

She stepped around his desk and wrapped her arms around him. "We did it." She sighed happily, feeling as though all of the puzzle pieces of her messy life had fallen into place. "Can I ask you something?"

"Anything."

"Do you still believe the legend is just that?" Hazel didn't. She believed in magic with her whole being. She'd seen what it could do with her own eyes. Felt it with her own heart.

He raised his eyebrows, holding her tight. "How could I

not? You came into my life, and everything changed for the better. Something special brought you here, Hazel. Magic. Fate. Destiny. Whatever it was, I'll be grateful for it for the rest of my days. Magic is real, and the magic is you."

EPILOGUE

Six months later

THE AIR WAS fresh and warm, the trees budding with green as Adam wove his fingers through Hazel's. Up ahead, he could hear the rushing of the falls and the burbling creek, thawed now that spring had officially taken hold.

The past six months had been, without a doubt, the best of Adam's life. Not long after the gala, Hazel had moved in with him. She'd found a sublet for the remaining months on her lease, and then when it was up, she'd sold or donated most of her stuff, only moving a handful of things with her to Gossamer Falls. On her first night as an official resident of Gossamer Falls, they'd had celebratory drinks at Pour Decisions with his entire family along with the friends she'd made. That night, he'd whispered "welcome home," as he'd slid inside her.

The draft of the book, which they'd titled *Through the Mist*, was in Daisy's hands, and they'd been going back and forth with edits and changes and additions. It was slated to be published the following year, and there was already talk of movie and TV rights being a hot commodity. More than anything, he was proud of the book they'd written together. And he'd be forever grateful to Hazel for giving him back a part of himself he thought he'd lost forever.

He'd also pulled back on his hours at the hotel, delegating more responsibilities to Autumn so that he could spend more time writing and with Hazel. Autumn was happy to take on more, even if it meant she'd given those damned ghost hunters permission to film at their hotel. Then again, maybe they were onto something. He didn't know how he hadn't noticed it before, all the subtle signs that the hotel was home to more than just guests, but now that he'd seen it, felt it, it couldn't be unseen.

Surprisingly, he found that he didn't mind.

The path crunched beneath their boots as they walked, the roar of the falls growing louder. The water was thick and fast with winter runoff, the mist in the air landing on his hands and face.

"Show me exactly where you stood," he said, nerves kicking to life in his stomach. Hazel had told him about her experience at the falls under the full moon, and even he'd had to admit that it sounded pretty magical.

"Um, okay," she said, giving him a strange little look. He had a feeling that she suspected what he was up to, but was willing to play along. She led him further down the path and then onto the rocks on the edge of the creek. "It looks a little different right now—different time of day, different season— but I think it was right about here."

He slid his arm around her waist and held her close as they looked up at the majestic falls together.

"Here's where it all started," she said, leaning into him. His heart felt like it was going to burst. "That night changed my life in the best possible way. I learned about the legend, which in turn inspired the book. But more importantly, I made a wish that led me to you. This place brought us together." Her voice grew soft at the end, her eyes bright with emotion.

He took a deep breath, his hands shaking, his heart hammering wildly in his chest. "Which is why it feels right to do this here." He stepped away from her, pulled the small velvet box out of his jacket pocket, and dropped to one knee. "Hazel," he said, taking her hand in his. "Before I met you, I didn't believe in magic or legends. I only believed in what I could see with my own eyes. But then you came along, and you showed me that magic is very, very real. It's the things we see not with our eyes, but with our heart. And what my heart sees is you. I love you, and I want to spend the rest of my days loving you." He exhaled a shaky breath. Hazel was shaking too, tears streaming down her cheeks as she stared down at him with her whole heart in her eyes. "I wish I could give you the world. I can't obviously, but I can give you this ring." He flipped open the box to reveal the ring he'd picked out with Autumn's help. Hazel pressed her fingers to her lips, and he swore he could feel the joy radiating off of her. "Hazel Rebecca Woodward, you are the most incredible woman I've ever met. Will you marry me?"

He'd barely gotten the last syllable out before she was nodding and crying, "yes!". He hastily slid the ring on her finger, rose to his feet, and pulled her to him.

As they kissed, the mist intensified, clinging to their hair, their skin, even the tips of their eyelashes. A feeling of wholeness so complete it took his breath away washed over Adam, and he knew there was only one thing left to say. He held Hazel tight, his chin on her head as he looked up to the sky and the crest of the falls.

"Thank you," he whispered.

THE END

Thank you so much for reading Hazel and Adam's story! I sincerely hope you enjoyed it. If you want another dose of Hazel and Adam, join my newsletter to get access to a scene that got deleted because it was just a little too dirty for the book. You can sign up here: www.tara-wyatt.com/newsletter.

Want to take another visit to Gossamer Falls?
Watch for ONE ENCHANTED EVENING,
Jack's story, coming in winter 2024.
(Don't forget to join my newsletter to stay in the loop!)

ABOUT THE AUTHOR

Tara Wyatt is a contemporary romance and romantic suspense author. Known for her humor and steamy love scenes, Tara's writing has won several awards, including the Golden Quill Award and the Booksellers' Best Award. In 2018, she was a RITA® Finalist for her novella, *Until the Sun Sets*.

When she's not hanging out with your next book boyfriend, she can be found reading, bingeing something on Netflix, and drinking wine. Tara lives in Hamilton, Ontario, Canada with her husband, daughter, and the world's cutest dachshund.

Don't miss out on a sale or new release!
Join Tara's newsletter: www.tara-wyatt.com/newsletter

For regular updates and to stay in the loop, follow Tara on Facebook: www.fb.com/tarawyattauthor

Visit her on Instagram:
www.instagram.com/taradwyatt

Follow Tara on BookBub:
www.bookbub.com/authors/tara-wyatt